A SCANDALOUS WINTER WEDDING

Marguerite Kaye

MILLS & BOON

First Published in Great Britain 2018
by Mills & Boon, an imprint of HarperCollins*Publishers*
1 London Bridge Street, London, SE1 9GF

© 2018 Marguerite Kaye

ISBN: 978-0-263-93323-9

MIX
Paper from
responsible sources
FSC® C007454

This book is produced from independently certified FSC™ paper
to ensure responsible forest management.
For more information visit www.harpercollins.co.uk/green.

Printed and bound in Spain
by CPI, Barcelona

Prologue

London, February 1819

Kirstin Blair curled up in her favourite arm-chair in front of the fire and poured herself a cup of fragrant tea. It was a new blend, a gift from one of her oldest friends, the Marquis of Glenkin, but while the smoky brew was undoubtedly as refreshing as any Ewan had previously supplied, tonight she might as well have been drinking dishwater. As she settled in her seat, the rustle of the letter secreted in her dressing gown pocket proved too difficult to resist.

She opened the missive once again, staring down at the bold, decisive masculine handwriting. The maelstrom of emotions she had been keeping at bay all day overtook her, making the delicate Sèvres teacup shake in its saucer. She set it down, closing her eyes, lying her head back on the wings of her chair.

She'd never seen his script before. She'd had no inkling, when she broke the seal this morning in her office, of the explosive contents of that single sheet of expensive pressed paper. Scanning the signature first, as she always did, she'd thought her eyes deceived her, but a second appraisal of it left no room for doubt.

Cameron Dunbar. There could not be another with that particular name.

The shock hit her afresh as she stared at the letter. It was not that she'd thought him dead, more that she had so effectively written him out of her life it was as if he had never existed. She rarely permitted herself to recall any detail of that fateful night.

As she struggled to repress the confusing and almost unprecedented smart of tears, years of practice allowed her to draw a thick black curtain over the memory. She would not cry. She had barely shed a tear in the darkest of times. She had taught herself to concentrate wholly on the positive, to look forward not back.

'Onwards and upwards,' she whispered to herself now, but the words which had so often inspired her, and many of the women she had aided, failed to work their magic on this occasion.

Cameron Dunbar. He was unquestionably an outrageously handsome man, but it was not his classical good looks which had drawn her, it was his smile. He had one of those intimate smiles, a smile seemingly intended only for her. Despite the fact that they had been surrounded by strangers, that the carriage had been pungent from the succession of boiled eggs one passenger had consumed at regular intervals, and ripe with the sweat from another, and regardless of the fact that they had been sitting diametrically opposite each other, that smile had enveloped them in a bubble of their own. She'd found herself smiling back, something quite alien to her reserved nature. It should have been a warning that most certainly should have been heeded.

Kirstin's eyes snapped open. Cameron Dunbar's easy charm was of no interest to her. On the other hand, the letter which lay in her lap, whatever its mysterious request turned out to entail, might prove to be a very lucrative business opportunity. If she chose to accept it. Not that she would. She would be a fool to have anything to do with the man who had, albeit unwittingly, come so close to destroying her. She had saved herself, living by her considerable wits, reinventing herself, working hard to create the myth behind which she now flourished, to establish the flawless reputation she now enjoyed. There was no need to conjure up this ghost from her past.

On the other hand, business *was* business. Despite the fact that her alter ego was besieged every day with enquiries, such was the complex nature of her extremely discreet and niche service that only a very small percentage of these commissions could be accepted. Making the impossible possible required her to ensure that she never failed, but the need to make a handsome living that would safeguard her future meant she was not in a position to reject any approach out of hand.

But this particular prospect she most decidedly could not investigate, far less take on, for she could not possibly meet Cameron Dunbar face-to-face.

Yet it was impossible to deny that she wanted to, given the incontrovertible evidence that he was alive. She found herself intensely curious as to how his life had turned out, more than six years on, and what his circumstances were. And she wanted to know what desperate bind he had found himself in that he was compelled to seek her expensive and exclusive assistance. Not that he could have any idea at all who it was he'd actually written to.

Which thought gave her pause. A small smile

played on her lips as she poured herself a fresh cup of tea. Taking a sip, she nodded with satisfaction, relishing the smoky blend of this second cup. Cameron Dunbar had written to her alter ego. Even if he remembered Kirstin from that one night over six years ago, he had no reason to connect the two of them. And, actually, there was a reasonable chance that he wouldn't even remember that night, for a man as handsome and as charming and as charismatic as Cameron Dunbar must surely have had many such nights since. That illusion of intimacy between them, that feeling she'd had, the reason she'd allowed herself to be carried away, that *she* was special, that his behaviour was every bit as out of character as hers was exactly that, an illusion.

Seeing him again would change nothing, Kirstin told herself, but the logical approach which ruled her life, a legacy of her mathematician father, failed to hold sway. Her world was quite perfect, as far as she was concerned, and most importantly of all it was *hers*. She had no desire whatsoever to change it, and plenty of reasons to protect it from the eyes of the world. So it made no sense to her that from the minute she'd opened that letter a persistent niggling voice had been urging her to meet the owner of its signature.

Relentlessly analytical, Kirstin probed deeper into her own motives. It was not only blind curiosity which drove her, though that did play a small part. She wanted to prove to herself that the path she had chosen was the correct one. That her defiance of convention had been vindicated. That the smooth, impenetrable face she presented to society was the best form of protection from the judgement of the world for those she held most dear, allowing the life of splendid isolation which existed behind the façade to blossom.

There was no place there for Cameron Dunbar, but nor was there any room for doubts. Thanks to this letter, he'd temporarily escaped from the mental prison she'd locked him in. She needed to see him one more time, to assure herself that he was completed business, then put him back in his cell and this time throw away the key.

Besides, from a business perspective she had an obligation to meet him, at the very least to discover what it was he sought and whether she could provide it. If she could, well and good. She would match a deserving subject to his requirements and there would be no need for them ever to meet again. If not, there would be no harm done.

Kirstin set down her empty teacup. She folded

up the letter. All she had to do was to find a way for them to meet once, a meeting that would allow her to see him, to question him, but which would grant him no such reciprocal privileges.

The Procurer always dressed in black. Understated but expensive, her working clothes could be those of a rich widow or a discreet and exclusive Covent Garden madam—there had been a deliberate irony in Kirstin's choice of her assumed title. She was also aware that black outfits, severely tailored, suited her particular form of beauty. Though the notion of using seduction to achieve her goals repelled her, she would not be such a fool as to deny the power of a pretty face. It was unfair, but there were times, especially before her reputation was fully established, when her good looks had worked to her advantage, opening doors which might have otherwise remained firmly closed.

Today, despite the fact that her appearance was irrelevant, for Cameron Dunbar would not see her, she dressed with great care, scrutinising herself in the mirror. The black velvet military-style full-length pelisse with its double row of braid, tight sleeves and high collar showed off her tall, slim figure to perfection. Black buttoned half-boots, black gloves, a poke bonnet

trimmed with black silk and a large black velvet
muff completed her outfit. What little showed of
her face was pale, save for the pink blush of her
full lips, and the grey-blue of her heavy-lidded
eyes which even today betrayed nothing of the
turmoil raging in her head.

Kirstin smiled the enigmatic smile of The
Procurer, relieved to see her alter ego smiling
back at her. Cameron would not see her, but if
he did, he'd see what everyone did: The Procurer, a beautiful, aloof and powerful woman,
with an air of mystery about her, a woman with
a reputation for making the impossible possible.

Satisfied, she made her customary farewells
and left her house by the discreet side door. It
was a short walk to Soho Square, to a very different world from genteel Bloomsbury, though
The Procurer, whose business relied upon her
being extremely well connected, had several
dubious contacts who lived nearby. St Patrick's
Church was located on the corner.

Kirstin checked her enamelled pocket watch.
Five minutes to eleven, the appointed hour and
the first test she had set Cameron Dunbar, insisting he be prompt. This first hurdle she had,
with an unaccustomed nod towards letting fate
decide, set herself. If he was too early, or was

already inside the church, their meeting was not meant to be.

She waited, ignoring her racing heart, standing in the shade of one of the churchyard's leafless trees, a location she had earlier selected for its excellent view of the entrance porch. She would give him just five minutes' leeway. Her pocket watch gave off the tiny vibration which alerted her to the hour, but before she could begin to manage her disappointment at his failure to materialise he appeared.

From this distance, Cameron Dunbar looked unchanged. Tall and ramrod-straight, he still walked with that quick, purposeful stride which made the capes of his dark brown greatcoat fly out behind him. He wore fawn pantaloons, polished Hessians, and a tall beaver hat which covered his close-cropped hair so that she couldn't see if it was still as black as night.

He stopped at the steps of the church to check his watch, thus unknowingly passing her first test, and the breath caught in her throat at seeing his face in profile, the strong nose, the decided chin, the sharp planes of his cheekbones. He was still the most ridiculously handsome man she had ever seen. She was relieved, for the sake of her ability to breathe, that he was frowning rather than smiling as he snapped shut the cover of his watch, returned it to his pocket and entered the church.

Kirstin stood rooted to the spot, staring at the large wooden door of St Patrick's. Her heart was beating so fast she felt light-headed, her stomach churning, making her thankful she had decided against attempting breakfast. He was here. He was, even as she stood watching, making his way down the aisle, following her precise instructions, oblivious of the fact that she and The Procurer were one and the same.

Part of her wanted to flee. She had not expected this meeting to feel so momentous. She was afraid that she might betray herself with all the questions she dared not ask.

Did he remember that night at the posting house? Did he ever think of her? Did he ever wonder what had become of her? What direction had his own life taken?

This last question she, with her many contacts, could have easily found answers to, but until that letter had arrived she had preferred to know nothing, to persist with the illusion she had created that he did not exist.

But now! Oh, now she was afraid that this myriad of feelings she couldn't even begin to unravel, which she'd had no idea had been so long pent-up, would rise to the surface, would be betrayed in her voice. She was afraid that she would not be able to maintain her façade. She was afraid that he would recognise her. She was even more afraid that she would, in her emotional turmoil, spill out enough of the truth for him to guess the rest.

No! A thousand times no! The consequences could not be contemplated, never mind borne. She would never, ever be so foolish. The knowledge calmed her, allowing her rational self to take charge once more. She would satisfy her curiosity. She would learn enough of the man and his situation to ensure that there could never in the future be any seeds of doubt. She would decide whether his case could be taken on and, if so, she would find him a suitable helpmeet. Then she would never see him again.

The Procurer now firmly in charge, Kirstin squared her shoulders and made her way inside the church.

Cameron Dunbar stood in front of the baptismal font set in an alcove off a side aisle. The church appeared to be deserted, though the sweet scent of incense and candle wax from the morning mass hung in the air, along with the faint tang of the less than genteel congregation. Feeling slightly absurd, he made his way to the confessional boxes ranged on the left-hand side of the aisle, entering the last one as instructed.

The curtain on the other side of the grille was closed. He sat down in the gloomy confined space and prepared himself for disappointment. The Procurer's reputation for discretion was legendary, her reputation for being elusive equally so, but he had, nonetheless, expected to meet the woman face-to-face. Part of him questioned her very existence, wondering if she wasn't some elaborate hoax. Even if she was more than a myth, he wasn't at all convinced that he could bring himself to explain his business, especially such sensitive business, in such circumstances.

Sighing impatiently, Cameron tried to stretch his legs out in front of him, only to knock his knees against the door of the wooden box. If he had been able to think of another way to proceed, any other way at all, he would not be here. He hadn't even heard of the woman until two days ago. Max had assured him that everything said of her was true, that her reputation was well-deserved, but Max had also refused to divulge a single detail of his own involvement with her, save to say, primly, that the matter had been resolved satisfactorily.

Cameron trusted Max, and his problem was

urgent, becoming more urgent with every day that passed.

How long had he been sitting here? The blasted woman had been so precise about his own arrival she could at least have had the decency to be punctual herself. On the brink of breaking another of her list of instructions by peering out of the confessional into the church, he heard the tapping of heels on the aisle. Was it her? He listened, ears straining, as the footsteps approached. Stopped. And the door on the other side of the confessional was opened. There was a faint settling, the rustle of fabric as The Procurer sat down—assuming it was she and not a priest come to hear his confession.

The curtain on the other side was drawn back. It made little difference. Cameron could see nothing through the tiny holes in the pierced metal grille save a vague outline. But he could hear her breathing. And he could smell the damp on her clothes and the faint trace of perfume, not sickly attar of roses or lavender water, but a more exotic scent. Jasmine? Vanilla? What kind of woman was The Procurer? Max hadn't even told him whether she was young or old.

'Mr Dunbar?'

Her voice was low, barely more than a whisper. Cameron leaned into the grille and the shadow on the other side immediately pulled back. 'I am Cameron Dunbar,' he said. 'May I assume I'm addressing The Procurer?'

'You may.'

Again, she spoke softly. He could hear the swishing of her gown, as if she too was having difficulty in getting comfortable in the box. The situation was preposterous. Confessional or no, he wasn't about to spill his guts to a complete stranger whose face he wasn't even permitted to see.

'Listen to me, Madam Procurer,' Cameron said. 'I don't know what your usual format for these meetings is, but it does not suit me at all. Can we not talk face-to-face, like adults? This absurd situation hardly encourages trust, especially if I am to be your client.'

'No!' The single word came through the grille as a hiss, making him jerk his head away. 'I made the terms of this meeting very clear in my note, Mr Dunbar. If you break them—'

'Then you will not consider my case,' he snapped. Cameron was not used to being in a negotiation where he did not have the upper hand. But this situation was in every way unique. 'Very well,' he conceded stiffly, 'we will continue on your terms, madam.'

Silence. Then her face moved closer to the

grille. 'You must first tell me a little about your-self, Mr Dunbar.'

Though he must know nothing of *her*, it seemed. It stuck in his craw, but he could not risk alienating her. She would not, he sensed, give him a second chance, and if there was any possibility that she really was as good as Max averred, then he had no option but to play the game her way.

'If you're concerned that I can't afford your fee,' Cameron said dryly, 'then let me put your mind at rest. Whatever it is—and I've heard that it is anything from a small fortune to a king's ransom—then I have ample means.'

'A king's ransom?' the woman on the other side of the grille whispered. 'Now, that is an in-teresting proposition. What would you pay, Mr Cameron, to release the current King from his incarceration?'

'A deal more than I'd pay for his son were it he who were locked away. I'd much prefer a madman on the throne to a profligate popinjay. Though the truth is I doubt I'd put up a penny for either.'

'You are a republican, then, Mr Dunbar, like our friends in America?'

'I'm a pragmatist and a businessman, and I'm

wondering what relevance my politics can possibly have to the matter under discussion?'

His question caused her to pause. When she spoke again, her tone was conciliatory. 'I take many factors into consideration before agreeing to take on a new client. I was merely trying to establish what sort of man I would be dealing with.'

'An honest one. A desperate one, as you must know,' Cameron replied tersely. 'Else I would not have sought you out.'

'You have told no one about this meeting? Not even your wife...'

'I have no wife. I have spoken to no one,' Cameron replied, becoming impatient. 'You are not the only one who desires the utmost discretion.'

'You may trust in mine, Mr Dunbar.'

'So I've heard. You must not take it amiss if I tell you that I prefer to make my own mind up about that.'

'You are perfectly at liberty to do so. Though I would remind you that you came to me for help, not the other way around.'

'As a last resort. I am not a man who trusts anyone but himself with his affairs, but I cannot see a way to resolve this matter on my own. I desperately need your help.'

Her silence spoke for her. He must abandon his reservations, must throw caution to the wind and confide in this woman, no matter how much it went against the grain, else he would fail. The consequences of failure could not be contemplated.

'You must believe me when I tell you I do not exaggerate,' Cameron said. 'This could well be a matter of life and death.'

Many of the people who sought The Procurer's help thought the same, but there was a raw emotion in Cameron Dunbar's voice that gave Kirstin pause. Hearing his voice, knowing that the man who had quite literally changed the course of her life was just inches away, had been more overwhelming than she could ever have imagined.

The urge to throw back the door of the confessional, to confront him face-to-face, was almost irresistible. She had not expected the visceral reaction of her body to his voice, as if her skin and her muscles remembered him, and the memory triggered a longing to know him again.

She was frustrated by the grille which kept her identity concealed, for it kept him safe too, from her scrutiny. Images flashed into her mind when he spoke, vivid, shocking images of that night that brought colour flooding to her cheeks, for the woman in those images was a wanton who bore no relation to the woman she was now. This had been a mistake. She could not help Cameron Dunbar, yet she could not force herself to walk away.

'I will listen,' she found herself saying. 'Though I make no promises, I will hear you out.'

And so she did, with a growing sense of horror, as Cameron Dunbar told his story.

When he came to the end of it, Kirstin spoke without hesitation. 'I will find someone suitable who will assist you. Tell me where you may be reached.'

Chapter One

Handing her portmanteau to the hackney cab driver, Kirstin gave the address of the hotel where Cameron Dunbar had taken up residence. It was by no means the grandest establishment in London but it was, she knew, formidably expensive, not least because it had a reputation for offering the utmost discretion, which suited certain well-heeled guests. She wondered how Cameron had come to know of it. The friend he had mentioned, Max, who had recommended The Procurer's services, no doubt. She remembered Max. A difficult, but ultimately satisfying case, and the first one in which Marianne had been involved.

The cab rattled through the crowded streets and Kirstin's heart raced along with it. It was not too late to turn back, but she knew she would not. Her farewells had been said.

'We'll be fine,' Marianne had told her with a reassuring smile, and Kirstin hadn't doubted it, having come to trust her completely over the years in both business and personal terms. But it had been a painful parting all the same, astonishingly difficult to pin a smile to her face, to keep the tears from her eyes. 'Go,' Marianne had said, shooing her out through the door, 'and don't fret. Concentrate on completing this case, which sounds as if it will require all of even your considerable powers. It will be good for me to have the opportunity to be in charge, stand on my own two feet.'

Marianne, discreet as ever, had refrained from asking why Kirstin was taking on this case personally, something she had never done before, though it was Marianne who had, albeit inadvertently, put the idea into Kirstin's head, when she had pointed out that Kirstin possessed exactly the attributes the client had specified.

As The Procurer, Kirstin could have found another suitable female, she always did, but it would have taken time, and Cameron had none to spare. It therefore made perfect, logical sense for her to make the momentous decision to step into the breach, she told herself as the cab neared her destination. It was clear to her, from the sketchy information Cameron had provided, that the situation, though not necessarily a matter of life and death at present, could, if unresolved, easily become one.

Though had it been any man other than Cameron Dunbar who had come seeking her help would she have acted in a similar fashion? No. Kirstin's habit of being brutally honest with everyone, including herself, was ingrained. She would have moved heaven and earth to find a suitable female candidate, but she would not have dreamed of offering her own services. She was here to help Cameron Dunbar resolve his terrible predicament, but she was also here for her own reasons.

It meant depriving another woman of the opportunity to make a fresh start for herself, but after their wholly unsatisfactory meeting the day before yesterday, Kirstin had been forced to acknowledge that she too needed a fresh start. Far from letting her close the door on the man, it had merely served to let him stride through. She had to know more about him, and she had a very legitimate reason for needing to do so. The time would come when she could no longer field questions with feigned ignorance, and it was not in her nature to lie.

More than six years ago she had taken the decision to be true to herself, to live her life in her chosen way, independent of everyone, answerable to no one. In order to continue to do so she must reassure herself that her decision was the correct one, which meant excising Cameron Dunbar from the equation.

And keeping him completely in the dark while she did so.

Kirstin smiled grimly to herself. It was hardly a difficult task for one who made a living from extracting information while offering none in exchange. She must assume that Cameron would remember Kirstin Blair, but he would have no idea that she and The Procurer were one and the same. The Procurer's own unbreakable rules that no questions could be asked, no personal history need be revealed, would protect her, and the notion that she would ever confide in him of her own free will—it was ludicrous. Kirstin, as Marianne had once said, could give lessons in discretion to clams.

Reassured, confident in her decision, as the cab came to a halt and the hotel porter rushed to open the door, she turned her mind to the coming reunion, telling herself that her nerves were everything to do with her determination to prevent the matter becoming one of life and death, and nothing at all to do with the man she was going to be working with in close proximity.

In accordance with the letter from The Procurer, which had arrived yesterday, Cameron had reserved a suite of rooms in the name of Mrs Collins. He had instructed the Head Porter to inform him when this lady, whom he was to claim as an old acquaintance, arrived, and to issue her with an invitation to take tea with him.

His own suite overlooked the front of the hotel. Unable to concentrate on the stack of business letters which had been forwarded from his Glasgow office, Cameron had spent the last two hours gazing out of the window, monitoring every arrival.

He had no idea what to expect of Mrs Collins, though he had formed a picture in his head of a smart, middle-aged woman with faded hair, a high brow, intelligent eyes. The relic of a man of the church, perhaps, who had worked in London's slums, or with London's fallen women, and was therefore no stranger to the city's seamy underbelly, but who had also solicited London's society for alms. At ease with the full gamut of society, Mrs Collins would be tough but compassionate, not easily shocked. The type of woman who could be trusted with confidences and who would not judge. Since her husband had died, she would have been continuing with his good works, saving lost souls, but she'd be finding her widowed state confining, he reckoned, and since she'd always had a penchant for charades, which they'd played in the vicarage every Christmas, the need to assume various disguises would appeal to her.

Cameron nodded with satisfaction. An unusual combination of skills, no doubt about it, which made it all the more surprising that The Procurer had found someone to suit his requirements so quickly.

He leant his head against the glass of the tall window, impatient for her to arrive. The ancient female dressed in a sickly shade of green matching the parrot she carried in a cage, whom he had watched half an hour ago emerge from a postchaise, could not be her. Nor could this fashionable young lady arriving with her maid, one of those ridiculous little dogs that looked like a powder puff clutched in her arms. A hackney cab pulled up next, and a slim female figure emerged, dressed in a white gown with a red spencer. She had her back to him as she waited for her luggage to be removed, yet he had the impression of elegance, could see from the respect she commanded from the driver and from the porter rushing to meet her, the assurance with which she walked, that she was a woman of consequence.

Intriguing, but clearly not his Mrs Collins.

Cameron turned his back on the window, inspecting his pocket watch, debating with himself on whether to order a pot of coffee. A rap on the door made him throw it open impatiently, thinking it was the arrival of yet more business papers.

'I've been sent to tell you that your acquaintance has arrived,' the messenger boy said. 'She's happy to hear that you are staying in the hotel, she says, and she would be delighted to join you for tea.'

'Are you sure? When did she get here?'

But the boy shook his head. 'Nobody tells me nuffin', save me message. Head Porter says to expect her with the tea directly,' he said. 'If there's nuffin' else...?' He waited expectantly.

Cameron sighed and handed over a shilling. He must have missed Mrs Collins's arrival. Or perhaps there was a side entrance.

A few minutes later there was another soft tap on the door. He opened the door to be confronted with the elegant woman who had emerged from the hackney cab.

His jaw dropped, his stomach flipped, for he recognised her immediately.

'Kirstin.'

He blinked, but she was still there, not a ghost from his past but a real woman, flesh and blood and even more beautiful than he remembered.

'Kirstin,' Cameron repeated, his shock apparent in his voice. 'What on earth are you doing here?'

'I wondered if you'd recognise me after all this time. May I come in?'

Her tone was cool. She was not at all surprised to see him. As she stepped past him into the room, and a servant appeared behind her with a tea tray, he realised that *she* must be the woman sent to him by The Procurer. Stunned, Cameron watched in silence as the tea tray was set down, reaching automatically into his pocket to tip the servant as Kirstin busied herself, warming the pot and setting out the cups. He tried to reconcile the dazzling vision before him with Mrs Collins, but the vicar's wife of his imagination had already vanished, never to be seen again.

Still quite dazed, he sat down opposite her. She had opened the tea caddy, was taking a delicate sniff of the leaves, her finely arched brows rising in what seemed to be surprised approval. Her face, framed by her bonnet, was breathtaking in its flawlessness. Alabaster skin. Blue-black hair. Heavy-lidded eyes that were a smoky, blue-grey. A generous mouth with a full bottom lip, the colour of almost ripe raspberries.

Yet, he remembered, it had not been the perfection of her face which had drawn him to her all those years ago, it had been the intelligence slumbering beneath those heavy lids, the ironic twist to her smile when their eyes met in that crowded carriage, and that air she still exuded, of aloofness, almost haughtiness, that was both intimidating and alluring. He had suspected fire lay beneath that cool exterior, and he hadn't been disappointed.

A vision of that extraordinary night over six years ago flooded his mind. There had been other women since, though none of late, and never another night like that one. He had come to think of it as a half-remembered dream, a fantasy, the product of extreme circumstances that he would never experience again.

He wasn't at all sure what he thought of Kirstin walking so calmly back into his life, especially when he was in the midst of a crisis. Were they to pretend that they had no history? It had been such a fleeting moment in time, with no bearing on the years after, save for the unsettling, incomparable memory. Cameron supposed that it ought to be possible to pretend it had not happened, but as he looked at her, appalled to discover the stirrings of desire that the memories evoked, he knew he was deluding himself.

'Cream or lemon?' Kirstin asked.

'Lemon,' he answered, though he habitually drank his tea black and well stewed, a legacy of his early days on-board ship.

He held out his hand for the saucer, but instead she placed it on the table in front of him, drawing an invisible line between them and bringing him to his senses. Whether they acknowledged their history or not, it had no bearing on the reason she was here now.

'Are you really the woman chosen for me by this infamous Procurer? Do you know what it is I need from you? What has she told you of me? The matter—'

'Is one of life and death, you believe,' Kirstin answered gravely. 'To answer your questions in order. Yes, I am here at the behest of The Procurer. She has outlined your situation, though I will need to hear the details from you. I know nothing of your circumstances, save what you have told her.'

'She has told me nothing at all of you. Is Collins your married name?'

'My name is what it has always been. Kirstin Blair.'

'You're not married?' Cameron asked. It was hardly relevant, yet when she shook her head he was unaccountably pleased as well as surprised. Because it would be impossible for them to proceed if there was a husband in the background, or worse in the foreground, he told himself. 'I'm not married either,' he said.

She nodded casually at that. Because she already knew from The Procurer? Or because she had deduced as much from his appearance? Or because she was indifferent? This last option, Cameron discovered, was the least palatable.

He began to be irked by her impassive exterior. 'You do remember me, I take it?' he demanded. 'That night...'

The faintest tinge of colour stole over her cheeks. She did not flinch, but he saw the movement at her throat as she swallowed. 'This is hardly the time to reminisce.'

Their gazes snagged. He could have sworn, in that moment, that she felt it, the almost physical pull of attraction, that strange empathy that they had both succumbed to that night. Then Kirstin broke the spell.

'It was more than six years ago,' she said pointedly.

'I am perfectly aware of how many years have elapsed,' Cameron snapped.

He had never disclosed his reasons for having made that journey to anyone. He had been interested only in trying to forget all that he had left behind during the trip south, and he had succeeded too, temporarily losing himself and his pain in Kirstin. He'd thought the mental scar healed.

It had been, until Louise Ferguson had written to him as a last resort, begging for his help in the name of the very ties she'd so vehemently denied before. Compassion for her plight diluted his mixture of anger and disappointment that she should turn to him only *in extremis*. He was long past imagining they could be anything to each other, but it forced him to acknowledge that he had, albeit unwittingly, been the root cause of her past unhappiness. There was a debt to be paid.

Doing what she asked would salve his conscience and allow him to put the matter to bed once and for all. He wouldn't get another opportunity, and he needed Kirstin to help him, so he couldn't afford to allow their brief encounter to get in the way. It was the future which mattered.

Cameron swallowed his tea. It was cold, and far too floral for his taste. He made a mental note to stick to coffee, and set the cup down with a clatter.

'I recall, now, that your Procurer's terms specify that there should be no questions asked, either you of me, or me of you. It's a sensible rule and allows us to concentrate on the matter that brought us both here,' he said, deliberately brusque as he leaned back in his seat, crossing his ankles. 'However, I am paying a small fortune for your assistance. I think that gives me the right to ask what it is about yourself that makes The

Procurer so certain you will suit my extremely demanding, if not unique, set of requirements.'

Kirstin poured herself a second cup of tea, deliberately avoiding Cameron's gaze. It was more taxing than it ought to be to maintain her poise, but she was determined he would not see how much this face-to-face encounter was affecting her. Those eyes of his, such a deep, dark brown. She could feel them on her now, sense his rising impatience. An understandable emotion, in the circumstances. Extremely understandable, she thought guiltily.

Determined to keep her mind focused on the matter at hand, she peeled off her gloves and untied her bonnet. Cameron had every reason to question her suitability. Her first task was to reassure him—which fortunately she could easily do, by telling him the truth.

'I have worked closely with The Procurer for many years. I know her and her business intimately,' she said. 'She requires the utmost discretion from her employees, and has never had the slightest cause to question mine. As her trusted assistant, I have access to her extensive network of contacts. I am required to mix with a most—eclectic, I think would be the best description—range of characters, in a number of guises. I have the facility to win over the most unlikely people, from all walks of life, and extract confidences from them. You could call it the quality of a chameleon.'

She permitted herself a thin smile.

'Whatever you wish to call it, the net result is that I am expert at finding people who do not wish to be found. I am also, as you requested, a woman of good standing, and so able to enquire after the whereabouts of a young and innocent girl without it being assumed my purpose is nefarious—something you could not do. Though I must ask you, Mr Dunbar, if you have considered the possibility that she has already encountered another with just such nefarious intent?'

Across from her, Cameron was frowning deeply. 'I have not said as much to the young lady's mother, but it seems to me, unfortunately, a possibility which must be investigated.'

'I am relieved to hear that you have not discounted this.'

'I'm more or less a stranger to London, but I'm a man of the world.'

'Then we shall deal well together, for I am a woman who prefers that a spade should be called a spade.'

He laughed shortly. 'Though you look like a woman whose sensibilities are very easily offended.'

'Precisely my intention when I assumed this guise. I have dressed as a lady of quality, because only a lady of quality would be accepted as a guest in this hotel, Mr Dunbar. One should not judge by appearances, though fortunately, for the success of our mission, many people do.'

'Do you think we'll be successful?'

Though he asked her coolly enough, there was just a hint of desperation in his tone. With difficulty, Kirstin resisted the urge to cover his hand, one of the few gestures of sympathy she ever allowed herself to bestow. It was even more difficult to resist the urge to reassure him, but that was one rule she never broke.

'I will do everything in my power to help you, but it has been over a week now. You must face the fact that the damage may already have been done.'

The pain in his eyes told her he had already been down that path, far further than even she had. 'We must succeed,' he said. 'Mrs Ferguson is relying on me to find her daughter.'

'She cannot possibly blame you if you fail.'

'Believe me, she will, and she won't give me another chance.'

Kirstin frowned, wondering if she had missed something significant he had said in the confessional two days ago, but her memory was prodigious, she missed nothing. 'Another chance to do what?'

'Pay my dues.' Cameron dug his hands into the pockets of his coat, looking deeply uncomfortable. 'The woman believes that I owe her, and in all conscience I think she has a point. If I can restore her daughter to her then we can both get on with our lives unencumbered.'

Only now did his mode of address strike her as odd. She should have noticed it before. She tried to recall what Cameron had told The Procurer in the confessional, and realised he'd said nothing at all of his relationship with Mrs Ferguson and her daughter, save to inform her of the blood tie.

'You don't know your sister well enough to call her by her first name, yet she turned to you when her daughter disappeared?'

Cameron got to his feet, making for the window, where he leaned his shoulder against the shutter. 'Mrs Ferguson is only my half-sister, making Philippa my half-niece, if there is such a thing.'

'You do realise that a failure to disclose salient facts renders your contract with The Procurer null and void?'

He rolled his eyes, but resumed his seat opposite her. 'It's a long story, and I can't see how it's relevant, but until Philippa disappeared I had met her mother only once. I've never set eyes on Philippa myself. This is her.' He produced a miniature, which depicted an insipid girl with hair the colour of night. 'There's no portrait of the maid, but according to Mrs Ferguson she is a pert chit with ginger hair, from which we can infer a pretty redhead.'

'You think that if you can restore Philippa to her mother, your sister will be grateful enough to—to nullify some previous debt?'

'It's not about money.'

No, nothing so simple, Kirstin deduced from the slash of colour in his cheeks. She would have liked to question him further but, like Cameron, she was bound by her own rules. There was a very big difference between history which had a bearing on this case, and bald curiosity.

'And if you fail?' she asked carefully.

'I cannot fail. I've never met the girl, but having seen the mother—she's in a terrible state— I can't let her down. Can you imagine what she must be feeling, to have her only child disappear like that, from right under her nose?'

A shiver ran down Kirstin's spine. 'No,' she said, catching herself, 'I do not want to imagine, and nor does it serve any purpose. What we must do is try to put an end to her suffering. That is why I'm here.'

'I was, as you'll have noticed, somewhat taken aback when you turned up, but I'm very glad you did, Kirstin—Miss Blair—Mrs Collins. Curse it, I've no idea what to call you.'

He smiled at her then. It was a rueful smile. A smile that acknowledged their brief shared history, and acknowledged, too, that it was exactly that. History. Yet that smile, the warmth of it, the way it wrapped itself round her, brought it all back as if it were yesterday...

December 1812, Carlisle

He had boarded, as she had, at the White Hart Inn in the Grassmarket at Edinburgh, jumping into the coach at the last minute, squashing himself into the far corner, apologising to the stout man next to him, though it was he who was overflowing both sides of his allotted seat. The new arrival was swathed in a many-caped greatcoat, which he was forced to gather tightly around him. His legs were encased in a pair of black boots with brown tops, still highly polished, no mean feat having navigated Edinburgh's filthy streets. When he took off his hat, clasping it on his lap, the woman sitting next to Kirstin gasped. The man looked up—not at the woman whom Kirstin had decided must be a housekeeper en route to a new appointment, but directly at Kirstin. In that brief glimpse, before she dropped her gaze deliberately to her lap, she saw enough to understand the housekeeper's reaction, but she was irked and no little embarrassed, mortified that he might think the involuntary reaction had emanated from her. He was handsome, far too handsome to be unaware of the fact, and no doubt accustomed to having women of all ages gasping at him. Kirstin wasn't about to add to their number.

But as the coach lumbered across the cobblestones of the Grassmarket towards the city gate and the road south, she found herself sneaking glances at the Adonis in the far corner. He sat with his head back on the squabs, his eyes closed, but the grim line of his mouth told her, as did the rigid way he held his body, that he was not asleep. His hair was black, close-cropped, the colour like her own, showing his Celtic origins. He had a high brow, faintly lined, his skin tanned, not the weather-beaten hue of a Scot who worked outdoors in the assorted forms of rain which dominated the four seasons, but a glow borne of sunshine and far warmer climes. His accent had been Scots, west coast rather than east, she thought, it was difficult to judge from his few terse words, but he obviously spent a deal of his time abroad. To his advantage too, judging by his attire, which was expensive yet understated. A businessman of some sort, she conjectured, discounting the possibility that he was a man of leisure, for such a man would certainly not travel on a public coach. This gentleman was obviously accustomed to it, managing to stay quite still in his seat despite the rattles and jolts of the cumbersome vehicle that had everyone else falling over each other.

She wondered what it was that he was thinking to make such a grim line of his mouth. Was he in pain? Angry? No, his grasp on his hat was light enough. Upset? There was a cleft in his chin, which was rather pointed than square. It was the contrasts, Kirstin decided, which made him so handsome—the delicate shape of his face, the strong nose, the sharp cheekbones. His brows were fierce. She was speculating on the exact colour of his eyes when they flew open and met her gaze. Dark brown, like melting chocolate, Kirstin thought fancifully before she caught herself, and was about to look away when he smiled directly at her, and she had the most absurd sensation that they were quite alone. She smiled back before she could stop herself. It was the housekeeper's disapproving cluck which recalled her to her surroundings.

For the next few miles, Kirstin doggedly occupied herself with weaving histories for the other passengers, a game she'd played to pass the time ever since she was a lass sitting at the back of her father's mathematical lectures, too young to understand the subject matter which would later enthral her, for she had inherited his logical brain, so instead occupying herself by studying his students. The tiniest details were her raw materials: the type of pencil they used to take notes or the paper on which they wrote; whether a muffler was hand-knitted or silk; which young men wore starched collars and cuffs, and which wore paper; those who fell asleep because they'd spent the night revelling, and those who struggled to keep their eyes open because they worked all hours to pay for their studies.

As the coach proceeded on its journey south, this pastime kept Kirstin's eyes directed anywhere but at the far too handsome and interesting man for the most part, though several times, when she strayed, she met his studied gaze. She was used to men looking at her, admiring and lascivious in equal measure, but this man seemed interested in a different way. Was he speculating about her reasons for making this long journey unaccompanied? Was he wondering who she'd left behind, who was waiting at the other end to meet her? No one, and no one, she could have told him. He wasn't really interested, why should he be, it was wishful thinking on her part, but she decided to indulge in it all the same, because what was the harm, when her entire life now lay before her, waiting on her choosing her path?

She had taken the bold step of quitting Edinburgh, with no ties to keep her there now that Papa had given up his long struggle with illness. She had nothing save his small legacy and her wits to live on, and only the kernel of an idea, a chance remark made by her friend Ewan, who was now so happily married to Jennifer. She'd laughed, dismissing their praise for her matchmaking skills, for she had never intended them to make a match, and had seen them merely as the ideal solution to each other's practical problems. Was she a fool to think that she could assist others in a similar fashion?

Her excitement gave way, as it had regularly done since she'd started planning this new life of hers, to trepidation. How was she to go about setting up such a bespoke service? With neither reputation nor references, save the unintended one she'd extracted from Ewan, how was she to persuade anyone to employ her? She closed her eyes, reminding herself of the qualities which would make her successful, reciting them like an incantation. Trepidation gave away to anticipation once more. She opened her eyes to find the handsome man staring at her brazenly and this time she responded, smiling back, because there was no harm in it, and because they'd never see each other again after today, and because it gave her the illusion that she was not completely and utterly alone.

They had crossed the border from Scotland into England well over an hour ago. It was a mere ten miles from Gretna Green to Carlisle, but the snow was falling thick and fast now, making progress excruciatingly slow. Through the draughty carriage window she could see the huge flakes melting as soon as they touched the ground, for it was not cold enough for snow to lie, though it was making a quagmire of the road, a white curtain obscuring the driver's view.

The coach hit a rut, rocked precariously, jolted forward, rocked the other way, then came to a sudden halt, catching everyone by surprise, throwing them all from their seats. Save, Kirstin noticed dazedly, the Adonis, who was wrenching the door open and leaping lithely down. Seconds later her own door was flung open and she was pulled from the chaos in the coach into a pair of strong arms.

He did not set her down immediately. He held her high against his chest, carrying her bodily away from the coach, from the plunging horses and the frightened cries of the passengers, to the side of the road. And still he held her, the snow falling thickly around them. 'Are you hurt?' he asked, frowning anxiously down at her.

Kirstin shook her head. 'No, and I'm perfectly capable of standing on my own two feet, thank you very much.'

He let her go reluctantly, it seemed to her, though her irrepressibly logical brain told her she was being foolish. His hands rested on her arms, as if she required his support, and though she was quite unshaken and perfectly capable of supporting herself, she made no move to free herself as she ought. It was possible, she discovered with some surprise, to think one thing and to do quite another. 'How soon, do you think,' she asked, 'will we be able to resume our journey?'

He shrugged his shoulders. 'Depends on the damage, but probably not till morning. Luckily we're only a short walk from the next posting house. They have rooms there—not smart, but clean enough.'

'You've stayed there before?'

'A number of times, travelling on business. Likely they'll be able to repair any damage to the coach there too, and you'll be on your way in the morning.'

'Won't you be travelling with us?'

'I'm Liverpool bound. I have a ship waiting— though it won't wait, that's the trouble. I'll have to hire a private chaise if I'm to get there in time now.'

'So you are a businessman with foreign interests,' Kirstin said, nodding with satisfaction. 'I had guessed as much.'

'Am I so transparent?'

'Only when you choose to be, I suspect. And I am, if I may be so bold, a very good reader of small clues. Your clothing, your tan, your familiarity with public transport, though I'm not sure, now I think about it, why you should be taking a coach from Edinburgh to Liverpool. Assuming you had just concluded business in the port of Leith, would it not have been quicker to go by boat?'

'Now there, your logical assumptions have let you down, I'm afraid. I had no business in Leith.'

'Oh.' Kirstin felt quite deflated. 'I was so sure—what then brought you to Edinburgh? Your accent is faint, but I am pretty certain it is Glaswegian, Mr—I'm sorry, I don't know your name.'

'Dunbar. It is Cameron Dunbar,' he answered,

but his attention was no longer on her. He was frowning, the tension she had noticed when first he boarded the coach thinning his mouth.

'I beg your pardon if my question was unwelcome,' Kirstin said. 'I didn't mean to sound so inquisitive.'

He blinked, shook his head, returned his gaze to hers. 'It was a—a personal matter, which brought me to Edinburgh.' He forced a smile, a painful one. 'I'd rather not talk about it.'

'Of course not. I'm very sorry.' Embarrassed and at the same time disappointed, Kirstin stepped away, turning her back on Cameron Dunbar and her attention to the coach, where the remaining passengers were being helped out by the driver and the groom. 'We should go and help them, let them know that there's an inn nearby.'

'Leave them to it.' He spoke brusquely, caught her arm, then dropped it with a muttered apology. 'Excuse me. I only meant that there's no need for you to become embroiled. The coachman is more than capable. Come, I'll walk with you to the inn, then you can have your pick of the rooms before the rush.'

'Thank you, Mr Dunbar, that is very thoughtful.'

'It's not really. I'm being selfish, for it means I can have your company to myself for a little longer. I don't mean—I beg pardon, I didn't mean to presume—I only meant…'

He broke off, shaking his head, looking confused. Whatever this personal business of his had been, it had unsettled him. 'I suspect you're not quite at your normal self-assured best,' Kirstin said, tucking her hand into his arm.

'No.' She was granted a crooked smile. 'I'm not.'

'No more am I, to tell the truth. This journey to London I'm making, it's going to be the start of a whole new life for me, and there's a part of me absolutely terrified that I'll make a mess of it. Though of course,' Kirstin added hastily, 'my feelings are perfectly logical since the odds are stacked against me.'

Cameron Dunbar laughed shortly. 'Has anyone ever told you that you're a very unusual woman?'

'I think you told me so just a moment ago. Though actually what you said was that I was surprising.'

'You are both. And a very welcome distraction too, if you don't mind me saying.'

'Compliments are most welcome, just at the moment.'

They walked on in the growing gloom, through the sleet and the mud. She could not read his ex-

pression, though she sensed he was frowning.
Twice, he gave the oddest little shake of his head,
as if trying to cast off unwelcome thoughts. Re-
lating to this painful personal business of his, she
assumed. It seemed that beauty in a man was no
more a guarantee of happiness than it was in a
woman. There was, of course, no reason to assume it would be. She had not thought she could
be so facile.

As they approached the welcome lights of the
inn, and a dog started barking, Cameron Dunbar stopped, turning towards her. She assumed it
was to bid her goodnight. He once again proved
her wrong. 'Since you are in the market for compliments, I find your conversation both endear-
ing and distracting, and I'm very much in need
of distraction right now. Would it be too much
of a liberty to ask you to take dinner with me?'

It would be wrong of her to dine alone with
a complete stranger, she knew that. But she too
was a complete stranger to him. And he was not
the only one in need of distraction. 'I'd like that
very much,' she said simply.

'Thank you, Mrs—Miss—I'm sorry, I haven't
even asked your name.'

'It is Blair. Miss Kirstin Blair.'

Chapter Two

London, February 1819

Kirstin shook herself from her reverie. Now was categorically neither the time nor place to recollect the past. Cameron was staring at her, his brow lifted quizzically. 'I'm sorry,' she said, 'what did you ask me?'

'How should I address you?'

'Kirstin will be fine, at least while we are alone. In company—well, it very much depends on the company, and that is likely to be rather varied.'

The wintery sun streaming through the windows of Cameron's hotel suite illuminated the dark shadows under his eyes, the furrow of lines between his brows, the grooves at the sides of his mouth. His skin was drawn tight around his eyes. Pity stirred in her breast. She knew little of him, but such a successful businessman as he must be finding his helplessness difficult to endure. Another man would have blundered on, useless if determined, too proud to ask for help, but Cameron Dunbar had quickly put his own ego aside. She admired him very much for that.

Once again, the urge to touch his hand was overpowering but it was not sympathy he needed. 'We must devise a plan,' Kirstin said briskly. 'Though I do not recommend you share the details with Mrs Ferguson, you will want to reassure her that you are taking decisive action. But first, let us review what you know.'

'I know nothing more than what I've already told The Procurer, and I presume she has already passed that on to you?'

'Of course, but it is my experience, Mr Dunbar, that details often emerge in the retelling that have been overlooked.'

'Can't you bring yourself to call me Cameron?'

No, she wanted to say, because it implied an intimacy she didn't want to acknowledge. But if she refused, he'd wonder why and she didn't want him speculating. So Kirstin shrugged, as if it mattered not a whit. 'Very well, *Cameron*, let us start with your initial involvement in this matter. Mrs Ferguson wrote to you, I believe?'

'An express delivery to my main office in Glasgow. The one piece of good fortune in this whole sorry affair is that her letter found me there. I spend a great deal of my time abroad, looking after my various business concerns, though Glasgow is my home, in as much as any place is. I set off for London immediately, catching the mail coach which had delivered my letter on its return journey, but even so, it has now been over a week since Miss Ferguson disappeared with her maid from the Spaniard's Inn at Hampstead, the last stop on their journey south. Unlike me, Mrs Ferguson's preference is to travel in easy stages, and she certainly wasn't going to take the risk of crossing the heath at night. Little did she know it would have been safer to risk a highwayman than...' He cursed under his breath. '...than whatever befell the pair of them. Two young lassies with not a clue of the ways of the world. It doesn't bear thinking of.'

'Then don't, for it serves no purpose save to upset you. Let's concentrate on the cold hard facts.'

Cameron grinned. 'A woman after my own heart.'

Caught unawares, Kirstin only just bit back her answering smile. 'A woman after saving your niece's life, and that of her maid,' she said tersely. 'Recount for me now, as accurately as you can, what Mrs Ferguson told you of the events of that night.'

'She dined with Philippa in a private salon. She had a headache from the day's journey. Philippa saw her to her room and brought her a sleeping draught.'

'Did Mrs Ferguson request that she do so?'

'She did. She was in the habit of taking one every night. Apparently she is a very poor traveller. If Philippa planned to run off,' Cameron said, grimacing, 'she could easily have done so, knowing she could rely on her mother being comatose. A possibility Mrs Ferguson is all too alive to.'

'And which must be consuming her with guilt,' Kirstin said. 'If she'd been awake, she might have heard that something was afoot, yes?'

'Her exact words.'

'I will need to hear them from her own lips,' Kirstin said. 'If you are more or less a stranger to her, it's possible there are salient facts she's unwilling to reveal to you.'

'Even though it might jeopardise my chances of finding her daughter?' Cameron shook his head.

'I'm sorry, but it is vital that we are blunt with each other—you don't know her, Mr—Cameron. She could be concealing something.'

He got to his feet to shovel a heap of fresh coals onto the fire. 'You're right, I don't know her, but I'm a fair judge of character. Her desperation to find Philippa is genuine. If she's concealing anything then she's completely unaware of the fact. Which was your point, I know,' he added ruefully. 'Very well. Item one on our list, a meeting with Mrs Ferguson. She's lodging at a friend's house—the friend is in Paris—as she regularly does, apparently, on her shopping trips to London.'

'Thank you.'

'But let me make something clear, Kirstin.' He sat down again on the sofa beside her, his knees brushing her skirts. She inched away from him, an action he noted with a sardonic lift of his brow. She'd forgotten that he was as observant as she. 'I need your help. In your areas of expertise, I will bow to your experience. That is what I'm paying for. But ultimately, I am in charge.'

She stiffened. 'I am aware that you are the client.'

He laughed, shaking his head. 'A client who trusts your professional judgement implicitly.'

'In certain areas.'

He tilted his head to one side, studying her as if he was seeing her for the first time. She stared back at him, her brow faintly raised, subjecting him to her well-practised piercing look which never failed to intimidate. Until now. 'Being given orders does not sit well with you,' he said.

'Nor you, I suspect.'

'Your suspicion would be well founded. We will work most effectively if we collaborate, but the final decision will be mine. Those are the rules of engagement I agreed with The Procurer.'

'Then those are the rules we will abide by.'

'I am relieved to hear you say so. Have you always worked for her? Since coming to London, I mean? You never did tell me what your plans were, though you told me you had some.' Cameron held up his hands. 'I know, I know, no questions.' He sighed. 'Look, this situation might be familiar territory for you, charging to someone's aid, taking control, doing whatever it is you do, but I feel as if I've walked into someone else's dream. Or nightmare, more like.'

'Thank you kindly for the compliment.'

'You know what I mean, Kirstin.'

She could tell him it was the same for her, but it was hardly what The Procurer would call a salient fact. Instead, she finally allowed herself, for just a fleeting second, to touch his hand. 'You realise the odds suggest that, even if we find the girls, they may not be unscathed.'

Cameron flinched. 'You take a very grim view of the situation.'

'I find that it is better to err on the side of pessimism.'

'Sparing yourself the possibility of disappointment? So you prefer to stack the odds? Isn't it against your mathematical principles to do so?'

This time it was she who flinched. That Cameron had recognised her was not really surprising. That he recalled anything at all of their conversation though—now, that was unsettling. She didn't want him to remember her, unguarded, confiding, such an aberration of her character before and since. As to her mathematical principles, she had discovered for herself that life was no respecter of those. 'It is not a question of disappointment, rather one of preparing to deal with the worst,' Kirstin said.

Cameron slumped back on the sofa, looking quite exhausted. His eyelids fluttered closed. His lashes were coal black, shorter than hers, but thicker. Though he had shaved this morning, there was already a bluish shadow on his chin. A lick of hair stood up from his brow, marring the smooth perfection of his crop and in doing so managing to make the perfection of his countenance even more breathtaking. In repose, his lips looked sculpted. They had been soft, the first time he'd kissed her. Gentle. Persuasive. She had tried other kisses since, but none compared with the memory of his, so she'd stopped trying. At her age and in her circumstances she ought to be past wanting any kisses. Looking at Cameron's mouth, those perfectly moulded lips, Kirstin found to her horror that she was wrong.

She looked away hastily as he opened his eyes. 'You are understandably weary. We will continue this conversation later, when I am settled in my own suite.' She made to get to her feet, but he was too quick for her, grabbing her wrist.

'I *am* tired, and the many dire possibilities regarding what fate befell Philippa and Jeannie, her maid, *are* grim indeed. I've contemplated them, Kirstin, trust me. But life has a way of defying the odds. I will find them. I have to find them, because failure is not an option. So we will keep searching until we do. Those are my terms. Under The Procurer's rules, you are obliged to adhere to them. Go away, unpack, think about it. And if you aren't willing to make that commitment, then you can pack up again and go.'

Cameron closed the door on Kirstin, and immediately rang the bell. He needed strong coffee, and a good deal of it. If ever there was a time for ordered thoughts, calm thinking, it was now, and his head was all over the place. Retreating to his bedchamber, he splashed cold water over his face, automatically smoothing back the cow's lick in his hair. His face gazed back at him in the mirror as he rubbed himself dry with a towel. He looked a good five years older than his thirty-five years, thanks to the tribulations of the last week, while Kirstin seemed hardly to have aged at all since he'd first met her.

A knock on the door heralded his much needed coffee. He sat down to inhale the first cup in one scalding gulp and immediately poured another, the perfect antidote to the flowery water that passed for tea in this hotel. Though Kirstin had seemed to enjoy it, and by the way she'd oh-so-delicately sniffed the leaves, it would seem she considered herself a bit of a connoisseur. What age would she be now? Thirty-one, -two? It didn't seem possible, but he clearly remembered her telling him the night they met that she was twenty-five.

She *had* changed. She had not aged, precisely, there were no lines marring the perfection of her skin, but there was something about her, an edge to her that hadn't been there before. Experience, he supposed—though what kind? She was not married. It could not possibly be for want of being asked. More likely her very obvious desire to do no one's bidding but her own had kept her single. Bloody hell, but she was as prickly as a hedgehog. It would take a brave man to get anywhere near her. She'd been very different that night. Excited, anxious, elated, frightened in turn. In extremis.

As had he been, for very different reasons— emotionally battered, the hopes which had been so recently raised, quite devastated. He'd barely had a chance to come to terms with what he'd read in that letter, only to be told that there could be no coming to terms, no answers to his questions. Not ever. The future had taken on a bleakness he'd not known since childhood. Kirstin had been like a beacon of light, smiling at him across the coach. He couldn't exactly credit her for turning his thinking around, but she'd been a respite that night, and her enthusiasm, her desire to embrace her future—yes, some of that had rubbed off on him. He'd used the memory of their moment out of time as a talisman in the months that followed. It had sustained him through some dark times.

What would she say if he told her so? She'd be too dumbfounded to say anything, most likely. They had quite literally been ships that passed in the night. She had made it very clear this afternoon that she didn't want to remember anything about it. Yet still she had come here, at The Procurer's behest, knowing she'd be meeting him. Was she simply indifferent, intent upon doing a job for which she would be handsomely rewarded? She was expensively garbed. She had done well for herself, which wasn't surprising. He'd never met any woman, before or since, quite like her. She was exactly what he needed. What's more, he was confident that she'd do exactly what she promised, everything in her power to help him. If she chose to stay.

Cameron cursed. He shouldn't have issued her with an ultimatum, it was guaranteed to rile a woman like her, so reluctant to take orders from anyone! Yet he'd been right to say what he did, and he had the right, it was written into his contract with The Procurer. If he must have an accomplice, and he was long past the stage where he refused to acknowledge he did, then his accomplice must be wholeheartedly committed to finding Philippa and her maid. Whatever state they found them in, they *would* find them.

He poured himself the treacly residue of the coffee. There was a plate of biscuits on the tray. He bit into one, screwed up his face, coughing as he forced it down. Coconut. He couldn't think of a flavour he detested more, though he must be in a minority, judging by the small fortune he'd made importing the dried version of it in the last year. If they were using it here for the biscuits, it must be getting even more popular. He made a mental note to ask his agent to organise another shipment, then he retrieved his leather-bound notebook from the stack of business papers and set his mind to reviewing his notes. Every little detail mattered, Kirstin had said. When she returned, when she accepted his terms, as she must do, for he could not fail at this first hurdle, then he would be as well-prepared as it was possible to be. Unlike all those years ago.

December 1812, Carlisle

The snow, Cameron saw with relief, was turning to rain outside the window of the private salon. On top of everything else, missing his ship from Liverpool would be the final straw. These last few weeks, since that life-changing letter had finally reached him, having followed him halfway round the world and back again, he felt as if he'd been through the mill. And in the end it hadn't turned out to be a life-changing letter after all. Not a new chapter in his life, but a book closed for ever.

'Ach!'

It wasn't like him to be so fanciful. Leaning his head against the thick window pane, he screwed his eyes shut in an effort to block out the memory, but the words echoed in his head all the same.

You cast a blight over my childhood. You were responsible for making my father's life a misery. I don't want to see you or hear from you ever again.

It hurt. Devil take it, but it hurt. All the more because he hadn't had a clue, until he'd met her, of just how unrealistic his hopes had been. The desire to belong he'd buried so deep for so many years had resurfaced. He wasn't sure he was up to the task of digging a new and final grave for it.

'Mr Dunbar? Excuse me, but perhaps you'd rather take your dinner alone after all. You don't look like a man fit for company.'

Cameron opened his eyes, turning away from the window. Miss Kirstin Blair was hovering in the doorway, a vision of loveliness in a grey wool travelling gown, looking not at all discomfited by his obvious distress, but instead eyeing him in what he could only describe as an assessing way, as if he were some conundrum she wished to resolve.

'I've not changed my mind.'

'There's no need to be polite,' she said. 'An idiot could see that you are troubled.'

He couldn't help but laugh at this. She had a

very singular way of expressing herself. He held out his hand. 'Come away in, please. I won't pretend that I've not got a lot on my mind, but I can say in all honesty that now you're here I'll be able to forget about it for a while. I've ordered dinner. Will you take a glass of sherry while we wait for the food to arrive?'

'Thank you, I will.'

She sat herself down on one of the chairs by the fireside, stretching her boot-clad feet towards the hearth with a contented sigh. He'd known her for an extraordinary beauty from the moment he'd set eyes on her. Without her bonnet to shade her face, her cloak to conceal her figure, by the bright glare of the candelabra on the mantel Cameron could not detect a single flaw. Yet she had none of the airs of a beautiful woman, that assumption they all shared that they would be looked at and admired. He couldn't believe, however, that she was oblivious to her charms.

He handed her a glass of rather cloudy sherry, taking the seat opposite her. She inspected the drink, taking a suspicious sniff and immediately setting the glass aside.

'I would advise against it, Mr Dunbar. It is either the dregs of a keg, or the leavings of a decanter left open too long. It will be revoltingly sweet, if I am not mistaken, for the sugar has crystallised.'

'I'm sure you are right, Miss Blair,' he answered, 'but it is all they have, and I am in sore need of a drink.'

'You'll be in sore need of a restorative in the morning if you drink too much of that muck.'

'I'll take my chances. Believe me, I've drunk a great deal worse. I have not your delicate palate.'

'Obviously not.'

There was a glimmer of a smile in her eyes that brought to mind what it was that had first drawn him to her when he'd first boarded the coach. 'You prefer your sherry to match your wit, Miss Blair.'

'If you mean dry, then you are quite correct, Mr Dunbar.'

He laughed, tipping back the glass and swallowing the contents whole. It was, as she had predicted, far too sweet, and quite disgusting, but it served its purpose and warmed his gullet.

He poured himself another. 'I hope the wine I've ordered will be more to your taste.'

She raised a sceptical brow. 'Do you know anything at all about wine?'

'I ought to. I do a deal of trade in it.'

'Then I must presume your customers are not particularly discerning.'

'Aye, well, it's true. I reckon most of them prefer quantity to quality.' He settled back in his chair, making no bones about studying her. She did not flinch, she did not blush, she returned his gaze evenly. 'What are you doing, travelling alone on the public coach, may I ask?'

'You may, but I'd far rather you told me first what you *think* I'm doing?'

'By using my powers of deduction, as you did? Is that a game you like to play, Miss Blair?'

'I do, though it's usually a game I play for my own amusement.'

'Ah, now, there you've given me another clue, though a surprising one. A woman as beautiful as you cannot possibly lack company.'

'True, if I was inclined to value company because the company valued only my face, and nature must take the credit for that.'

'A great deal of credit, if you don't mind my saying so.'

'It is simply a matter of ratio and proportion. What Luca Pacioli called *de divina proportione* and Leonardo da Vinci used to great effect. Of chin to forehead. The spacing of the eyes. The alignment of the ears with the nose. The symmetry of a profile. If any of those factors vary from the optimum, then beauty is skewed. My face has no variation, thus it is, mathematically speaking, perfectly beautiful. I hope you are not going to make the obvious mistake of assuming, however, that what is on the outside reflects what is on the inside?'

'Nor am I going to join the ranks of your admirers who, I assume, make the mistake of feigning interest in what goes on behind that perfect visage. Lovely as it is, and I will not deny that I do find you very lovely, would you believe me, Miss Blair, if I tell you that it was rather your air of—it is not aloofness exactly. I'm not sure how to put it, but you strike me as one who coolly observes, if that makes sense?'

To his astonishment, she blushed, and, judging from the way her hand flew to her cheek, she was just as astonished as he. 'My father taught me that observation and deduction are the key cornerstones of any scientific field.'

A tap at the door announced that dinner was served. As the servants set the table with steaming dishes and decanted the wine, Cameron took the opportunity to study his dinner guest. She had spoken impassively, but he was not fooled. His inadvertent compliment had touched her, and her discomfort touched a chord in him.

His own dark looks had been the source of endless whippings in his early years, an unnecessary effort to forestall any vanity taking root.

Taking their lead from those who had wielded the whip, his peers had turned on him, forcing him to become tougher, to use attack as the best form of defence. As an adult, when those same dark looks had attracted a very different kind of attention from women, he'd been first incredulous and then—yes, just as Miss Kirstin Blair was now—he had resented it. No one looked beyond his appearance. Save this most surprising woman, now helping herself from the dish of mutton stew with undisguised hunger.

'Dare I ask if you wish to try the wine?' Cameron poured her a half-glass and handed it to her.

She took a cautious sip and nodded her approval. 'It is not that I am a connoisseur, as you suggested,' she said, smiling at his obvious relief, 'it is simply that I have a very sensitive palate.'

'Another gift from nature. Is there no end to her bounty?'

Miss Kirstin Blair chuckled. 'I have no talent for drawing, no ear for music and no patience for fools.'

'You can't blame nature for that.'

She considered this as she took another sip of wine. 'It is an interesting question, isn't it? How much we are formed by nature and how much we form our own nature. Would I be mathematically inclined were it not for my father? I would like to think so, but since I cannot wipe my mind clean and start afresh it is impossible to be certain. Do you take your business acumen from your own father, Mr Dunbar?'

'I doubt it,' Cameron replied shortly.

'He was not business-minded?'

'I have no idea.' Nor ever would have now. The vast wasteland that was his heritage would remain empty for ever.

Kirstin Blair was studying him above the rim of her wine glass dispassionately. 'I seem to have the knack of inadvertently touching on what you least wish to discuss,' she said. 'Though it seemed a natural enough question, given the direction of our conversation…'

He was obliged to laugh. 'As I recall, our conversation began with you asking me to tell you what I have deduced about you.'

'Yes, I did, so feel free while I help myself to some of this excellent capon.'

'Firstly, you are not afraid to defy convention, since we've already committed several social *faux pas*, two complete strangers, dining alone together.'

Her eyebrows shot up. 'Really? You think me a rebel?'

'Not exactly.' Cameron pushed his half-finished plate to one side. 'You do not, I think, set out to be different, but your combination of clear thinking and the expression of that thinking without any attempt to moderate it makes your personality even more singular than your looks.'

'Singular? That is not, I think, a compliment. It might be construed as meaning *odd*.'

'It's the unvarnished truth, just as you prefer it. Am I right?'

'You are.' She propped her chin on her hand. 'Tell me more.'

'You cannot be too much in the habit of socialising, else this habit of yours, of speaking your mind, would have been curbed—unless you are in the habit only of socialising with similar-minded people.' Cameron frowned at this. 'Since you've told me that you take your mathematical inclinations from your father, then I wonder if he is perhaps a professor at the university in Edinburgh?'

Her half-smile faded. 'Was.'

'Oh, I'm so sorry.'

Kirstin shook her head, looking studiously down at the table to avoid his eyes. 'He had been ill for some time and died peacefully in his bed, as he wished to do, a month ago.'

She met his eyes again, almost defiantly, making Cameron think the better of offering his condolences. 'I presume,' he said instead, 'that this loss is the reason for you setting out on this new life of yours, then? You have no other ties to keep you in Edinburgh?'

Her expression softened, and he knew he'd said the right thing. 'Very good. My mother died when I was a child. I've no other kith or kin. Go on.'

But Cameron shook his head. 'I'll quit while I'm ahead, if you don't mind. Aside from guessing your age, which I'd say was three or four and twenty…'

'I'm twenty-five.'

'There, you see, I should have held my tongue. As to this new life of yours, that you're excited about and afraid of in equal parts, all I can say is that it must be something like yourself—unconventional—and nothing so predictable as a post as a governess or a teacher. Unless you've found an institution which accepts female mathematicians?'

'I did not even attempt to look. Aside from the fact that few men believe women capable of understanding even the most rudimentary forms of logic, I do not have any formal qualifications. Being a female. It is a vicious circle.'

'Aye, I can see that it is.'

'I'll tell you the truth,' Kirstin said. 'I've no complete idea myself of what this new life of mine will be, save that it will be, as you said, unconventional. You are an excellent observer.'

'A high compliment, coming from one such as yourself.'

'Are you teasing me?'

'I wouldn't dare.'

She laughed at that. 'Beneath that very handsome exterior—and don't pretend you don't know how very handsome you are—there lurks a personality which could, I suspect, be very intimidating if you chose. I think you would dare almost anything, Cameron Dunbar.'

'Do you now?' he said, taken aback by this. 'You don't seem particularly intimidated, if I may say so.'

'No, but that is because you have not tried to intimidate me, being in need of my company to distract you.'

'And because I've taken a liking to you, let us not forget that. I've never met anyone like you.'

'The feeling is entirely mutual.'

'Do you believe in fate?'

'It is not a logical concept.'

'No, but sometimes we humans defy logic.'

Kirstin smiled at that. 'You think it was fate which brought us together today?'

'If it was mere chance, then it was a very fortunate one. I would not have liked to miss this opportunity to get to know you, however briefly.'

'And you have,' Kirstin said, 'or do—know me, I mean—better than most of my acquaintance, even though we've barely met and are no sooner getting acquainted than we must part. It must be getting late.'

Cameron consulted his watch, exclaiming in astonishment at the hour. 'It's after ten.'

'Why haven't they been to clear the table?'

'Reluctant to interrupt us, I suppose, and plenty else to keep them occupied, looking after the rest of our coach party.'

'They will probably all be abed by now. We make an early start in the morning.' Kirstin pushed back her chair. 'We should bid each other goodnight.'

Cameron too got to his feet. 'We should, though I'm loath to do so.'

'Lest your demons return?'

'You've well and truly banished my demons. I'm much more likely to be kept awake thinking of you, if you want the honest truth.'

He hadn't meant to speak so bluntly, but the words were out before he could stop them. Yet instead of looking affronted, Kirstin widened her eyes as they met his, and in that instant the

mood between them changed, became a meeting of minds subsumed by a rush of unmistak-
ably mutual desire.

Chapter Three

I will find her. I have to find her, because failure is not an option. So we will keep searching until we do. Those are my terms. Under The Procurer's rules, you are obliged to adhere to them.

Kirstin replayed Cameron's words over and over in her mind. As he had pointed out, these were The Procurer's rules of engagement—her own rules. She'd assumed they would protect her from Cameron asking awkward questions, but she hadn't counted on them working against her.

Were they too onerous? She thought back to the women who had played by those very rules over the years, women who had, by doing so, saved themselves, bought themselves independence, a new life, a fresh start. Their success had been richly rewarded, but at what cost? She had never considered this aspect of her vocation. She took account only of the facts: that the woman had the appropriate skills, a determination to succeed and too much to lose to fail.

Those had been the foundations of her own success. She had assumed those other women would be similarly driven and willing to do whatever it took, no matter the collateral damage.

Except she was now the one in the firing line. Had she demanded too much of them? Cameron had the right to keep her here until his search was successfully completed. Kirstin, staring at her unpacked portmanteau, wasn't at all convinced she could commit to that, no matter how urgent and worthy the cause.

Though there were actually two causes, she reminded herself, his and hers. If she left now, there could be no turning back, no other opportunity to know him and to use that knowledge to ratify the life she had chosen.

He had disconcerted her so far. It wasn't only that she still found him fiercely attractive, it was the man himself, so honourable, so assured, and so—so *likeable*. Dammit, he even had a sense of humour!

If only he'd been different. Arrogance, a common trait in many men as successful as Cameron, would have provoked an instant dislike. Even if he'd been less inclined to listen to her, more determined to have his own way, it would have helped. Instead, to add to all his other disconcerting qualities, he was happy to accept her advice and solicit her opinion. Though he was paying through the nose for it, she knew from past experience it did not necessarily mean he would take it. There was steel at the core of him that made it clear he would not hesitate to take control should he deem it necessary.

Which thought made her shudder, for if he knew the truth, and had the inclination to act, a man as powerful as Cameron Dunbar could easily realise her biggest fear. So he must never, ever guess the truth.

Did this mean she should leave, disappear for ever from his view, to protect her secret? And by doing so learn to live with the questions his reappearance had raised? Impossible. Kirstin sat down on the bed and undid the buttons of her spencer. She had no choice but to stay here and do what she had commanded all those other women to do.

All or nothing. It would be challenging, but when had she ever shirked a challenge? It required her to commit herself wholeheartedly, to lay aside her other responsibilities for the first

time in six years. Marianne would relish the
challenge of taking charge. It might even prove
oddly liberating.

A knock at the door heralded the delivery of a
note from Marianne. Scanning it, she smiled to
herself. In the grand scheme of things this was
welcome good news.

Kirstin opened her portmanteau and began
to unpack.

'I have decided to stay and abide by your
terms until we find Philippa and Jeannie,'
Kirstin said brusquely as she took a seat once
again in Cameron's sitting room an hour later.

He sat opposite her, making no effort to disguise his relief. 'Thank you. Any delay while
The Procurer finds someone to replace you could
prove fatal to my chances of success.'

'But what if they are never found?' she asked
gently.

'I prefer to operate on the assumption that
they will be. For what it's worth, I am convinced
Philippa is alive. I feel it. Here.'

Cameron put his hand over his chest. Kirstin
knew where his heart was. She'd laid her cheek
on his chest and listened to it as she'd watched
dawn come up through the post house bedroom
window, the solid, regular beat counting out the

seconds and minutes until they must part. She'd thought him asleep until he'd slid his hand up her flank to cup her breast, until he'd whispered, his voice husky with passion, that there was still time for...

She dragged her mind back to the present. 'Your instincts in this case are correct.'

'What do you mean?'

She permitted herself a small smile. 'As soon as I accepted your offer I took the liberty of getting in touch with a man who, quite literally, knows where the bodies are buried in London and its environs. I have received word from Mar—my assistant that he has been in touch. There have been no suspicious deaths fitting the description of your niece and her maid. Trust me, if there had been, this gentleman would know. So we can safely assume that they are alive, for the time being.'

Cameron stared at her in astonishment. He laughed, an odd, nervous sound. He shook his head. And then a smile of blessed relief spread across his face. 'Thank you,' he said fervently.

'That does not mean—'

'I know, I know. But still.' He dragged his fingers through his hair, staring at her in something of a daze. 'It's a very positive development.'

'Yes.' She permitted herself another small smile. 'Yes, it is.'

He had taken off his coat and rolled up his sleeves. There were fresh ink stains on his fingers, though the stack of papers on the desk seemed to her undisturbed. Either he was very neat, or he had been working on something else. The fact that he was no longer tense, and seemed more relaxed to her presence, patently in charge of the situation, led her to the conclusion that the 'something else' was his notes. She was quietly pleased when he proved her correct by opening the leather-bound notebook on the table in front of him.

'I've been thinking...'

'As indeed have I,' Kirstin intervened. 'Before we proceed, I have some questions for you.'

Cameron closed his notebook on his lap, rested his arm on the back of his chair and angled himself towards her. 'Ask away.'

Kirstin took out her own notebook. 'Your half-sister, Louise Ferguson,' she began in clipped tones. 'Firstly, how did she know where to contact you, given that you'd had only one previous encounter?'

'I'm not difficult to find, Kirstin, my name is well-enough known in trade circles. She wrote to my main place of business in Glasgow, as I said, and fortunately for all concerned I was there.'

'But why you, Cameron? You are, by your own admission, a virtual stranger to her.'

'Because her husband is dead and she has no other close male relatives. Because she doesn't want anyone she knows involved. Because she knows enough of my reputation, it seems, to be sure that I have the means that she does not, to pull whatever strings are necessary. And because,' he concluded with a bitter smile, 'she was pretty certain that I'd leap at the chance to help her. As I said, and as she pointed out, I owe her.'

'You do not resent the fact that she turned to you in her time of need when she'd previously estranged herself from you?'

He had not flinched at her bald statement, but she was watching him very closely. There was the tiniest movement, an involuntary tic at the corner of his mouth. It did hurt him that the woman was using him. Of course she couldn't exactly be blamed for doing so, she was a mother in desperate fear for her child's life, but all the same it didn't cast her in a particularly favourable light. While Cameron— There could be no denying that Cameron was a very honourable man.

'I was angry, of course I was, but I can't blame

her,' he said, unwittingly echoing Kirstin's own thoughts. 'She's desperate. Not only to find Philippa, but to keep her daughter's disappearance quiet. When I suggested getting the Bow Street Runners involved she almost had a fit.'

'Why? Surely publicising her daughter's disappearance would make finding her easier.'

'Aye, but it would also mean that everyone would know, and Mrs Ferguson isn't sure that either of them would recover from the scandal of it—whatever it turns out to be.'

'So she turned to you, knowing you would help, knowing that you had the means, as you call it, to do whatever was necessary, and knowing that you'd have no option but to be discreet, being unknown to any of her family and friends?'

'My desire for discretion in this matter has nothing to do with my social circle or the lack of it,' Cameron replied tersely, 'and everything to do with my desire to protect the reputation of an innocent young girl, her maid and her mother.'

'My own desire is to understand the circumstances of this case. It was not my intention to upset you.'

'You did not,' Cameron retorted. Though it was clear that she had.

'It is in the nature of these contracts that the

client—in this case yourself—is forced to reveal a good deal of his life and his personal circumstances,' Kirstin continued carefully. 'Sometimes things which he would prefer to keep to himself.'

'I am aware of that, and I am doing my best to be candid with you. I am also very much aware that the obligation is not reciprocal.'

'For very sound reasons. You can have no idea of the circumstances under which my—' Kirstin broke off, astounded to detect a quiver in her voice. 'It is a very necessary term of all The Procurer's contracts,' she repeated coolly. 'My—our—The Procurer's aim is to protect the women whom she employs from judgement, from assumptions, from any sort of knowledge which could be used against them.'

'Are they always women?'

When Kirstin remained silent, Cameron rolled his eyes.

'Fine, forget I asked.'

'Yes,' she answered, surprising herself, 'The Procurer chooses always to employ women. Those in need of a blank slate, deserving of a fresh start, who have been judged and found wanting through no fault of their own. I dare say there are many men in such a situation, but it is her experience that woman have fewer opportunities to re-establish themselves.'

'I had no idea that The Procurer was a philanthropist.'

'She is not,' Kirstin snapped, confused by having confided even this much. 'In her view, women don't want charity, they simply want the opportunity to earn a second chance.'

'And you clearly agree with her?'

'Yes.'

'It's an admirable ethos. You are fortunate to work for such a like-minded woman, though I must admit I'm surprised that you work for anyone. When we first met—'

'As I recall, I was not specific at all about my plans.' She waited, allowing the silence to serve as her rebuke, before continuing. 'What was the purpose of Mrs Ferguson's trip to London?'

'To purchase her daughter's trousseau. Philippa has, I understand, made a very good match, one heartily approved of by her family.'

'And one which would be endangered if it were discovered she had run off—*if* she has run off. Has it occurred to you that the two might be connected?'

Cameron wrinkled his nose. 'That the match is to her mother's rather than to Philippa's taste? Certainly Mrs Ferguson is mighty keen on it.'

'Do you know how Philippa feels about the match?'

'Mrs Ferguson says she is perfectly content with the arrangement.'

'Though you don't know Mrs Ferguson well enough to be sure she's not either lying or in denial?'

Cameron sighed. 'You're in the right of it there. I don't. And the lass is just seventeen, hardly old enough to know her own mind, let alone be married.'

'Perhaps she does know her own mind but has not the strength of character to defy her mother. What type of person is Mrs Ferguson?'

'You'll be meeting her in due course, would you not prefer to form your own opinion?'

'I will, but I am interested in yours.'

'Even though I hardly know her?'

'You are a good judge of character and, as a businessman, accustomed to making rapid assessments. Your powers of observation,' Kirstin said with a wry smile, 'are almost as acute as my own.'

'A high compliment indeed! Mrs Ferguson struck me as a forthright woman, not one given to outright lies, though very sure of her own opinion. If her daughter is unhappy, either with her choice of husband or with the idea of such an early marriage, then she has either said nothing to her mother or her mother has discounted her daughter's views as having less value than her own. But I'm only surmising, Kirstin.'

'It is all you can do for the present. Do you have any notion of what the girl's relationship with her mother may be?'

'Better than the relationship Mrs Ferguson had with her own mother, I hope,' Cameron retorted. Seeing Kirstin's surprise at this, he shrugged. 'Mrs Ferguson certainly cares for her daughter. Her distress, I am sure, is genuine. I'd guess the relationship is dutiful rather than loving. It could be the daughter is keeping secrets from her mother. Aye, it could easily be the case.'

'It is likely to be the case. May I ask what you meant when you said—?'

'No!'

The single word was spoken like the crack of a whip, making Kirstin flinch.

'It has no relevance to this matter.' Cameron tempered his answer. 'Now, if you have finished with your questions, I'd like to discuss my ideas on how we should proceed.'

She'd guessed from the start that he could be intimidating, but she'd had no idea until now that she would be susceptible to it. She had no clue as to how he did it, for he was not scowling, was not looming over her, it was rather that he seemed to have turned into a version of himself carved from granite.

Kirstin resisted the impulse to shiver and forced a small smile. 'Please do,' she said. 'You have my full attention.'

Cameron picked up his notebook with relief. As he recalled it had been exciting, that night they'd met, playing a guessing game of who they were and what their stories were. But now Kirstin's powers of observation and deduction, as she called them, were making him uncomfortable, and the feeling was obviously mutual. It was not surprising, given the time that had passed, that they both had secrets they didn't want to reveal. It was odd, he'd felt he'd known her that night, but the reality was, despite what had occurred between them, they were all but strangers.

'Philippa and Jeannie disappeared from the posting house overnight,' he said. 'Naturally Mrs Ferguson was distraught when she woke to find the pair of them gone. The landlord made enquiries, but no one saw them leave. He offered to contact the authorities, but Mrs Ferguson demurred. By this time she'd calmed down and had begun to think through the consequences. Believing the disappearance would turn out to be the result of girlish foolishness, she told the landlord some tale of forgetting that alternative arrangements had been made and continued her journey, thinking that the girls would turn up themselves at the house in Mayfair, suitably repentant. Unfortunately she was wrong, and the girls did not turn up.'

'So Mrs Ferguson turned to you?'

Cameron nodded, tapping his pencil on the cover of his notebook. 'Obviously we must go to the Spaniard's Inn and make discreet enquiries ourselves, one or both of us. I've not done so yet simply because I didn't want to prejudice things—frighten someone off, or even alert them to the fact that a search is being made, making our task more difficult.'

'Yes, that was wise of you.'

'Philippa could have run off. She could have eloped. She could have been lured away by one of those dubious persons who haunt the inns on the outskirts of the city in search of innocent flesh.' Cameron winced. 'Or she could have been abducted for some other reason. I think that covers all the options.'

'I think we must also assume that, wherever they are, Philippa and her maid are together.'

Cameron shuddered. 'I sincerely hope so. It's bad enough trying to follow one trail, let alone two.'

A faint frown straightened the line of Kirstin's brows. Her eyes were intent, focused completely on him. He had a flashing memory of that same intent gaze fixed on him as she lay naked beneath him, but he pushed it ruthlessly away.

'Then a visit to the posting house is top of our list, I reckon,' Cameron said. 'I think that must take priority over anything, even your meeting with Mrs Ferguson.'

'I agree. Two young girls with no knowledge of London cannot have disappeared into thin air without assistance. Whether they planned to run off, or whether they were forced into it, someone at the posting house must have seen something.'

'So we travel there tomorrow. In what guise?'

'We'll need to think carefully about that.' Kirstin tapped the end of her pencil against her bottom lip. 'It seems to me that we have a number of questions to ask Mrs Ferguson before we can begin to eliminate any of the possibilities. Whether Philippa had another beau, for example. Or what possible reason there could be for abduction—are Mrs Ferguson's family wealthy? Is Philippa herself an heiress?'

'I don't think so, but I don't actually know.' Cameron winced. 'We can add that to the list of questions to ask Mrs Ferguson, but aside from that I'm afraid I don't know what else we can do until we've visited the Spaniard's Inn.'

'After which I hope that some of my contacts will be able to help us.'

'More of your dubious sources? You'll write to them?'

Kirstin gave a snort of laughter. 'They are not the type to commit what they know to paper. I doubt some of them even know how to write. I will contact whichever of them I think can help, and I will let you know if there is anything to report.'

'If you're going to meet them…'

'Then I must do so alone. It's not that I don't trust you, but they will not. My contacts tend to be cagey, suspicious of strangers, and with good reason.'

'I don't want you risking your neck.'

'It's my neck, and you are paying me very well to risk it.'

'No,' Cameron said flatly. 'I'm paying you to help me, but not at any cost.'

She sighed, rolling her eyes theatrically. 'Allow me to know my business. I have been running it successfully for more than six years.'

'Running it?'

'Running my part of it.'

'For more than six years? Since you first came to London, then. You have worked for The Procurer all this time?'

'Yes. Now, if we are done here, I would like some time to order my thoughts, so if you'll excuse me.' She got to her feet.

'You'll join me for dinner?'

Kirstin looked as startled by the invitation as Cameron was in issuing it. 'I don't see that we have any more to discuss until—'

'There is the matter of how we are to set about our enquiries in Hampstead.' He hesitated. 'Though we could resolve that matter in the morning, if need be. It's not that. We're going to have to work very closely together. I thought it would be a good idea to have a companionable dinner together, that's all, but if you prefer to dine alone then please don't feel obliged to join me.'

He had the sense that she was weighing up a list of pros and cons, though her expression remained bland enough, making it impossible for him to guess which way the decision would fall until she shrugged.

'Very well, I will join you for dinner. At least I can be certain that the sherry provided by this establishment will be drinkable.'

Kirstin was not surprised to discover a note from Marianne in response to her own earlier missive, assuring her that all would be taken care of for however long she must be away, and that regular updates would be sent. Though she knew it was illogical to require reassurance, since she had been gone less than a day, she was reassured.

Feeling foolish, but unable to stop herself, she kissed the footnote before hiding the papers in the lining of her portmanteau.

Business done, Kirstin turned her mind to dressing for dinner. She had a weakness for beautiful clothes, one of the few guilty pleasures she indulged, and consequently owned a great many more gowns than she had the opportunity to wear. As The Procurer, her various toilettes were designed to be unmemorable, and though she could afford to have them beautifully made in the most expensive of fabrics they were, nevertheless, her work clothes, worn by her alter ego not her true self.

Her true self stared back at her in the mirror as she prepared to dine with Cameron, wearing a crimson evening gown that was far too elaborate for the occasion but which, now she had put it on, she could not bring herself to change.

The plain silk slip was narrow, falling straight from the high waistline, making the most of her tall, slim figure. The overdress of sarcenet had a fuller skirt, weighted down with a border of silk, adorned with a bunch of blowsy crimson

silk appliqué poppies. A narrow sash was tied
at the back, where the tassels were designed to
swish provocatively when she walked. The scal-
loped edges of the décolleté were both demure
and inviting against the swell of her bosom, and
there were just a few inches of her upper arm
showing bare between the puffed sleeves and
her long white kid evening gloves. Her hair was
piled high on her head in a severe arrangement
which drew attention to her neck and her shoulders. She had darkened her lips with carmine,
thickened her lashes with kohl.

Studying herself in the mirror with her accustomed detachment, she was satisfied with
the overall result. Allowing her disguise to slip
for a second, Kirstin smiled gleefully, executing
a little twirl which sent her skirts and the tas-
selled belt whirling out. She had designed the
gown herself, and as ever the discreet Madame
LeClerc had brought her drawings to life with
flair and French chic. It was a preposterous purchase, justified by a vague notion of wearing
it to the opera, which had never been fulfilled
nor was ever likely to be, but she was glad of it
now. The sophisticated yet alluring woman in
the mirror was utterly unlike the Kirstin Blair
of six years ago.

Doubt assailed her once more. Her contrariness confused her. Her dress was provocative, but she had no wish to provoke, and certainly no intention of this dinner ending as the last one with Cameron had.

Her ruthless honesty forced her to admit that this was not entirely true. At a very base level she still desired him in a way that she'd never wanted any other man. Was the solution to indulge that passion? Was that why she had dressed herself thus? To tempt him to make love to her in the hope that it would be a failure, in the hope that she would discover her memory at fault?

With a frustrated growl, Kirstin turned away from the mirror. It was a ridiculous idea, and utterly illogical. Of course she wasn't thinking such a thing. Nor did she care, not one whit, whether Cameron found her attractive or not. She wanted to make a good impression—yes, she would admit that much, it was a reasonable enough ambition. She was wearing this gown because it flattered her, because she loved it, and because she wasn't likely to get an opportunity to wear it again soon, and there was nothing more to it than that.

'I have no idea what type of food you prefer,' Cameron said apologetically as he held Kirstin's chair out for her. 'I think I might have ordered far too much.'

'Provided you did not order porridge and bannocks, in tribute to our joint heritage, I am not particularly fussy.'

He laughed, pouring her a glass of red wine, having dismissed the servants. 'I was raised on gruel rather than porridge, and it never came with a bannock as far as I remember. May I carve you some of this guinea fowl?'

'Please.' Kirstin took a cautious sip of the wine before giving a little nod of satisfaction.

'I am pleased to see that my taste in wine meets with your approval.'

'Knowledge you must have acquired later in life, if your origins are as humble as you imply.'

'I fared no better nor any worse than everyone else in my situation.'

Kirstin helped herself to some artichokes. Her hand hovered over the dish of peas, but she decided against them with a wrinkle of her nose and instead took some of the parsley buttered carrots.

'I forgot to ask, what age is Mrs Ferguson?'

Cameron wasn't at all fooled by her casual manner. He spooned some of the disregarded peas onto his plate beside the pigeon to buy himself some time. He could tell her he didn't know, which was true—he had no idea at all of Louise's exact age—but that would only encourage Kirstin to probe further, and her probing into his past was not his notion of getting to know one another.

He cut into his pigeon, which he noted with satisfaction was cooked through. He didn't care for bloody meat, though he knew in some eyes it made him a culinary heathen, when in fact it signalled the pauper he had been, for whom meat had been a rare treat, boiled for hours to provide stock for soup, providing another meal. Some might call it thrift, for him it had kept belly from backbone.

He lifted his glass again, and found Kirstin's eyes upon him. 'You wish to know whether my half-sister is older or younger than I?'

'Older, is what I would hazard. If Philippa is seventeen, unless Mrs Ferguson was also a child bride...'

'You have guessed correctly.'

Kirstin studied him for a moment longer, making it clear that his brusque tone was noted, before forgiving the peas their wrongdoings and taking a spoonful. 'You don't wish to talk about your family.'

It was a statement, not a question, and she was

right, which irked him. 'Why don't you tell me about yours instead?'

'There is little of any note to talk about,' she answered, with a little downturned smile. 'I never knew my mother, who died when I was very young. I have no siblings, older or younger, known or unknown to me. Until I left Edinburgh I lived a singularly unexciting and somewhat secluded life.'

'Though there must have been someone, surely, an aunt, perhaps, who had a hand in raising you?'

'No—at least I suppose there must have been a nurse when I was an infant, but I have no memory of any other females save the servants. It was always just Papa and myself.'

Which explained a great deal, Cameron thought. 'So you never missed your mother?'

'One does not miss what one did not have.'

No, but it didn't stop you imagining what you were missing, and idealising it too. 'You were lucky,' he said, 'to have a father willing to take on the rearing of you on his own.'

'He was my father. He loved me.'

'The one does not follow automatically from the other. Not every man considers a bairn a blessing.'

She flinched at that. 'What about you?'

He shrugged. 'I've never wanted a wife, never mind weans. The life I lead is not one that lends itself to fatherhood, and I've no desire to change that life.'

'Would you have to change it so completely?'

'Aye, I reckon.' He smiled wryly. 'Your father and I would be in accord on this, if nothing else. If you go to the trouble of bringing a child into the world, then you've a duty to do the very best you can to take care of it. In my mind, that means being there, not disappearing off abroad for six months or a year at a time in search of new commodities and trade deals.'

Cameron picked up his wine glass, swirled the contents thoughtfully, then set it down again untouched. 'That's my life, Kirstin, and I love it. If I had to give it up I'd come to resent it, and that's the truth.'

'So you've no interest in having children?'

'I've no room for them, and no desire to make room,' he said vehemently, 'but, judging from that fierce frown you're casting in my direction, I assume you think differently.'

She started, looked momentarily confused, then made a conscious effort to smooth her brow. 'I find your honesty refreshing on a subject so many people equivocate about.'

'Maybe so, but that's not all you were thinking. Do *you* want children?'

She smiled, the Sphinx-like smile that she used, he now realised, when she had no intention of revealing a single one of her thoughts.

'I am not married and, like you, have no desire to change my single state.'

He threw back the remnants of his wine, choosing to accept the non sequitur at face value. 'It's a strange profession you've chosen, if such it can be called, though I remember you said, didn't you, that you were set on an unconventional life? It seems you've achieved that, all right. Has it proved, unlike your Edinburgh days, to be exciting?'

Kirstin, clearly as happy as he to change the subject, laughed. 'It could not be more different.' She poured herself another glass of wine, pushing the decanter across the table to him, twirling the crystal glass between her fingers. 'Is your life exciting? Trading in—? I don't even know what you trade in, save wine.'

'Spices, perfumes, precious stones, mined gold, tin and copper. Coconut. Coffee. Cocoa. Whatever there's a market for. The more exotic the better—I enjoy the challenge of being ahead of the pack in what I can supply. Although I've had my share of disasters. A Greek wine flavoured with resin called *retsina*, which I quite liked, did not go down well with the wine merchants I trade with. And my experiment with a dried spice made from the chilli plant was not very well received either—one of the men who sampled it claimed he could taste nothing else for a month.'

'I am hazarding a guess that you found this chilli spice rather tasty,' Kirstin said.

'Aye, I did, which is just as well, for I've enough of the stuff in my warehouse in Glasgow to season my food for the rest of my life and then some.'

'Did you lose a great deal of money over it?'

Cameron shrugged. 'Where's the fun in playing safe? I make far more than I lose.'

'Your ships must travel across the globe to trade in such exotic goods.'

'And I with them. Persia, Algiers, St Petersburg, Naples, Constantinople, Damascus.' Cameron grinned. 'The more exotic and the more dangerous the better, as far as I'm concerned. I'm not the type to sit in his office at the Trades Hall waiting around to see what goods are unloaded.' He laughed. 'I'd die of boredom. So, to answer your original question, my life is quite exciting. I enjoy the fact that I am my own man.'

'You are fortunate that you can be.'

'I've worked bloody hard, Kirstin, to get where I am.'

'Then that is something else we have in common.'

He studied her under the guise of taking a sip of wine. 'I reckon we've more in common than you think. Variety must be the spice of life in the work you do for The Procurer.'

She smiled at that. 'Very true, and it is one of the things I enjoy most—expecting the unexpected.'

'For me it is the thrill of the chase, closing a deal that everyone else thought impossible. Which, now I come to think of it, is what your employer claims to do, doesn't she? Make the impossible possible?'

'It is a well-founded claim.'

'I'm sure it is. You've no need to get so prickly.'

'I wasn't.'

He raised an eyebrow at this. She was forced to smile. It wasn't much of a smile, but it was enough to make him catch his breath. He'd been trying very hard not to stare at her, at the smooth, beguiling expanse of cleavage revealed by her gown, at the way the filmy fabric clung to her, the way the colour complemented the crimson of her lush lips.

She had painted them with carmine. It was a

shocking thing for any lady to do here in England, though he'd seen it used to some effect in other countries. It made her seem exotic. He wondered if it was a foible of hers, or whether she'd done it for some other reason. She had made it so clear she didn't want to be reminded of that night, yet what else was he to think of now that he had allowed himself to look? Now that she was looking back at him and the air between them seemed to crackle with the memory?

The urge to touch his own lips to hers was almost irresistible, but he could not risk losing her. Cameron pushed back his chair and rang the bell to summon a servant to clear the table. 'We still have to make plans for tomorrow.'

Kirstin got to her feet and went to the window, pushing back the curtains, leaning on the ledge to gaze out. The little tassels on the belt of her gown flicked provocatively against the curve of her bottom. For a woman so slim, he remembered she had a delightfully round bottom.

Cameron groaned inwardly. *Don't think of her bottom!*

'When I was waiting for you to arrive,' he said, 'I pictured Mrs Collins as a vicar's widow.' He tried to conjure her again, that smart, middle-aged relic of the church with faded hair. Comely. A bit wrinkled.

Kirstin turned around. Beautiful. Smooth.

Her hair black as night. And her mouth curved into that cool, mocking smile that was so very deceptive, because her kisses weren't at all cool. 'Were you disappointed?'

'You were certainly not what I was expecting.' He told her what he had expected, describing the imaginary Mrs Collins in detail, in an attempt to distract himself.

It didn't work. His description amused her. And intrigued her. Her eyes sparkled. Her lips curved into a half-smile. 'It's an excellent solution.'

'What is?'

'A cover story for tomorrow, our visit to the Spaniard's Inn. The Reverend Mr Collins travelling from Scotland with his wife en route to a new life in America, stopping off in the metropolis to stay with—with…'

'The Archbishop of Canterbury?'

Kirstin burst into a peal of laughter. 'I was imagining the reverend as a man of the High Kirk.'

'A wee bit too strict and zealous even for the archbishop, you mean? A fire and brimstone man, is he, who disapproves of singing so much as a psalm?'

'And who thinks that dancing is a sin only second to fornication.'

'Oh, no, dancing is much worse, for it is done in public.'

Kirstin's lip curled. 'It would be funny were it not true. Though they are a dying breed, there are still a fair few of those hypocrites preaching, determined that we shall all be punished and go to hell for our sins, determined that no good can ever come of what they see as an evil world, full of temptation.'

There was an edge to her words that took him aback, though it also struck a chord. 'I must confess I gave up on the church at an early age, thanks to one such man.'

'Yes? I wonder if I was more or less fortunate for it to have taken more than a quarter of a century for my illusions to be shattered,' Kirstin said. 'My father's faith was of a gentle sort, but I found, in the end, that even the gentler sort will not forgive a sin which is unrepented.'

He could ask, though she would not answer, what this sin was. He had the impression that she had entrusted him with something momentous, that her doing so was some sort of challenge. It was the way she was looking at him, defying him to question her, and yet—and yet there was something else. She had surprised herself.

'I don't think our Reverend Collins is such a man,' Cameron said gently. 'I think our Reverend Collins is a kind man who does not judge, who inspires his congregation rather than terrifies them.'

He was rewarded with a tremulous smile. 'And Mrs Collins,' Kirstin asked, 'is she a little church mouse, or...?'

'Oh, no, Euphemia is—'

'*Euphemia!* Oh, Cameron, surely not?'

He grinned. 'You don't like it?'

'Euphemia...' She considered this, biting her lip. 'Actually, I think it is perfect. She is not a church mouse, no, not at all, but a rather formidable woman, I think.'

'With a heart of gold, surely?'

She chuckled. 'And a light touch with a sponge cake. Though I beg you not to put that to the test, for I am one of those women who can burn a boiled egg.'

'Which explains your slenderness.'

'And my appetite, when faced with a repast such as you have provided tonight. For which I should have thanked you before now.'

'I merely ordered it. I didn't cook it.'

'Can you cook?'

'Yes, believe it or not, I can. I learnt through necessity, in my early days aboard ship.'

'You were a ship's cook?'

Cameron chuckled. 'I was a cabin boy.'

'From cabin boy to one of the country's leading merchants?'

'I would not say that, exactly.'

'Because you are modest. If you were not one of the country's leading merchants, you could not afford my fees.'

'The Procurer pays you well, then?'

To his surprise, Kirstin looked uncomfortable. 'Yes.'

'There's no shame in it. A man—and even a woman, in my radical opinion—should be proud to be able to make their way in the world by their own ingenuity, and you, I reckon, are particularly ingenious.'

'I will happily admit to that. I'd even go so far as to admit that we have that in common too. I am proud of having made my own way, just as you are, though I have not reached the heady heights of success you have attained.'

'I'm a man. It's much harder for a woman to excel.'

'Though very unusual for any man to recognise that fact.'

'That sounds like The Procurer talking.'

'We speak, on the whole, with one voice.' Kirstin smiled at him. 'And you and I have spoken enough for tonight, I think. It's getting late.'

'It is.' Though he didn't want her to go, didn't

want to lose this cocoon which they'd somehow wrapped themselves in, of confidences and understanding. He was a man who neither needed nor sought company, but Kirstin's company was different.

'So it is settled, then. Tomorrow we will travel to the Spaniard's Inn as the Reverend Collins and his wife, Euphemia.'

'It is settled.'

Their eyes held. The air seemed to tense. He took a step towards her. His arm reached for her of its own accord. Her hand grabbed his wrist, halting him in mid-air, and he heard the sharp intake of her breath.

'Cameron.'

He had no idea what she meant. A warning? An invitation? He could not breathe. She lifted his hand to her mouth, touched his knuckles with her lips.

There was a sharp rap on the door. They sprang apart as the servant he had summoned arrived with a tray and Kirstin, looking utterly appalled, turned and fled in a flutter of red, leaving him staring down at his hand and the crimson imprint of her kiss.

Chapter Four

~~~~~~~~~~~~~~~~~

Kirstin slammed the door of her suite shut and turned the key before rushing towards her bed-chamber, turning the key in that door too, and leaning against it, as if she were trying to keep a demon at bay, which in a way she was.

Her heart was beating wildly. Her cheeks were flushed, not only with shame but with shameful desire. Dear heavens, she couldn't believe what had happened and, even more mortifying, she couldn't believe that she was standing here wishing that it had not stopped there.

With a noise that sounded ridiculously like a child denied a longed-for treat, and completely unbecoming for a thirty-one-year-old woman, she began to undress, fumbling with the fastenings and ties that had been so cunningly designed for a female without a maid, finding them infuriatingly complicated. She had to be out of this dress, and now. A tearing sound made her curse, but she struggled on regardless. Serve her right for wearing the damned thing. Hadn't she known the effect it would have on Cameron? And hadn't she hoped it would have exactly that effect?

Tugging the gown down over her hips and stepping out of it, Kirstin cursed again. Stupid of her not to take account of the fact that it might have that same effect on her. Though it hadn't been the damned dress, had it? It had been bloody Cameron Dunbar!

'Oh, God.'

She slumped down on the bed, tugging at her hairpins. If only he hadn't looked at her like that. If only she hadn't returned that burning gaze of his. She ought to have remembered how it had been before. That look, the heat of it, and the rush, like some sort of fatal chemical surging through the brain. Desire. Every bit as fatal. It had happened that first time, and it had happened again. Though this time they had not kissed. Not like the last time...

December 1812, Carlisle

'You've well and truly banished my demons,' Cameron said. 'I'm much more likely to be kept awake thinking of you, if you want the honest truth.'

The honest truth was that she was like to do the same, Kirstin thought, though she'd never have dared speak so plainly.

Her mouth went dry. She couldn't take her eyes off him, for his words changed everything between them, turning what had been lightly flirtatious into something weightier, more dangerous. Desire. Though she'd never felt it before, she recognised it for what it was, rooting her to the spot, coursing through her blood, a dark, delicious temptation that whispered seductively in her ear that it should not be denied because the opportunity would never present itself again. She knew it was wrong, she knew it made no sense, but as she stared into Cameron's eyes and saw them darken, reflecting exactly what she was thinking, Kirstin cast caution to the four winds.

She stepped into his arms and his arms wrapped themselves tightly around her even before the distance was closed. She could hear his breathing, rasping, fast and shallow, just like hers, could see from the rigidity of his mouth, of his hands on her waist, how close to losing control he was, and it was, heaven help her, the most heady, powerful feeling, knowing that she could make him take that final step.

And so she did. One hand on his shoulder. The other hand resting on his hip. She lifted her face for his kiss, parting her lips, closing her eyes. There was a second when he resisted. And then his mouth claimed hers and she was lost. Lost without words, without reason, surrendering to the sensation of his mouth on hers, the heat between them, his tongue touching hers, setting her alight, his hand cupping her face, his fingers tugging through her hair, his other hand roving over her body, her back, her bottom, her waist, her arm, brushing the side of her breast.

She was a quivering, gasping, moaning creature, following his lead, running her fingers through his hair, feeling the roughness of it where it was short-cropped at his nape, his skin hot to her touch, and the unexpected silkiness of it where it was longer. She could feel his muscles tensing beneath his coat, under her flattened palms. She traced the line of his spine down to the indentation at the base, and as his hands curled over her bottom, pulling her tight against him, she felt her hands on the tightness of his rear and the thick, astonishingly hard length of his arousal against her belly.

She had never lost herself like this before, and sought only to lose herself further, the wanton creature that must have been dwelling inside her waiting to be released, making her nip at his bottom lip, shiver when he moaned in response, making her arch her back, pressing herself more urgently against him, through all the layers of her travelling gown and her petticoats, a primal instinct to press the insistent thrum of her own arousal against his.

He swore violently, a word she had heard only in the stables, and pushed her away.

'I did not mean—you must believe me when I tell you that I did not—do not...' He shook his head, his eyes dark, his lips swollen from their kisses. 'You'd better go to bed before we do something we'll both regret.'

'Will we?' She was already beyond regret. Her body was like a racehorse, mid-race, at full tilt towards the finishing line and unstoppable. 'Is it what you truly want, Cameron?'

'No.'

'No more do I.'

'Kirstin, do you know what you're saying?'

Her lie was instinctive. 'Yes.'

'Are you sure?'

This time there was no need to lie. 'Certain,' she said.

Hampstead, February 1819

The Spaniard's Inn, situated opposite the toll house, had reputedly once been the haunt of Dick Turpin amongst many other notorious highwaymen. Less than two hours' travel from London, it was an extremely popular posting house, for many travellers the last stop before the metropolis. The Reverend Mr Collins and his wife Euphemia arrived at a relatively quiet time, in a hired post-chaise in the middle of an unseasonably sunny morning.

Cameron was dressed in a shabby black coat patched at the elbows, with breeches, woollen stockings, heavy boots, his adopted profession's requisite neckcloth and a shallow-crowned hat bare from brushing. The outfit, acquired that morning by Kirstin at a second-hand market, exuded an odour which made him wrinkle his nose, though he did not, as she had first feared, refuse to don it, insisting only on his own linen.

The correspondingly shabby brown gown and grey jacket which she wore came from the same market, as did the oversized poke bonnet which obscured her face, and the truly hideous plaid shawl woven in what she could only describe as shades of rotting straw, which she'd draped around her shoulders. What little of her hair showed had been greyed with powder, while her face was the colour of a woman who spent much of her time outdoors, skilfully achieved with greasepaint.

As the chaise pulled up at the front of the inn,

Cameron grinned. 'Are you quite ready, my dear Euphemia?'

'Indeed,' Kirstin said primly, rummaging in her cavernous bag, knitted by an unknown and highly unskilled hand in a shade which she had named seaweed. 'But you, Reverend, are not. Put these on.' She handed him a pair of pince-nez. 'And, pray, if you can, refrain from smiling.'

He put the glasses on his nose, eyeing her over the top with his brows raised. 'I thought I was to be a jovial man of the cloth.'

Kirstin couldn't repress a snort of laughter. 'Kindly, not jovial. Sober, verging on the funereal.'

Cameron put his hands together, casting both his mouth and his eyes downwards, and let out the heavy sigh of a man who had lost a sixpence and found a penny. 'Like this?'

'Much better,' Kirstin said, stifling a giggle. She produced a bible from her bag. 'Put that in your pocket. I am sure you will find an appropriate opportunity to consult it.'

'You think of everything. May I say that you look quite—quite Euphemia-like?' Cameron said. 'It requires only a scowl—ah, perfect.' He swung open the door and leapt down, turning to help her. 'What *is* that smell coming from my coat?' he asked, as she stepped onto the cobblestones beside him. 'I've been trying to put a name to it, but for the life of me cannot place it.'

'Wet dog,' she told him, making a show of straightening his waistcoat in a wifely manner as their empty chaise trundled round the corner to the stables. 'If only you would hang your coat up as I have time and again asked you to, my dear, then our hound would not have the opportunity to make his bed on it.'

She could feel him shake with laughter, but she dared not meet his eyes lest he see her own amusement. Though she had not for a moment lost sight of the reason they were here, and the urgency of their mission, she was enjoying herself, relishing the role she was playing and the playing of it alongside Cameron.

'Goliath,' he said to her as he held out his arm for her to take.

'I'm sorry?'

'The name of our hound, my dear. How can you have forgotten when you named him yourself, don't you remember? Even as a puppy he was so very large.'

'And so very smelly.'

'The disadvantage of having such a very sensitive nose, my dear Euphemia. It is to be hoped that the landlord is not similarly endowed, or he will be in no way inclined to prolong our little chat. Shall we?'

The Spaniard's Inn was a square building of three storeys with two tall chimneys and a shallow roof. The windows on the ground floor were shuttered, and those on the second adorned with window boxes which were at this time of year empty. The narrow hallway which they entered was panelled with dark wood, the bare boards scuffed and pitted. A glimpse into the taproom on the left showed a large chamber similarly panelled, empty save for two draymen propping up the bar.

'Landlord's out back, Reverend,' one of them informed Cameron. 'George!' he bellowed. 'There's a vicar here to see you. Hope you aren't going to confess to watering down your ale!'

The summons was not needed, for the landlord was already bustling down the hall, drying his hands on his apron. A tall spare man, with a thin band of grey hair which made his tonsure look like an egg rising from a scarf, he had a mournful moustache to match and would, Kirstin thought, have made an even better man of the cloth than Cameron.

'Reverend.' The landlord, assimilating Cameron's appearance with the eye of a man who made his living from such lightning assessments, sketched the shallowest of bows. 'How may I be of service?'

'Collins is the name, and you can help me with a wee cup of tea for myself and my wife, my good man,' Cameron said in a thick Glaswegian accent. 'Have you a room fit for my good lady, sir?'

'If you'll come this way, madam… Reverend Collins. I'll have my wife tend to you.'

Clearly concluding they were not worth his valuable time, the innkeeper abandoned them in a small room at the back of the inn looking over the stable yard, clad in the ubiquitous dark wood panelling. A fire smoked sulkily in the grate, above which a watercolour of the Spaniard's Inn hung.

'Dick Turpin and Bess, I presume,' Kirstin said, eyeing the one-dimensional figure on a horse depicted, pistol raised, in the foreground of this dubious masterpiece. 'Though it could just as easily be Bessie the cow he's sitting on. I've never seen such a bovine horse.'

Cameron, pulling the bible from his pocket and setting it down on the one table the room possessed, looked up at this. 'I would refrain from saying so, however. I suspect the artist must be kin to the landlord. Why else would a work of art worthy of a five-year-old be on display?'

'A five-year-old would at least have got the number of windows right,' Kirstin said, joining Cameron on the wooden bench set into the wall behind the table, which was the room's only seating. 'Even I could have done better than that.'

Opening the bible, Cameron clasped his hands together and lowered his head, as if in prayer. 'And you, by your own admission, have no talent for art.'

'No.' Kirstin eyed him curiously. 'Have you?'

'What?'

'A talent for drawing?'

'As a matter of fact I do, though I'd call myself a draughtsman rather than an artist. I like to draw maps. Not sure where I get it from. Why do you ask?'

She wished she had not, now, for it forced her to recognise what she had always known, yet never allowed herself to acknowledge. A person was made up of two halves, inheriting traits from both sides of their heritage.

'Kirstin?'

And this person, seated beside her, unlike almost every other person she encountered, had a most unnerving ability to read her thoughts.

She gave herself a shake and picked up the bible. 'Shall we pray together, my dear?'

'What for? A decent cup of tea?'

His irreverence made her smile, but the quizzical look he drew her made it clear he knew she was equivocating.

'Not that I'd know a decent cup of tea, mind,' Cameron added, showing an even greater understanding of her character by choosing not to pursue the matter, a fact that was a relief and a worry at the same time.

Fortunately for Kirstin, the landlady chose this moment to arrive with the tea, decent or otherwise. 'Reverend... Mrs Collins, I am sorry to keep you waiting,' she said, putting the tray down. 'I am Mrs Crisp. I've brought you a piece of my currant cake, but if you'd prefer something more substantial...'

'No, no, Mrs Crisp, this looks affie good,' Cameron said, getting to his feet and resuming his broad accent. 'If you can spare us a wee minute of your precious time, my wife and I would like a word.'

'You would?'

'Sit ye doon, sit ye doon. Why don't you take the second cup?' Cameron retrieved a chair from the far corner of the room and pressed the surprised Mrs Crisp into it. 'You pour, Euphemia, my dear. I'm sure this good lady will welcome the chance to get aff her feet for a moment.'

'Well. Thank you very much. May I get you an ale, or…?'

'Nae, nae. I'm fine, thank you, I'll just have a wee bit of cake. I'm right fond of cake, am I not, Euphemia? Though you'll not take it amiss, Mrs Crisp, if I tell you that my wife, in my most humble opinion, makes the very lightest of sponge cakes of anyone in all of the British Isles. The receipt is the most closely guarded secret in the parish we've left behind, but if you ask her nicely I'm sure she'll tell you.'

'Mrs Crisp is not interested in cake ingredients,' Kirstin said, biting her lip and kicking Cameron sharply under the table.

'Ah, but indeed I am,' Mrs Crisp said, taking the cup which Kirstin handed to her. 'Though I make a very good fruit cake, my own sponges often fail to rise. Do tell me, what is your secret?'

What did one make cakes with? Kirstin's mind was a complete blank. 'Why, nothing but air,' she replied.

'Air?'

'Good Scots air, Mrs Crisp,' she said firmly. 'That's the secret of a nice rise. Now, before my husband allows his stomach to make him forget his manners, I'll have him say a wee prayer.' She smiled sweetly at Cameron. 'Say grace, my dear.'

He bowed his head. He clasped his hands together. 'Grace,' Cameron said solemnly, and took a large bite of currant cake. 'Delicious, Mrs Crisp, quite delicious. I don't think we'll taste anything as good as this in the New World.'

'You are bound for America, Reverend?'

'Indeed we are, Mrs Crisp, a new congregation, a new country. We're fair excited about it.'

'Though one thing is bothering us,' Kirstin said, leaning confidentially towards the landlady. 'We've said our goodbyes to all our friends back home save one. A Mrs Ferguson. She's one of my oldest friends. I don't suppose, with so many people coming through this lovely inn, that you'd remember her? We missed each other, you see, and I'm worried that we'll miss each other again—that she'll have been and gone before we reach the city ourselves. A woman of my age, though much better dressed, she—'

'I remember her well, Mrs Collins.' Mrs Crisp looked decidedly uncomfortable. 'Did you say you are good friends with the lady?'

'Oh, aye, very good friends. The pair of us were at school the'gether.' Cameron was not the only one who could thicken his accent. Kirstin assumed a worried look. 'Don't tell me that something happened to her?'

'No, no. That is...' Mrs Crisp got up, checked the door of the parlour and came back to the table. 'I will be frank with you, Mrs Collins, Reverend Collins, my husband and I are rather at odds on this matter.'

'This matter? You are putting the wind up me, Mrs Crisp.'

'No, no. There is naught—at least that is what Mrs Ferguson assured my husband. For myself, I would have been inclined to call the authorities, no matter what she said, but she would have none of it, and one must assume that the woman knows her daughter well enough.'

'Her daughter?'

'This is a respectable inn.' Mrs Crisp crossed her arms over her sparse bosom. 'There are some,' she said, her voice lowered to a whisper, 'where young women are preyed upon, where young girls from the country are indeed— Well, suffice it to say that the work they are offered and the work they are given bear little resemblance to each other. You understand me, Mrs Collins, Reverend? I am sorry if I offend...'

'Och, not at all,' Cameron intervened, touching Mrs Crisp's arm sympathetically. 'Euphemia and I have long worked in the poorest of parishes. We are sadly very much aware of the vices young lassies can be drawn into. Though I do hope you are not going to tell us that Mrs Ferguson's lass...?'

'No, no. Goodness, no. What I'm trying to tell you is that she could not have been—nor her servant. We are most vigilant about keeping a respectable inn and a respectable courtyard.'

'Despite your historic associations with the highwayman standing guard over the mantel?' Cameron said, with a perfectly pitched smile.

'Oh, that thing. My husband's mother painted that.' Mrs Crisp returned his smile with a grim one of her own. 'A better judge of his fellow man than Mr Crisp there is not, but when it comes to his mother I'm afraid he is blind.'

As is his mother, if her artwork was anything to go by, Kirstin thought irreverently, as Mrs Crisp embarked upon a clearly long-suppressed description of her mother-in-law's many failings.

'Aye, you've many a cross to bear, but if you don't mind,' Cameron interjected as the landlady drew breath, 'I'd like to return to the subject of Mrs Ferguson's daughter.'

'Ca—Caleb! You forget yourself, my dear.'

Only by the faintest tremor did Cameron betray himself. 'My wife, Mrs Crisp, only uses my given name when she wishes to castigate me. And quite rightly too, my dear,' he said, with a soulful look at Kirstin. 'I spoke out of turn. I merely know how anxious you are yourself to hear more regarding your friend.'

'A perfectly understandable sentiment,' Mrs Crisp said, 'I'm sorry to have to tell you this, Mrs Collins, but I'm afraid that your friend's daughter has run off.'

'No!' Kirstin clasped her hands together in horror. 'What do you mean? Pray, tell me quickly.'

Mrs Crisp needed no urging, pouring out a highly coloured tale, though it was one which, Kirstin noted, varied very little from what Louise Ferguson had already recounted to Cameron.

'And yet,' Kirstin said, as the woman finally came to an end, 'you say my friend decided against calling the authorities? I find that most...'

'Strange? As indeed did I, Mrs Collins. One minute she's creating a right hullabaloo, demanding that my husband question our staff as if they were not to be trusted, and the next she's changed her tune entirely, and it's all, "Oh, I think I've made a mistake"..."Oh, I remember now, there was an arrangement!" Shall I tell you what I think?'

'Please do.'

'I think there *was* an arrangement, but it was made by the young lady herself, and her mother, though she might have had an inkling, certainly would not have been party to it.'

'You think an arrangement of a—a romantic nature, Mrs Crisp?'

'That I do, Mrs Collins, that I do.'

'But what makes you conclude that as an explanation for her disappearance rather than something more sinister? Though of course I do not doubt the respectability of your inn…'

'As indeed you should not, but I will allow it's a natural enough question. I will tell you why. It is because of Tom.'

'Tom?' Kirstin repeated blankly.

'One of the stable hands.'

'And what tale did Tom tell?' Cameron asked.

'That a man asked him to take a note to the young Scottish lady who was expected off that day's coach.'

Beside Kirstin, he stiffened, though his expression did not change. 'And did Tom do as he was bid?'

'He did, Reverend, I'm afraid to say. At least, he gave the note to the young Scottish lady's maid, and I must assume that she passed it on to her mistress—her young mistress, Miss Ferguson, I mean.'

'What did Tom suppose was the purpose of this note?'

'Tom is one of those boys who has a way with horses and not a thought for much else in his head,' Mrs Crisp retorted waspishly. 'I doubt he supposed anything much. In fact I know he did not, for when my husband questioned him, at Mrs Ferguson's behest, he never saw fit to mention the note. My husband, you see, asked only if anyone had seen either Miss Ferguson or her maid leave the inn, and Tom did not see them. He saw only the note.'

'Yet he thought to mention it to yourself— when, exactly?'

There was an edge in Cameron's voice now, that made Mrs Crisp's eyes widen. She swallowed, eyeing him less conspiratorially and with some fear. 'Reverend, you must understand Mrs Ferguson was adamant...'

'When, Mrs Crisp?'

'Two days later. Though my husband was content to let the matter drop...'

'His lips being sealed by a douceur, yes?'

'How did you—?'

'Please understand, Mrs Crisp, I am concerned only for the girls. Mrs Ferguson is a woman of some—some strength of personality. I understand that well enough,' Cameron said more gently. 'It's her way or the highway, as we say in Glasgow.'

'I've never heard that expression.' Mrs Crisp's lips twitched. 'It describes her perfectly.'

'So, although your husband let the matter drop, you were worried?' Kirstin prompted.

'The young lady seemed so nice, and the maid—well, she was cocky, as some of these girls are, when they are raised above their station, but I could see no real harm in her. A pair of country mice, that's what they were when it came down to it, and innocent as a lamb, the young lady was. I simply couldn't believe she'd run off with some man—but there, I was wrong. For when I asked around myself Tom remembered the note, and who else would be sending a note like that save a lover? So Mrs Ferguson was right after all, to try to hush the matter up. What a scandal! What that poor woman must be suffering. I don't know what would be worse, tracking the girl down before she is married or letting her marry in haste and repent at leisure.'

'You think they were headed to Gretna Green?'

'Where else?'

'Have you evidence to back that notion up, Mrs Crisp? Did one of your men actually see the carriage?'

'No.' The landlady shook her head. 'No,' she repeated, 'no one has said so.'

'But you suspect…?' Cameron said.

'But you think…?' Kirstin said.

'I think I've said more than enough. Speak to the farrier. He has been dropping all sorts of hints, in the hope of a reward, I'll wager. Whether there's any substance to his nods and his winks—well, I leave it up to you to find out.'

Mrs Crisp got to her feet. 'He's a big brute of a man, and one with a very high opinion of himself and of his worth too. He charges us well above the going rate for the work he does. Were it not for the fact that we could not do our business so well without him— There, but I've said more than enough. You are welcome to talk to him, though I doubt you'll get anywhere. I only hope that you being a man of the cloth, Reverend Collins, will prevent him taking his usual measures with those he doesn't wish to pass the time of day with. Don't say I didn't warn you.'

It was late afternoon when they arrived back at the hotel. The back stairs to which Cameron had been granted access, having duly greased the Head Porter's palm for the privilege, allowed the reverend and his wife to avoid the main reception area. His generosity had also resulted, he was pleased to note, in the arrival of a servant bearing a tray of refreshments within five minutes of their return.

Kirstin, looking genuinely grateful for the pot

of revoltingly fragranced tea, sank down on the couch and poured herself a cup. 'So it is clear, from what the farrier told you,' she said, 'that the two girls were abducted.'

Cameron helped himself to coffee and dropped down into the chair opposite her, stretching out his legs in their prickly woollen stockings. 'Very clear. He saw the maid waiting across the road at the toll booth. "Yon one with hair the colour of a cock's comb," is what he said, so it must have been Jeannie. Anyway, assuming it was a lovers' tryst, the farrier kept an interested eye. It was not until the coach pulled up that he became suspicious. For a maid to have a lover with a coach and a pair struck him as unusual.'

'Though he did nothing about it,' Kirstin said, undoing her shawl and pulling off Euphemia's bonnet. The movement released a puff of powder from her hair, the grey at the front making the rest look even more midnight glossy than ever.

'There was nothing to be done at first, he claimed.' Cameron cast off the reverend's hat and loosened his necktie.

'And when poor Jeannie cried out, while she was struggling to get away from the two men pulling her into the coach…'

'The farrier dared not intervene. He's a big brawny man, but he feared they would be armed,' he said, with a sneer as he recalled the man's initial bravado, and how easily it had been destroyed.

'If only Philippa had been as timid she would not have tried to save her maid, which is what I think must have happened.'

'Aye. That note which the landlady mentioned, the one intended for the young Scottish lass, it must have been for Jeannie, though who wrote it I have not an idea.'

'Whoever it was, Jeannie must have told Philippa, and Philippa was intrigued enough to follow her to catch a glimpse of this lover. Do you think Jeannie had a lover, Cameron? And if she did, what was he doing waiting for her at the Spaniard's Inn? If he followed her from Scotland—' Kirstin broke off with a sigh. 'It makes no sense. It is much more likely that Jeannie was meeting a relative, isn't it? Or perhaps a friend. Though why she should meet anyone in such a clandestine way...'

'Perhaps we'll get something from Mrs Ferguson when we meet with her tomorrow morning. We may have more questions than answers now, but we've made progress, of a sort. We know that what we're dealing with is definitely an abduction, and not a random one either.'

As he stretched across to set his coffee cup

down on the tray, the sleeves of his second-hand coat rode up, revealing the bruised and bloody knuckle which had, to his great satisfaction, so easily made the farrier crumble.

Kirstin gasped in surprise. 'You hit him!'

Cameron grinned. 'More than once. I find that with some people the direct approach is much more effective.'

'I thought you wanted me to stay outside so that you could talk with him man to man.'

'Which is exactly what I did, in his own language,' he retorted. 'It's nothing.'

'It's not nothing.' Kirstin jumped to her feet. 'I have some salve. Give me one moment.'

She was gone but a few minutes, bustling back in with a small tin of something and a washcloth. 'Let me see.'

He held out his hand meekly for her inspection, amused by her concern, but more than happy for her to make a fuss over his grazed and swollen knuckles if it meant her touching him.

It hadn't occurred to him that she might have misinterpreted his desire to talk to the farrier man to man. It had seemed so very obvious to him from the little the landlady said that the farrier would require roughing over rather than coaxing or bribing with coin.

Kirstin had poured the contents of the hot

water kettle into a saucer, and was now dabbing cautiously at his hand with the towel. 'Does that hurt?'

'No.'

'Is this your only injury?'

He chuckled. 'If I told you he'd thumped me on the chest and that I'd a huge bruise...'

Her head whipped up. 'Cameron, you have not— Oh, you are teasing me.'

He smiled at her. 'Do you mind?'

'I take it that the farrier came off the worse from your encounter?'

'He'll have been looking for a steak from the kitchen for his eye.'

'How revolting. A pack of ice would serve the purpose just as well.'

'It wouldn't, actually. A steak brings the swelling down much more quickly.'

'What on earth do *you* know of such things?'

Cameron shrugged. 'You don't learn to be handy with your fists without taking part in a few fights.'

'And you are? Handy with your fists, I mean?'

She was not revolted by this. Far from it, she seemed rather taken with the notion.

'Oh, very,' Cameron said airily, though the truth was he'd not had cause to hit a man for a long time, until today. But it seemed that a skill so hard-learned was not easily forgotten, and he was enjoying the effect of his toughness on Kirstin. Who'd have thought it?

'You should have seen the look on the farrier's face, when the Reverend Collins planted his fist on his jaw. *Just because I'm a man of the cloth*, I told him,' Cameron recounted in his best Glaswegian growl, '*it disnae mean that I can't take care of masel.*'

Her eyes were fixed on his. He was not imagining the flare of heat there, he was sure of it, and as he leaned towards her, she leant towards him.

'I suppose that working in such a rough parish as we did, you got into any number of fights.'

'And you, my sweet Euphemia, were always there to bind me up and kiss me better.'

The towel she'd been holding dropped onto the floor. 'I'm not so sure that Euphemia is sweet.'

'Och, but she is. She puts on a good front to the world, mind, but when they are alone Euphemia and—and...'

'Caleb,' she reminded him, with a smile that caught his breath. 'When they are alone...?'

'When they are alone...' He trailed his fingers down the line of her jaw to rest on her shoulder and she leant in, closing the tiny gap between them. 'She is the sweetest...' He kissed her brow.

'The very sweetest...' He kissed the tip of her nose. 'The very, very sweetest Euphemia you can imagine.'

He kissed her mouth. He meant it to be a simple kiss but as their lips met, and he felt the sharp intake of her breath, their lips clung, and their kiss turned into something much more complex.

She tilted her head, and her mouth opened to his, and his head whirled. There was an echo, the fleeting memory of their kisses all those years ago, and then it was gone and he was firmly in the present, drinking in the taste of her, his blood singing in his veins as their tongues touched, as their kiss deepened, as she twined her arms around his neck, as he felt the brush of her breasts against his chest, as he inhaled the odd mixture of powder and greasepaint and second-hand clothes and a feral, heated undertone that must be desire.

Blood surged to his groin as their tongues danced together, as their breaths mingled, shallow and fast, as they pressed themselves uncomfortably together on the sofa, not wanting to move lest they break the kiss, yet wanting so much more.

And then the wanting sharpened, and the kiss ended, and they were left gazing into one another's eyes, dazed, confused, letting each other go, reality coming back slowly as they sat up, as their breathing calmed.

Kirstin picked up the towel from the floor and folded it neatly in her lap. She reached for the little tin, opened it, and started spreading salve on his knuckles, concentrating only on that, the touch of her fingers light, determinedly impersonal, and the kiss faded like a dream.

'Put some more of this on tonight, before you go to bed,' she said, letting his hand go and snapping shut the tin.

'Thank you.'

She smiled at him awkwardly. 'I feel sure Euphemia would insist on binding your knuckles, but I feel equally sure that you would resist.'

'I reckon you're right on both counts.'

'And I reckon it's time we pack Euphemia and Caleb away, before they do any more damage.'

She got to her feet, shaking out her skirts. Despite the fact that she was still more or less in costume, she was no longer Euphemia but cool Kirstin. 'You'll likely need a bath to rid yourself of the smell of wet dog, so I'll leave you to it.'

Cameron opened the door for her, but as she made to step through, he caught her wrist. 'What did we do with Goliath? He was a smelly beast, but a loyal one, I hope he's not missing us too much?'

She smiled at that. 'I doubt he's missing us at all, living the doggie dream as he is now on your cousin's farm. I think you are missing Goliath more than he is missing you.' She touched his arm lightly. 'We'll get another dog in the New World. Something smaller. And sweeter-smelling.'

And with that she whisked herself away to her own suite, leaving Cameron smiling softly, thinking to himself that a collie would be a good substitute, before the whistling of a messenger boy in the corridor brought him back to reality and he shouted after the lad to bring water for a bath as soon as it could be arranged.

Chapter Five

As she ate a solitary breakfast alone in her suite the following morning, Kirstin realised, with disbelief, that this was only her third day at the hotel, a mere five days since her assignation with Cameron in the church. So much had happened it felt like weeks had passed.

Today she would meet Louise Ferguson, the half-sister who meant so much to Cameron that he would go to the enormous expense of employing The Procurer in order to help her, and yet who meant so little to him that he had no desire to see her ever again afterwards. What form of debt did he feel he owed her, since it was clearly not financial?

She poured a second cup of tea. The curious nature of Cameron's relationship with Louise Ferguson was none of her concern, though perhaps it was indicative of his general aversion to family ties? He had been quite unequivocal on the subject over dinner two nights ago. There was no place in his life for a wife, never mind a child.

She sipped her tea. They were the words of a man who knew himself very well, and was ruthlessly honest about what made him tick. Kirstin smiled thinly down at her empty plate and absent-mindedly began to butter another bread roll. A man after her own heart, in that sense.

But as she broke off a piece of the bread and popped it into her mouth, her smile faded. She had the proof she had sought. She had done the right thing six years ago, for all concerned, including Cameron, whose sense of honour would oblige him to do what he was not inclined to do if he ever found out. So he must never, ever find out.

For a moment, cold fear clutched at her heart, making her shiver violently, but Kirstin was not given to wild imaginings. She took a deep, calming breath. She reminded herself that she was The Procurer, the keeper of secrets, that there was no reason whatsoever to fear her secret might be discovered.

Her heart slowed. Her fingers unfurled their tight grip on the handle of her teacup. She had made the right decision. She need never question it again. The future she had planned was assured, and hers alone to shape. And so she could—not *enjoy* the situation, as such, given the circumstances, but relish it, knowing it was safe to do so.

She smiled. Now that the burden of her doubt was lifted she could admit to herself that she was not averse to spending some more time in Cameron's company. Free from other responsibilities, she could be herself, just for a while. It would be a novel experience. She would devote her energy to resolving this dreadful situation, and if, in the process, she and Cameron shared some laughter, a little danger, relished the thrill and the challenge of pitting their wits against this unknown abductor—well, then, where was the harm?

Soon enough they would go their separate ways. She might never get the chance to escape reality like this again. *Certainly not in the company of this particular man*, a little voice reminded her as she began to get dressed. But Kirstin brushed it aside, because that was precisely the point. This situation was a one-off.

She had rehearsed her argument that it would be best if she spoke to Louise Ferguson on her own, but when Kirstin tapped on the door of Cameron's suite an hour later he pre-empted her.

'I've already heard the tale straight from the horse's mouth, so to speak,' he said. 'A fresh pair of ears might pick up some undiscovered nuances.'

It was exactly what Kirstin had been about to say herself. From the moment Cameron had been forced to confide in her through the grille of the confessional he had placed Philippa's safe return above all else, but it struck her afresh how few men in his situation would have confidence enough in their own judgement, and indeed in hers, to delegate such a crucial task.

'I agree,' she answered, 'and I very much appreciate your sparing me the need to say so.'

He was sipping one of his endless cups of coffee, his gaze fixed firmly on her. It made her edgy, the way he looked at her as if he was reading her every thought, even though she knew that was preposterous. She would not think about that kiss yesterday. She would not allow a kiss to make things awkward between them, especially when it had been Euphemia and Caleb who had been doing the kissing, not Kirstin and Cameron.

'I am also hopeful that Mrs Ferguson may feel she can confide in a woman more easily than a man,' Kirstin said, trying to keep her mind fixed firmly on business.

To her relief, Cameron nodded, dropping his gaze. 'She knows why I've engaged your services. I won't deny she was dubious at first, terrified that you'd be indiscreet, but she made her own enquiries into The Procurer's reputation and seems reassured. It also helps that you come bearing the good news that Philippa is still alive.'

'As far as we know. I cannot give her any false hope.'

'Though you will not paint the picture blacker than necessary? She is a mother, and her only child—'

'I understand perfectly, I assure you—' Kirstin cut herself short, curling her fingers into her palm. 'I will not alarm her any more than absolutely necessary,' she said calmly, unfurling her fingers before Cameron could notice.

Louise Ferguson received Kirstin in the drawing room of her temporary residence in Mayfair. She was the kind of woman for whom the epithet *well-groomed* might have been invented. Tall, austere, in a grey-striped day gown. Kirstin could initially spot no resemblance to Cameron in her wide-spaced hazel eyes, fierce brows and rather prominent nose. It was the sensual mouth and the dimple in the centre of her chin which betrayed their common ancestry, as did the thick black hair which she wore in a complicated coiffure high on her head.

She rose slowly to her feet when the decrepit retainer announced Miss Blair, greeting Kirstin with a look which mingled surprise with trepidation. 'You will take tea,' she said, in a voice which brooked no dissent.

'Thank you.'

Kirstin took her seat on the opposite side of the table by the fire. The other woman's eyes were tinged with red under her skilfully applied powder. She had worried away at the skin at the side of her right thumb to the point where it was bleeding.

'I am pleased to report that your daughter,' Kirstin said without preamble, as her hostess began the process of pouring and measuring, 'is, if not safe, at least still alive, according to my sources.'

Louise Ferguson gave a little gasp, dropping the silver measuring spoon. 'How do you know? Are you sure?'

'I am afraid I can't tell you how I know, but I am as certain as it is possible to be. Philippa and Jeannie have not met an untimely death.'

Louise Ferguson's chest heaved. She clasped

her hands tightly together, tilting her head back, widening her eyes, but tears tracked down her cheeks untrammelled.

Kirstin watched helplessly as the woman tried to regain her composure, resisting the impulse to intervene, recognising in the compulsive swallowing, the shuddering breaths, the lips drawn tight into a grimace, all the signs of an iron will tested to its limits.

She knew implicitly, for she would have felt the very same herself, that Louise Ferguson would not appreciate sympathy. Accordingly, she busied herself with the making of the tea, noting with approval that the leaves were of excellent quality. Silently, she pushed a brewed cup across the table when, with a last shuddering breath, Louise Ferguson gave a little nod, dabbed her cheeks, and wetted her lips.

'Forgive me,' she said.

'A perfectly understandable reaction. Take some tea.'

The woman did as Kirstin bade her, adding a soupçon of milk with a relatively steady hand and sipping gratefully. Her cheeks remained pale, but the taut lines of her face softened as she nodded, accepting a second cup.

'Assuming that Mr Dunbar has explained the circumstances of my daughter's disappearance, Miss Blair, you will understand why I must shoulder the blame.'

'You certainly are partially culpable.'

A gasp and a small splutter of laughter greeted this remark. 'You do not mince your words.'

'You strike me as someone who, like myself, prefers her truth unvarnished,' Kirstin replied coolly. 'If you had not taken a sleeping draught Philippa would not have found it so easy to sneak out of the inn. Whether she would still have done so had you been awake or sleeping lightly is another matter, and a futile source of speculation. We cannot change what has happened. We can only aspire to repair the damage and get your daughter and her maid back safely.'

Such blunt talking might easily have estranged her from Louise Ferguson and destroyed any chance that Kirstin had of gaining her confidence, but since nothing could assuage maternal guilt, no matter how irrational, what Philippa's mother needed most was to feel that she was contributing to finding her daughter.

Kirstin was relieved to see that her strategy was the correct one. Louise Ferguson straightened her shoulders, clasped her hands on her lap and took a deep breath. 'What can I do to help, Miss Blair?'

'Please, call me Kirstin. May I call you Louise?' She waited for the other woman's assent before continuing. 'Now, tell me exactly what happened that night, omitting no detail, no matter how trivial or irrelevant you think it may be.'

'So you see,' Louise concluded, 'whichever way you look at it, I deserve a large portion of blame. I knew that Philippa was not nearly so keen on the marriage as I was, but I was certain that I knew what was best for her. She was, quite naturally, given her tender years, a little anxious about swapping the protection of a parent for a husband, but as I explained to her numerous times, it is the most natural thing in the world and has served society well for generations. I thought she had come to accept it. She was so excited about coming to London, about having a whole new wardrobe of gowns. But clearly I underestimated the strength of my own daughter's resistance.'

'You seem very certain that Philippa has run off to avoid an unwanted marriage.'

'It is the obvious conclusion, given the facts.'

'Your brother and I—'

'Half-brother.'

Which intervention told its own tale, and made Kirstin resentful on Cameron's behalf. But that was another irrelevance, for the moment.

'However you wish to refer to him, the point is that we paid a visit to the Spaniard's Inn yesterday, where a number of new facts emerged which change things somewhat.'

She proceeded to recount the salient details of what they had discovered. The effect on Louise was momentous.

'Philippa did not abscond? You are certain of this?'

'Completely.'

'That—that *blasted* Jeannie!' Louise jumped to her feet, wringing her hands. 'That pert chit wields far too much influence over my daughter.'

Perhaps because, Kirstin thought, Philippa had been starved of any other influence save her mother in her young life. She had never attended school, and seemed to have no friends of her own choosing, reading between the lines of all that Kirstin had heard today. She didn't question Louise Ferguson's love for her daughter, but it was clear that her certainty that she knew what was best might feel suffocating.

Kirstin's own conscience pricked her. Wasn't *she* just as guilty of such certainty? She dismissed this ruthlessly. The circumstances were radically different.

'Louise,' she said carefully, 'can't you see that Philippa acted with the purest of motives, from a desire to protect her maid, who is also her friend, without thinking of her own safety?'

'Would that she had thought first, we would not be—'

'But we are in this situation,' Kirstin said firmly. 'And now we must try to remedy it. It seems reasonable to me to assume that the note Jeannie received was not from a lover—unless some man followed her south from Scotland?'

'No, that does not make sense,' Louise said, frowning. 'She has been walking out with my neighbour's second footman for a few months now. It's a respectable match, and one that I understand from Philippa they are eager to formalise as soon as possible, much to my daughter's chagrin. Jeannie will most likely not be her maid once she is married.'

Louise set her cup aside. 'I've informed Kenneth—that is Philippa's betrothed—that Philippa has been somewhat under the weather and cannot write, in case you were wondering. Heaven forfend that I should force her into a marriage she truly does not want, but nor do I wish to close down the option should she change her mind. It is an excellent match. No matter what you think of me, I only...'

Louise's voice trembled. Kirstin allowed herself to touch her hand in sympathy. 'I am here to help you, not to judge you. If you could concentrate on what else you know about Jeannie, any connection at all with London…'

Kirstin sat quite still, her face a careful blank as Louise did so. Following a series of frowns, nods, and little shakes of the head, she finally looked up. 'Heather,' she said triumphantly. 'Heather Aitken.'

'Who the devil is Heather Aitken?' Cameron demanded, as Kirstin recounted her conversation with Louise some hours later.

'According to Louise, another cocky chit of a maid with ideas above her station. She and Jeannie started work for the Ferguson family on the same day. They are the same age, and bosom buddies, it seems. Heather had not the patience to gain the experience that would earn her promotion, so about a year ago she left Edinburgh for London. "In this city, demand is such that any servant, no matter how lazy, may easily be elevated"—I use Mrs Ferguson's own words here, you understand.'

'And she thinks that this Heather Aitken and Jeannie might have kept in touch?' Cameron said eagerly. 'Does she know where we might find her?'

'I'm afraid not, but that is of no consequence.

If she is in London, I will track her down easily enough.'

He looked suitably impressed. She treated him to The Procurer's trademark enigmatic smile, hiding the absurd little rush of pride his admiration gave rise to. She didn't need anyone to tell her how good she was at what she did, her reputation spoke for her. There had, over the years, been grateful letters thanking her, but she never permitted her clients or the women she matched with them to meet her once a contract was completed.

All the same, it was pleasant—very pleasant—to have her unique set of skills acknowledged face-to-face, as it were. Provided she did not become complacent or, worse, vain! And provided she remembered that this particular situation was unique and could never be repeated, for it contravened all The Procurer's well-established rules.

'Heather Aitken is, according to Louise, an ambitious young woman,' Kirstin said brusquely, dragging her eyes away from Cameron's answering smile. 'She will have set her sights on what is known as a superior household, and one therefore likely to use a well-established and respected employment agency. That will be my starting point. The world of domestic service is a close-knit one, even in a city as large as London. I have already set enquiries in motion.'

'How long…?'

'Impossible to say, but a day…two at the very most. My assistant is aware of the urgency of the matter, I assure you, and is making use of every resource at my disposal.'

'And there is nothing more to be done in the interim?'

'I don't think so,' Kirstin replied. 'This is our best—our only—lead.'

'I'm impressed with your efficiency. I take it, then, that you arranged all this with your assistant immediately after your visit to Mrs Ferguson? Presumably you have an office nearby?'

Cameron's tone was offhand, but Kirstin was not going to fall into the trap of revealing any details of her business. Many had tried to discover them and failed in the past.

'Until we can speak to Heather I'm afraid there seems to me very little else we can do to progress matters, other than have someone interview this under-footman whom Louise says is courting Jeannie.'

'Leave that with me. You are not the only one with contacts. What's more, mine happen to be in the right part of the country. I'll have an express sent to one of my men in Glasgow. I know it will take time,' he added as she opened her mouth to protest, 'but we can't leave any stone unturned. He's just the man for the job. His name is Tommy Devine. I have known him since we were boys. You could say he is the closest thing I have to a brother. We went our separate ways for a wee while, for he has no head for figures and was sent to work in a shipyard while I was learning to be a ledger clerk. But when I went into business for myself I sought him out, and he's been my right-hand man ever since. Is there anything else you'd like to know about him?'

'I only need to know that he has your trust and complete confidence,' Kirstin said stiffly.

'I'm offering you the opportunity to indulge your curiosity about me without needing to re-ciprocate.'

'I know you are. It's very magnanimous of you. Is this Tommy Devine taking care of busi-ness, then, while you are here?'

'As much as I allow him to,' Cameron an-swered wryly. 'It's not that I don't trust his judge-ment, I simply prefer to make my own decisions.'

'Now, that is something I do understand. When one has grown a business from the start, nurtured it, cared for it, it is very natural, I think, to be protective of it.'

'Is that how you feel?'

'I can't discuss business. The Procurer—'

'It's you I'm interested in, not The Procurer,' Cameron snapped, the teasing light fading from his eyes. 'Is that such a crime?'

Kirstin shook her head, feeling like a hypocrite. When Louise, highly relieved to have been able to be of some assistance in finding her daughter, had become voluble over a luncheon of smoked salmon and eggs scrambled with cream and chives, Kirstin had encouraged her to talk, telling herself that everything she could discover of the girl's home life was potentially of value. Once the subject of Philippa's short and rather mundane life had been exhausted Louise had turned to her own life, and it would have been so easy, by way of some skilfully placed questions, to lead her on to the subject of Cameron. Kirstin had resisted, but it had been a very close call.

She had tried, but had not been able to persuade herself that his history had any bearing on the case, though the fact that she had tried to twist the facts to satisfy her curiosity appalled her.

The question was, what to do about it? She could keep quiet, but her innate honesty made that option repellent. Guilt and shame made her want to hang her head, but she forced herself to look him straight in the eye. 'No, it's not a crime,

Cameron, especially when I cannot deny my own curiosity regarding you. I have to confess that I came very close to encouraging Louise to talk about you over luncheon.'

He stiffened. 'It would have been a futile exercise. Mrs Ferguson knows next to nothing about me.'

'Precisely.' Colour had flooded her cheeks. Now she felt it fade just as quickly. 'I wanted to understand how it is that you and your half-sister are strangers to one another.'

'The one topic on which I was not forthcoming,' Cameron said. 'It didn't occur to you that it is a chapter of my history I wish to keep private?'

'I have no excuse to offer.'

In fact she had one very valid excuse, but she would not use it, even to salve her own conscience. The questions she had almost asked had been to satisfy her own curiosity, and for no other reason. Cameron remained silent, giving her no clue as to his thoughts.

'I am deeply sorry,' Kirstin continued, striving to recapture her usual cool, professional tone. 'You may be assured that I will make no further intrusions into your personal affairs.'

He smiled faintly down at her then, shaking his head before touching her cheek lightly. 'Don't be so hard on yourself. You didn't pry when you could have. Anyway, I'm flattered.' Seeing her confusion, he broadened his smile. 'It proves that I intrigue you enough to make you interested in me. Which I suspect makes me an exception.'

Kirstin blinked up at him. 'You are an exception to almost every rule. But that does not mean I have any desire to—'

'But you do, don't you?'

He slid his fingers in a deliberately sensual movement up her arm, to rest on the bare skin at the nape of her neck. Though she tried to ignore it, she couldn't disguise her shiver of response.

'More than six years since that night,' Cameron said, 'and our desire for one another is every bit as powerful. You, who take such pride in being honest with yourself, should admit that much. But it's the only thing that's unchanged. We didn't know each other then. We barely know each other better now. We are both very different people.' He dropped his hand, stepping away from her. 'Till tomorrow, Kirstin…'

December 1812, Carlisle

Though Kirstin's kisses made his head spin, made his body thrum with desire, Cameron reluctantly tore his mouth from hers. 'You'd better retire to your room before we do something we'll both regret.'

'Will we?'

Her lips were swollen with his kisses. In the candlelight, it seemed to him that her eyes burned with the same desire which made him ache with wanting.

'Is it what you truly want, Cameron?'

He could not lie to her. 'No.'

'No more do I,' she said softly.

His mind was befuddled. Her words were so confident, seemingly so at odds with her experience—or lack of it. Had he misjudged her?

'Kirstin, do you know what you're saying?'

Her gaze did not falter from his. 'Yes.'

Yet still he sought further assurance. 'Are you absolutely sure?'

'Certain.'

She spoke with such confidence his conscience was salved. With a groan, Cameron pulled her into his arms again, kissing her deeply. She responded without hesitation, pressing her body against his, twining her arms around his neck, opening her mouth. Their tongues touched, sending such a flame of desire through him that he stopped thinking, surrendering completely to the frantic urging of their bodies.

He had no idea how they reached her bed-chamber, but as she closed the door, locked it, he asked once more, his voice hoarse and ragged, if she was certain she wanted this.

She laughed, a guttural, sensual sound that made the hairs on his neck stand on end and made his already throbbing shaft achingly hard.

'Far more than you, by the sounds of it.'

The challenge implicit in her words stripped him of the last vestige of self-control. He pulled her back into his arms, tight against him, leaving her in no doubt of the strength of his arousal.

'That's not possible.'

Kisses gave way to touch. Hands frantic, tearing at clothing, eager to find skin. His mouth on the hollow at the base of her throat, tasting the warm, feminine scent of her, while he undid the fastenings of her gown, sliding it down her arms, letting it drop to the floor, revealing her slim body sheathed in clinging undergarments.

The swell of her breasts above her corset and chemise made him catch his breath. He traced the shape of them with his tongue and his hands, then the delightful dip to her waist, the even more delightful shape of her bottom, her shallow breathing, her soft moans, rousing him further, urging him on.

She fell back onto the bed, pulling him with her. Her hands roved over his shoulders, his back, under his shirt, tugging it free from his breeches. He yanked himself free of it, eager for the sensation of skin touching skin, her eyes feasting on his body in an echo of the way he drank in hers, her hands echoing his touch.

Loosening her stays, the ribbon at the neck of her chemise, his mouth found the hard peak of her nipple. She arched under him as he sucked and licked, and he slid his hand up her leg, finding the opening in her pantaloons, the warm, soft flesh of her inner thighs and the damp, soft curls covering her sex.

She stilled under him for just a moment, but even as he hesitated in response she pulled him down towards her again, her lips meeting his in a drugging kiss. He stroked his way inside her, the wet, hot, tightness of her making his erection pulse and throb in anticipation. She was moaning beneath him, her body bucking under him as he stroked her to her climax.

This was no time for finesse, and he had no wish to delay completion for either of them. Her hands grabbed fistfuls of the bedcovers, her eyes closed as she came. The sight of her, unravelled and ecstatic under him, almost sent him over the edge. He kicked himself free of his boots and breeches…

London, February 1819

Cameron groaned, running his fingers through his hair. Why was he tormenting himself with the memory of that night? He poured himself a glass of port, wrinkling his nose at the cloying sweetness of it as he knocked it back in one draught. What he needed was a wee nip of whisky, but here in the south they considered the *uisge beatha* gut-rot, comparable to cheap gin, the tipple of the great unwashed.

Doubtless a great many of them would consider *him* a product of the great unwashed. There had been a time, way back, when he'd been trying to prove himself, when he'd have agreed with them. It made him smile now, the memory of those days, when the height of his ambition had been to return in triumph to Garrioch House, to parade the trappings of his success in front of those who'd been determined he was doomed to be a failure. He never had, thank God, realising just in time, on the eve of his planned visit, that the only person he needed to prove himself to was himself.

Cameron sighed, went to pour himself another glass of port then thought better of it. He didn't need to prove anything to Kirstin either, but he did want her to—to *understand* him, he supposed, with a wry smile. To know what made him who he was rather than rely on assumptions. He never talked of the past, and if Kirstin had

asked him outright he *would* most likely have
blanked her, but in time…

Time. Aye, and there was the rub. If he was
to get to know Kirstin at all he'd need time they
didn't have. And he did want to get to know her.
Now she'd walked back into his life, he wanted
to know if there was more to whatever it was
that drew the pair of them together than mutual
physical desire.

It had been a while since he'd been interested
in a woman, physically or otherwise. Too long,
now he came to think of it. There had been a
fair few women in his life, and there could have
been a lot more if he'd been so inclined. For
some reason the fairer sex had always liked his
dark looks, and his allure only increased when
it was supplemented by his success and personal
wealth. Trouble was, he'd become bored with
their attention. None of those women seemed
interested in who he was beyond good looks and
affluence.

Frowning out at the twinkling lights of the
city, he tried to recall his last affaire, and was
startled to discover that it had been at least a year
ago, more like two. He'd been starting to believe
himself past caring, that his business provided
all the stimulation he needed, but Kirstin was

proof that his appetites had merely been dulled, not extinguished.

Kirstin, who wasn't a whit interested in his looks, but who was, against her will, it seemed, interested in his life. She baffled him. If she'd wanted to forget that one night, why had she taken on the task of helping him find Philippa? It was all very well for her to claim that she was the best person to help him—and likely she was—but she had *chosen* herself for the role, for not even The Procurer could have coerced her. So why elect to meet him again, and then pretend that it was nothing more than coincidence?

Leaning his head on the window pane, Cameron closed his eyes. It wasn't that he'd been pining away for her for six years. He'd thought of her, but that night had, even at the time, seemed like a dream, the pair of them characters in some romantic drama, not real. He wasn't daft enough to think that Kirstin epitomised his perfect woman, and anyway, she was no more the same person she'd been six years ago than he was. But there was still something between them, and she knew it too, no matter how much she might want to deny it. They were two of a kind. Like drawn to like.

Well, one thing he'd always enjoyed was a challenge, and one thing he'd always been was persistent. He would take a trip to the docks tomorrow, see what was coming in, what was in demand. That way he wouldn't feel his day was wasted. And he'd ask her along. Show her a bit of his world and tell her where he came from, see if he could get her talking a bit about her own background.

With a satisfied nod, Cameron selected a sheet of writing paper and dipped a pen in the ink. He had an express to send to Glasgow.

Chapter Six

When she received Cameron's note early the next morning, Kirstin had barely started breakfast. He had decided to take an impromptu trip out to the docks, the missive informed her, and wondered if she would like to accompany him. Surprised and delighted to be able to escape the confines of the hotel, and for a reason entirely unconnected to their sombre task, she hurriedly finished her toilette, donning a full-length pelisse of crimson velvet braided with black, matching bonnet, black half-boots, and black gloves. A quick glance through the window revealed a winter sky the colour of pewter, and sent her back to the wardrobe for her black velvet muff before she hurried out of her suite.

'I reckoned we could both do with a diversion,' Cameron told her when he joined her in the hotel lobby, 'while we wait for Heather Aitken to be located. It's as good an excuse as any to take the pulse of London's current import market.'

He was dressed for the elements in a greatcoat and beaver hat. 'Ready?'

Pulling on his gloves, he made for the front door of the hotel, but when she stopped at the kerb, expecting him to summon a hackney, he shook his head. 'We'll walk down to the river, take a skiff from there.'

Though he was making an effort to slow his pace for her, she struggled to keep up with him as he led the way unerringly towards the river through St James's Park to Westminster Bridge, unable to disguise the fact that she was considerably out of breath when they arrived.

Cameron eyed her with some amusement.

'A lady, even one in my profession, is seldom called upon to run,' Kirstin said defensively.

He laughed. 'I've never run from anyone or anything in my life. I learnt very early in life never to turn my back on a fight.'

He turned away from her to the riverside steps, where a small skiff was waiting. He conferred briefly with the grizzled old salt in charge, before holding out his hand to help her. 'Be careful, the steps are slippery.'

Seeing her settled as comfortably as it was possible to be on the narrow seat in the stern, Cameron cast off, rock-steady despite the violent pitching of the small boat as their oarsman steered the boat out into the Thames.

'Why did you have to learn to fight so early in life?' Kirstin asked, as he settled beside her.

'I grew up in a place called Garrioch House, in the east end of Glasgow. It's a home for foundlings.'

It took a great deal to surprise her, but this admission made her jaw drop. 'Foundlings! But Louise—'

Cameron put a finger to her lips. 'Let's just enjoy the river trip.'

The sky was lowering. The surprising speed at which the little craft travelled made the hull lift out of the water then descend with a dull thud, and sent an icy spray into the air.

'*Enjoyable* would not be my first choice of adjective,' Kirstin said, as the boat crested another wave and would have jolted her out of her seat had Cameron not put his arm around her, smiling down at her as he anchored her against the shelter of his shoulder.

'I always think you see a city in a whole different light from the water. Stop thinking about whether you're going to lose your breakfast and look around you.'

'Fortunately, I did not get the chance to eat

breakfast,' she answered, trying to do as he suggested.

It *was* an odd way to see the city she knew so well towering above her, for the tide was very low. As they rounded a bend of the Thames, Somerset House came into view, and behind it the crowded district of Drury Lane could just be glimpsed. On the south side the buildings seemed an unstructured mass, a warren of lower-lying houses, wharves and offices contrasting with the more elegant architecture of the north bank and its plethora of church spires. There was the vivid green square of Temple Gardens, while all seemed brown on the other side, and though it must be a figment of her imagination even the air seemed gloomier, the chimneys belching blacker smoke.

The river itself was alive with traffic, from the smallest of rowing boats to skiffs like the one in which they travelled and bigger craft, all vying for space, their oarsmen calling to each other, their passengers too and even, in one passing yacht, a dog yapping in the prow.

'It is busier than Bond Street.' Turning, Kirstin found Cameron watching her. 'How is it that there are not more accidents?'

'There are too many as it is,' their oarsman interjected gruffly, glancing briefly over his shoulder. 'Young fools who don't know the tides, old lags who forget they're not as strong as they used to be, and rich fools, too drunk or in too much of a hurry to realise that the river has no respect for money or bloodline. But you're safe enough with me. I was born with the Thames flowing in my veins. You'll excuse me now, though, I need to concentrate. We're coming up to Blackfriars.'

The bridge spans seemed impossibly crowded but they negotiated their way through safely. St Paul's Cathedral loomed on the left-hand side, and on the right Southwark Priory. As the narrow, irregular arches of London Bridge came into view the skiff veered towards the north bank and Cameron got to his feet, ready to tie the rope to the iron ring on the wall by the foot of the stairs.

'It's far too risky to go any further downstream,' he explained, helping Kirstin out. 'The tide makes running under the spans of the bridge extremely dangerous.'

After tipping their oarsman, who was already negotiating a fee with someone looking to make the journey back to Westminster, he tucked Kirstin's arm in his. 'Stay close, and if you've a purse on you guard it well.'

It was on the tip of her tongue to tell him

that she had been in every dodgy district that he could dream of when she took a quick look around her and changed her mind. She thought of London, high *and* low society, as her world, but this environment was quite alien to her.

'I've never been here,' she said, gazing in awe at the mass of sailing ships jostling for space, tied up two, three abreast.

'It's known as the Pool,' Cameron told her. 'Every cargo must dock here to be inspected by the Excise men.'

'Thieving and pilfering must be rife here, given the temptation,' Kirstin said, looking askance at the rows of open warehouses, the stacks of goods waiting on the quayside to be moved. 'Is it similar at your wharves in Glasgow?'

'Smaller scale, but aside from that not much different. I've found that if you pay your men a fair wage temptation tends to be easier to resist.'

Kirstin chuckled. 'Don't bite the hand that feeds you? A shrewd tactic. I would expect no less from you.'

'Come, let's take a walk around, see what imports are doing well.'

They made their way towards the busiest part of the docks, past the Tower, weaving along quays and wharves, Cameron stopping every now and then to exchange words with a stevedore, with ships' crew and even with an Excise man.

He adapted seamlessly, Kirstin noticed, to each man, his manner, his speech and his accent modulated for each conversation, not enough to appear condescending but sufficient to gain respect. She was impressed, the more so for recognising the same chameleon-like technique she used herself. Though she was content to remain in the background and simply to observe, there was never a moment when Cameron was not aware of her, keeping a careful eye, watching her for signs of boredom.

The Procurer, she knew, was sometimes called The Sphinx. Cameron was the first person she had ever known who could read her most inscrutable expression. It was disconcerting, and made her at times deeply uncomfortable, yet today she felt it bound them, and she rather liked the novelty of it.

They wove their way along the docks towards Wapping, where Cameron steered them towards the large river basin.

'I had a brief acquaintance with this district of London last year,' Kirstin confided with a shudder. 'One of the few commissions which I regret taking on.'

'Because you failed?'

'No, but I will admit,' she said with a wry smile, 'that it was a close-run thing.' She surprised herself then, perhaps because Cameron did not press her, by telling him a little of the difficult nature of the case.

'What happened to the young woman?' he asked.

'I have no idea.'

His obvious astonishment made her hackles rise.

'Such women sign up for the opportunity to make a fresh start for themselves,' Kirstin said, unable to keep the defensive note from her voice. 'It is up to them what they make of it.'

'But aren't you curious?'

'I know, because The Procurer pays her fees promptly, that they have succeeded. I have no desire to know anything else.'

'If it was me,' he said, 'I'd want to know.'

'Well, I'm not you,' Kirstin said.

But he had once again made her uncomfortable by seeming to read her thoughts, since she *had* been wondering, since taking on this role herself, about those other women. What good would it do, though, to seek them out?

'What is that building?' she asked, pointing at the large edifice looming up in front of them, taking up most of one side of the massive, obviously recently created square dock.

'Tobacco Dock,' Cameron answered, his look telling her he was perfectly well aware that she was changing the subject. 'These are the warehouses for storing tobacco—as you can see from the size of them it's a very profitable trade, though not so much as a few decades ago. There was a time in Glasgow when the traders were known as the Tobacco Lords. I remember them, when I was wee, at the Exchange, mincing about in their scarlet cloaks, silver buckles on their shoes, looking down their noses at everyone as if they owned the place. Which I suppose they did, mind you.'

'Even when you were wee, then, you haunted the Clyde docks?'

'Not so much the docks but the river, the ships—it was a window onto the world.'

'Escape,' Kirstin said softly, deeply moved by the image this conjured up. 'Is that what you were after?'

'Aye.'

Cameron was staring off into the distance, perhaps picturing another dock, on another river, many years before. She tried to imagine him, a foundling, with heartbreaking good-looks, dreaming of another life, far from whatever brutal reality he'd endured, and her heart wrenched. 'Was it so very bad?'

He gave himself a shake, blinked, looked down at her with a twisted smile. 'I survived. No, more than that, I flourished against all expectations. You'd probably say I succeeded against the odds, and I wouldn't disagree with you in this case.'

'Will you tell me your story, Cameron?'

'Why do you want to know? As you've been at pains to point out, when we find Philippa we will go our separate ways once again. What difference would it make?'

Looking into his eyes, the strangest feeling took hold of her. Yearning. There was no other word for it. A longing for something she couldn't even begin to define mixed with a sharp, unmistakable and undeniable pang of desire. She forgot that they were standing in the middle of a crowded dock. Turning towards him, she reached her free hand up to caress his cheek. 'It makes all the difference in the world to me.'

He looked at her strangely, then caught her hand. He turned it over, pressing a fervent kiss to her palm. She could feel the heat of it even through her glove. He didn't kiss her mouth, but the look he gave her was enough to make her shiver as if he had.

Then he smiled crookedly, taking her arm again, and heading towards the tobacco warehouse. 'In that case, how can I possibly deny you? You'll need tea to sustain you, though. Come on.'

The Prospect of Whitby tavern lay at the far end of Wapping High Street, right on the Thames. Cameron secured an ornate wood-panelled private room on the top floor, with a view across the river to Rotherhithe and Bermondsey. It was, according to the landlord, the same room in which the diarist Samuel Pepys had once dined, a fact that Cameron found singularly underwhelming but which seemed to impress Kirstin. He ordered an early dinner to be delivered later, and coffee, tea and a platter of bread and cakes to keep them going in the meantime.

Kirstin, having discarded her coat and hat, warmed her hands at the roaring fire, leaning over just enough to give him a delightful view of her rear, and the desire which had caught him unawares a few moments before gripped him again. What was it about this woman that made him want her so much? Was it simply the result of his months of abstinence?

What did it matter? he thought impatiently, hurriedly glancing away from the enticing view as she stood upright and made for the tea tray. What mattered was that he did, and the feeling was mutual. What they would do about it—if anything—he had no idea. But he was damned if it would be nothing.

The coffee she poured for him was like tar, the way every sailor liked it. The landlord knew his clientele. Cameron took a happy gulp, wincing as it burned its way down his throat and into his gut. Kirstin, waiting for her tea to do whatever alchemy it did in the pot, shook her head at his impatience and poured him a second cup.

'Garrioch House?' she prompted, when they had been sitting opposite each other for a few silent minutes.

'Aye, Garrioch House. My home. For the first twelve years of my life, at any rate.'

Now that it came to it, although he wanted to talk about it, there was so much he didn't want to remember, aspects he preferred not to recall, details his memory had coloured and distorted over the years.

He decided to stick to the bare facts. 'A home for foundlings, it was—and still is to this day, like enough. I was handed into their care when not more than a few days old. Whoever left me gave them my name and a small purse of money, but nothing else.'

'Whoever left you? You mean it wasn't your mother?'

He shrugged. 'Unlikely, given what I know

now. A nurse, a midwife, a maid, or simply some poor messenger paid to deliver me, it could have been anyone.'

'And there was no other information to indicate your identity?'

'From the minute I was handed over to Garrioch House, my identity was fixed. I was a bastard.'

'Cameron!'

'What would you prefer? Illegitimate?'

'I prefer— I prefer...' Kirstin swallowed. To his surprise, her eyes held a sheen of tears. 'I prefer not to use any such term. A child should not be condemned for the lack of a piece of paper declaring her—his parentage.'

'True, but unfortunately neither society nor the law would agree with you.'

'Then both are wrong,' she said fiercely. 'You should not be punished for an accident of birth, Cameron.'

'Though punished I was, nonetheless.'

'You mean physically? That's outrageous!'

'Physically, mentally. It's the way of the world, I'm afraid.'

'But not now, surely?' Kirstin leaned forward, her perfect brow deeply furrowed. 'Now you are a successful businessman, a man of status, your own man. You're not going to tell me being illegitimate still affects you now?'

Of course it didn't. That was what he'd have said to anyone else. But Kirstin wasn't anyone else.

'I have no family, no heritage, and in the eyes of society and the law I am stigmatised for ever by my illegitimacy. I cannot change that. I had come to terms with it though,' Cameron admitted reluctantly. 'It's why the letter knocked me sideways.'

'Letter?'

'From my mother.'

He leaned back, closing his eyes, fighting the gut-wrenching pain which the memory of that day could still elicit. His hands gripped the arms of the chair. For a moment he was back there, on the doorstep in Edinburgh's New Town, Louise Ferguson's words ringing in his ears.

Then there was a soft touch on his arm, the rustle of skirts, and he opened his eyes to find Kirstin kneeling beside him.

'I had no idea this would be so painful for you. I am sorry I asked.'

He sat up, covered her hand in his. 'I've never spoken of that day to anyone,' he said.

'You don't have to speak of it now.'

'I want to. The letter was from my mother. Sheila Ferguson.'

'Louise's mother?'

'She was married to Louise's father some

years before she had me, and remained married to him for over forty years despite my very unwelcome appearance. When she wrote, he'd been dead a year.'

He could see her beginning to piece the sorry little tale together, but she made no effort to speak, for which he was grateful, as he was grateful for the comfort of her hand, clasped so firmly in his.

'It didn't say much, the letter. Only that she was my mother, that she'd managed to trace me through the records at Garrioch House for they kept the name she'd given me. She wrote that I was the result of an "indiscretion", and though she'd been forced to give me up she'd never stopped thinking of me and wanted to meet me.'

'Oh, Cameron, that is— What did you feel?'

'Angry that she'd left it so long. Disappointed that I had incontrovertible proof that I was, as I'd always been told, a bastard. Wildly curious as to the other half of my parentage, and at the same time desperately determined to dampen any curiosity of any sort. I was thirty years old, a self-made man with my own business, content with my life—' He broke off to rake his hand through his hair. 'And yet I still needed to know. Does that make any sense to you?'

Her cheeks were flushed. He'd have put it

down to the heat of the fire had it not been for the fact that she had suddenly dropped her gaze to their clasped hands.

'What have I said?'

She shrugged and shook her head. 'It doesn't matter. Please carry on.'

'Sheila Ferguson—my...my mother—was ill when she wrote to me. Dying, though I didn't know it. The letter was sent to my offices in Glasgow, but I was abroad. It took many months to reach me. By the time I read it and made my way to Edinburgh—'

His voice cracked. He coughed. His eyes smarted. *Devil take it, after all this time!*

'She was dead,' Cameron finished baldly. 'I never got the chance to meet her.'

'But you met Louise instead?' Kirstin said ominously.

'Aye.' He managed a crooked smile. 'Louise, who informed me that I'd ruined her father's happiness and destroyed her parents' marriage.'

'How on earth did she come to such a conclusion?'

'I asked her that. She had grounds,' Cameron said, looking deeply troubled. 'It seems that my mother had an affaire. Or, reading between the lines of what Louise told me, something more than an affaire. She was planning to leave my father for her lover, but he abandoned her. She was expecting me. She had no one to turn to, nowhere to go. Her husband, Louise's father, agreed to keep her on, but the price she paid for respectability was to give me up.'

'Dear heavens. How absolutely awful. But why does Louise blame you?'

He sighed heavily. 'It's not so much that she *blames* me, Kirstin, as hates my guts. My mother wasn't only planning to leave her husband, she was leaving her daughter behind too.'

Kirstin's eyes widened in shock. 'So in Louise's eyes your mother chose you and her lover over Louise and her father?'

'Aye. You see now why I feel I owe her?'

'I certainly see now why she wants nothing to do with you. What I don't understand is how she comes to know such a thing? She must have been a child when it happened.'

'Her father, the good, saintly man, saw fit to enlighten her one day. He sounds like a right vicious— Well, whatever his reason, he told her.'

'Oh, Cameron, that is absolutely awful. So this is the debt that Louise claims you owe her, then? That is why you are so determined to move heaven and earth to find her daughter? Because by your innocent birth you ruined her childhood and made her feel rejected? Yet still, however she suffered, I can't help feeling it was nothing, *nothing* compared to what you endured. You have been economical with the details of your childhood, but I know it must have been utterly miserable.'

'It's not a competition to see who suffered the most.'

'No, because no matter what she suffered it does not compare to...' Kirstin caught his hand to her cheek. 'You are an honourable man, while Louise...'

'Is simply a mother desperate to find her child.'

'Yes. Yes, you're right,' she said looking stricken. 'I beg your pardon. I take it, then, that she wanted nothing to do with you?'

'I neither saw nor heard from her again until Philippa disappeared. It took me a long time to come to terms with it, but I do understand her feelings. And I've no expectations of them changing,' he added hastily. 'I don't want her to feel obliged or grateful.'

'But if she came to know you...'

'She made it clear that she would not make any such effort over six years ago.'

'Six years ago?' Kirstin's eyes widened. 'Cameron, do not tell me that it was that very day—' She broke off, frowning. 'I assumed you were in Edinburgh on business. I remember now you said you weren't.'

She got to her feet and made for the window, staring out at the Thames. 'You said then that I was a welcome distraction,' she said when he joined her. 'I had no idea that was what you needed distracting from. You must have been in turmoil.'

'And yet distract me you did. In fact you turned out to be far more of a distraction than I ever imagined. Kirstin, you do know that that night was— Ach, I don't know how to describe it, to be honest. I don't even know how it happened. Afterwards, I couldn't quite believe it had, and I had no way of finding you again. You never did leave me a note of your address as I asked you to.'

'I never thought for a moment that you were serious about wanting it. Besides, I didn't have an address at that point.'

'You could have found me, though, if you'd wanted to, couldn't you? It's how you make a living…finding people who don't want to be found.'

She flinched at this. 'That night, we both of us agreed, was a moment out of time, nothing more.'

She was right, and it was unfair of him to press her, yet it mattered. 'So you never thought of me?'

'You asked me that before.'

'You didn't answer.'

She continued to stare in silence at the view. A huge barge sitting low in the water due to its cargo of coal was making its precarious way against the tide.

Finally she turned towards him. 'I thought of you,' she said. 'Happy now?'

He was, suddenly. Happy to have unburdened himself. Happy to have had her as his confessor. Happy that she had taken his part, though he hadn't thought he cared one way or the other.

'I'm happy to be here with you, if nothing else,' he said.

She slanted him an odd little smile. 'Taking dinner alone with me in an inn. Again.'

'It's not the same. We're very different people.'

'You can have no idea how different.'

'Oh, I think I can. You're every bit as beautiful, you've not changed physically, but in every other respect—more than six years of making your own way in life, and making a success of it too. You're a very different woman from the one I met that night.'

'And you? Are you a very different man?'

'I'm my own man now, in every sense. We're both older and wiser, I reckon.'

He traced the gentle plane of her cheek, his

hand coming to rest on her shoulder. Though he didn't urge her to, she stepped into his embrace. Desire was like the insistent beat of a drum between them, impossible to ignore.

'I think fate has brought us together full circle like this.'

'And fate will send us spinning off back to our own lives, once our business is complete.'

'Do you think so, Kirstin?'

'I know so, Cameron.'

She spoke with such certainty, yet her eyes burned with the fire which smouldered inside him. He was not interested in arguing with her. Instead he bent his head towards her, pulling her gently to close the tiny gap between them. She could have resisted. She did not. With a soft sigh that gave him goosebumps she slid her hand up to his neck, pressed her body against him, and tilted her face for his kiss.

The touch of her lips on his made him shiver. He curled his fingers into the indent of her waist, striving for control. She went to his head like a good malt. And, like a good malt, she should be savoured slowly, treated with respect.

He kissed her. A deep, slow kiss. His tongue stroking along the tender flesh of her lower lip. He felt her shudder and blood coursed to his groin, and for long, delicious moments their kiss went on and time seemed to stop. Then she sighed again, her body moulding itself to his, her fingers in his hair, her hand sliding under his coat-tails to rest on the small of his back, and his own hand slid down to the curve of her bottom, and he was lost.

They kissed, his hands roaming over her body, cupping her breasts, the throaty moan she gave in response making him achingly hard. She pulled him tight against her, and his own guttural cry in response startled him. Still they kissed, staggering back against the table, where she braced herself, wrapping one leg around him, impeded by her skirts, driving him mad with frustration.

Her hands slid under his waistcoat, tugged his shirt free from his breeches, fluttered over the skin of his back. Her own clothes were a barrier to the yielding skin beneath. He yearned to tear them from her. And still they kissed, panting, clutching, until a sharp rap at the door sent them springing apart and the dinner Cameron had ordered, and neither of them could have given a damn about now, arrived.

The door finally closed on the waiter and Kirstin, who had been staring determinedly out of the window while the various dishes were laid out, turned around and burst out laughing.

Cameron had tucked his shirt in, but his necktie was askew and his hair looked as if he'd been standing in a gale.

'I suppose he might have imagined that you were shadow-boxing and lost,' she said.

Cameron grinned. 'Were it not for the fact that you were so obviously trying to look invisible. He's obviously well used to it, though, for not only did he knock very loudly, he waited for about five minutes before entering the room.'

'I cannot believe that we allowed ourselves to— I am thirty-one years old, for heaven's sake, well beyond such antics.'

'Well beyond? You don't mean that, surely?'

Flustered, she sat down in the chair he held out for her. 'I have not— I am not— I don't—' She concluded, mortified to hear herself sounding more like a fifty-year-old spinster than a mature woman of the world.

Cameron sat down opposite her, busying himself with lifting the lid from several platters. She knew that his silence was a tactic designed to force her to fill the gap. Well, two could play at that game!

'I will have some of that pie, if it is rabbit, please. And the winter greens.'

He served her, filling his own plate with the same food before pouring them each a glass of wine. Cameron raised his glass in a silent toast. She took a delicate sniff of hers before taking a deep swallow. He was eating with relish, not making a pretence as she was, and she was horribly conscious of his eyes on her, watching as she cut up a piece of rabbit saddle into tiny pieces.

She loved rabbit. The gravy of this pie was delicious, flavoured with mustard and thyme, and the crust a flaky golden brown. She lifted a piece to her mouth, then set it down with a resigned sigh.

'I have no difficulty in attracting men, but most men I meet are not interested in me, only in my looks.'

'Have you considered that some might be, but you refuse to let them see past that lovely exterior?'

Startled, Kirstin set down her knife. 'None of them has tried particularly hard.'

'Because you didn't want them to.'

He was right. It irked her that he was right. 'I am perfectly content on my own, Cameron.'

He poured them another glass of wine, though Kirstin didn't remember finishing her first one.

'Speaking for myself, I've been celibate for almost two years,' he announced.

Kirstin's jaw dropped, and Cameron laughed. 'So you kissed me out of desperation?'

'I was desperate to kiss you, but that's an entirely different thing. Why did you kiss *me*, Kirstin?'

She shrugged, pushing her almost untouched plate to one side. 'You kissed me, so I kissed you back.'

He reached for her plate, then stopped himself with a rueful smile. 'Force of habit. So you were just being polite?'

Force of habit. Because every scrap of food had mattered in Garrioch House. Which meant he must have gone hungry most nights. It hit her then, the true extent of his trust in her. He had confided details of his past which many would consider shameful, confident she would not judge him.

Deeply moved, she saw how insulting her own response was now, saw that she had been batting away his questions, thinking to protect herself, when all he was trying to do was to know her a little better.

'Good manners didn't enter into it. I wanted to kiss you, plain and simple,' Kirstin admitted.

Cameron had been about to take another sip of wine. He set his glass down carefully, but she held up her hand to prevent him from speaking.

'I wanted to know if it would be the same as before.' She twirled her empty glass on the tablecloth. 'That doesn't mean that I have been pining for you all this time. I thought of you. For a while. But then I—I had other matters to occupy me.'

'Your business?'

She shrugged. It was not a lie to fail to contradict something.

Cameron got to his feet. 'Come and see the view, now that the light is fading.'

She joined him at the window. The Thames was turning from brown to silver and pewter. Lights twinkled on the wharves over on the south bank. The river looked perfectly still, the few craft which remained at sail seemingly becalmed.

'The tide is turning.' Cameron took her hand. 'So you kissed me to see if it was as you remembered?'

She curled her fingers around his. She wasn't obliged to explain, but she found she wanted to—to offer a quid pro quo for taking her into his confidence.

'Not to discover if it would be as delightful as I remembered, but to discover if it would be as delightful as I imagined it would be.'

His hand tightened on hers. She saw the flare of heat in his eyes and felt the answering heat in her own blood.

'And was it?' he asked.

'The jury is still out,' Kirstin said, twining her arms around him. 'I think more evidence is required.' And with that she pressed her lips to his.

Lying alone in her bed much later that night, Kirstin touched her hand to her mouth, closing her eyes, shivering at the memory of those kisses. There had been none of their earlier urgency, none of that frantic clutching, the quest for more intimate contact.

Those kisses had been slow, lingering, passionately restrained. It wasn't that they hadn't wanted to make love, but neither of them wished history to repeat itself. And so they had kissed. And talked. And kissed. And then they had taken a hackney back along the river and across the bridge, and now she lay here alone, still tingling and aroused, but in a strange way sated.

It meant nothing, of course, Kirstin's irrepressibly logical mind reminded her. She sat up in bed, suddenly anxious. Of course it meant nothing. She didn't want it to mean anything, couldn't allow it to. Most likely that was why Cameron had resisted attempting to make love to her properly too. The whole point of her coming here, taking this commission on, had been to eradicate any trace of him from her life because...

Kirstin inhaled sharply. There it was. The root of her anxiety. She reached for Marianne's latest missive, still lying on the nightstand, and lit a candle. The footnote was short, but beautifully printed in pencil. Eilidh had bestowed three kisses this time. One more than yesterday. Did this mean her daughter was missing her more?

It had only been four days. Coming up for five. But they had never been apart for more than a few hours before. Guilt washed over her. For long stretches of these past few days she had not thought of Eilidh at all.

Eilidh. The light of her life, the *raison d'être* for everything that she had achieved, her biggest, best achievement of all. From the first moment she had held her in her arms Kirstin had been overwhelmed with a love so profound that it scared her. For more than five years she had thought of her daughter as unique, special, loved all the more for having only a mother, with no need for a father. But today, listening to Cameron's description of his own illegitimate childhood, had given her pause for thought.

But no! A thousand times no. She would never, ever think of Eilidh in that way.

Though society would. Which was why an insidious, persistent voice had urged her to keep Eilidh hidden from society, wasn't it? And why she had, whenever the child had asked her, avoided every question about her parentage. Kirstin screwed her eyes shut but the tears flowed anyway. It didn't matter that she would not countenance that her child, conceived out of wedlock, was tainted. Others would condemn her for that, if they ever found out.

So they must not find out. If necessary she *would* lie to Eilidh. And she would continue to lie to Cameron, because heaven knew what his sense of honour, and the memory of his own childhood, would compel him to do if he ever found out. He'd want to give his daughter a name. A home. A life of his choosing. And Kirstin knew him well enough now to be afraid that he'd find a way of making it happen, no matter what she wanted. Or he.

Marianne's note was crumpled in her hand. A tear had blotted one of Eilidh's precious kisses. Kirstin sniffed, scrubbed at her eyes, and carefully folded the note away. She was The Procurer, a woman who made a living out of keeping secrets.

With a heavy sigh of relief she blew out the candle. This secret, her most vital secret, was safe.

Chapter Seven

'It turns out that Heather Aitken's move to the metropolis was not an unqualified success. As a consequence, Mar—my assistant struggled to track her down,' Kirstin informed Cameron the next day. 'Though she did indeed find employment as a chambermaid in a reputable household, she was dismissed for what the employment agency describes as "overfamiliarity with the eldest son of the house".'

'I suspect it will have been the other way around,' Cameron said dryly. 'Regardless, it will have cost her not only her livelihood, but her good character. A fatal blow to her employment chances.'

Kirstin eyed him with surprise. 'What do you know of such things?'

'I do have house and staff of my own.'

'Is it a very large house, then?'

'It's not a cottage.' Cameron shrugged. 'I don't know what you consider large. It's a manor, I suppose you'd call it, with a home farm, gardens—a lot more gardens and land than I've been able to do much with so far. Set in the outskirts of Glasgow, to the east.'

'I can't imagine you as lord of the manor.'

'I don't spend much time there, in all honesty. The farm and gardens provide employment for graduates of Garrioch House and other similar establishments. The options for foundlings are limited unless they have a particular facility, like I did for numbers, which is why they sent me to learn accounts.'

'A skill which has stood you in very good stead, I presume?'

'Very, though I hated sitting in an office totting up numbers in a ledger.'

'Did you run off to sea, then, and become a cabin boy?'

'I used to help the purser, and things just developed from there.'

'To the extent that you now have your own fleet? Tell me, do you take on orphans to crew your ships as well as to farm your land?'

'Aye, but don't go thinking I'm some sort of noble philanthropist. I give them a fair chance. It's up to them what they make of it.'

'A philosophy I can certainly empathise with.'

'Aye.' Cameron was frowning. 'Talking of wasted opportunities, where has this Heather Aitken ended up?'

'Deep in debt to an infamous moneylender.'

He cursed softly under his breath. 'Stupid wee lassie. She should have stayed in Edinburgh. God knows what will become of her.'

'I think we both know what's most likely,' Kirstin said brusquely. She could never be hardened to such cases but she had become reconciled, a long time ago, to the fact that she could only help a select few of them. 'She is living in St Giles, one of the most notorious rookeries in London. I think we will arouse less hostility there if we enter in the garb of the Rev and Mrs Collins. I'm afraid that you will have to put up with smelling of wet dog for a few hours.'

'Goliath,' Cameron said, with the ghost of a smile. 'It's a small sacrifice if it leads us closer to Philippa. Am I to assume that you know your way around this place?'

'I've been there before, quite recently, actually. I had a guide then, but I think I remember enough not to have to pay for another. If you will excuse me, I will go and get into costume. I suggest you do the same. I'll be back in fifteen minutes.'

* * *

The odour of Goliath, Reverend Collins's mythical hound, wafting from Cameron's coat, was as nothing compared to the stench rising from the gutters of St Giles's rookery. The worst of Glasgow's slums bore no comparison to this place, where the tall, ramshackle buildings lowering over them looked too rotten and decrepit to support any sort of life, other than the verminous kind.

Beside him, Kirstin was looking steadfastly ahead, ignoring the interest their presence was arousing, but Cameron's hackles were rising. The sharp stares from the gaunt men drinking from pewter tankards outside the rookery's many gin shops were blatantly challenging.

Instinctively, he stared back, with the hard, stony look he had used over the years to face down the bigger, more brutish boys in Garrioch House, the rougher sailors on board the clippers where he had first served, and the brigands who haunted the docks where he did business. If it came to using his fists, he would. Clenching them in readiness, he moved closer to Kirstin, keeping very slightly behind her, the optimum position from which to defend her from attack.

The alleyway they were following narrowed. Fetid air escaped from the cellars, where the hatches had been flung open in search of air, having discharged clutches of small, pale and undernourished bairns who sat, wide-eyed and impassive. Cameron's heart wrenched. He had a purse with him, full of coins, but it would be folly to dispense them now. On the way back, he promised himself.

'I know,' Kirstin said, slanting him a sympathetic smile. 'Only one in a hundred, perhaps less, has any prospect of escaping from here. I came in search of one such. Becky, her name was. A card sharp on the run from the law.'

'And did you save her—? I beg your pardon, did she save herself?'

He waited for the usual rebuff, but it did not come.

'I believe she will, and in rather spectacular style, though I have not yet heard. I sent her to Venice.'

'Venice! I am impressed,' Cameron said.

She permitted herself a tiny smile. 'You are meant to be.'

'I know.'

Another smile greeted this remark, but as they reached a crossroads between two alleyways, her expression became serious. 'It is here, I think. First door, second floor, by the sign of the Laughing Dog tavern.'

'I'll be right behind you, but it might be best if you speak to her first. She'll trust a woman before a man.'

'You read my mind. Are you ready?'

Kirstin mounted the rotting steps, leaving Cameron to check over his shoulder. As he'd thought, a small shadow had parked himself across the way. He waved at the lad, spinning a sixpence high in the air. It was expertly caught, the message acknowledged with a wink. Another sixpence when they left would ensure that they were not set upon.

Hurrying to catch Kirstin, he found her already at the door on the second floor.

'I mean you no harm, Miss Aitken,' she was saying. 'My name is Mrs Collins. I come as a friend, to talk to you of a mutual friend.'

'What friend?'

The door opened a crack. Quick as a flash, Kirstin inserted her foot into it, allowing Cameron to push it open and let the pair of them through. Heather Aitken had retreated, cowering against the furthest corner of the tiny room. A wraith of a girl, with the milk-white skin of one who rarely saw the sun, and a straggle of straw-coloured hair emerging from a dirty cap, she was clutching her hands against her breast, wide-eyed with terror.

'He promised I'd done enough to clear what I owed,' she said. 'Please, I don't...'

'Miss Aitken, we are not here at the behest of Mr Watkins.' Kirstin spoke firmly, approaching the girl as one would a frightened and cornered animal.

'How do you know about him if he didn't send you?'

'I can't tell you that, but you may trust me. I am here for quite another reason.' Kirstin cast her eye about the dingy room. 'Is it too much to hope that you have the makings of some tea?'

'Tea!' Heather Aitken exclaimed. 'Who in the name of the devil do you think you are, to push your way in where you're not welcome and demand a cup of tea?'

'No tea, then. Let us at least sit down and speak civilly.'

Cameron bit back the wholly inappropriate desire to laugh, for there was just a hint of relief in Kirstin's voice. He wondered how many cups of tea she'd forced down her delicate palate in the course of business. A good many, he reckoned, and what was more it was an effective tactic, for Heather Aitken, no longer looking terrified, but slightly baffled and a little bit intrigued, was doing as she was bid and taking a seat at the table. Obviously moneylenders, thieves and murderers did not demand anything so mundane as a cup of tea.

Kirstin took the chair opposite her. There was none for Cameron, but he wouldn't have taken it anyway. Best to keep out of it and let her deal with the lass. He rested his shoulders against the door and watched, fascinated, as she did so.

She took her time, coaxing Heather into recounting what they already knew of her dismissal. The girl's honest outrage at the accusations thrown at her confirmed what Cameron and Kirstin had already surmised, that Heather was an innocent victim.

'They had my name struck off the register at the agency,' she said, 'and the agency made good and sure every other agency knew it. I had to go calling round at doorsteps, but all I could get was daywork, and that doesn't even cover the rent on this place. I know what you're thinking, it's not much of a place, but the door locks and I don't have to share with— Well, Mrs Collins, most of the lassies here, they use these rooms for—for entertaining, if you know what I mean?'

Heather's pale skin flushed scarlet. Kirstin leaned over to pat her hand. 'And you are a good girl, aren't you?'

Heather bit her lip, her colour heightening. 'I'm not so sure about that.'

'Because you borrowed money from Mr Watkins to help with the rent?'

'One of the footmen at the last place I was working introduced me to him.'

'Did he, now? No doubt for a fee.'

'You think?'

'I know,' Kirstin said grimly. 'And Mr Watkins's terms sounded fair to you at first, I expect.'

'I didn't really understand them. I've no head for figures. By the end of the week I owed more than I'd borrowed, but he said it didn't matter, he'd let me carry the payment over, and then...' A tear splashed onto the wooden table.

'Then there came a time when he insisted that you give him all that you owed him,' Kirstin prompted gently. 'And it was a very large amount, quite beyond you?'

Heather nodded. Tears streamed unchecked down her cheeks. The colour had fled, leaving her skin ashen. 'Who sent you here, Mrs Collins? You said you'd come about a friend.'

'I think you know who, Heather, don't you?'

'Is it—is it Jeannie?'

Cameron, who had been quite unable to imagine what this scrap of a lass could possibly have to do with Philippa's disappearance, felt the hairs on the back of his neck rise at this whispered connection. He forced himself to keep very still, for Heather seemed to have forgotten all about his presence, though he wanted to leap across the room and shake the truth out of her. It did not need Kirstin's slanted warning glance to keep him quiet, however.

'Jeannie and you were good friends, I know,' she said, with an encouraging smile at the poor wretch. 'I'm sure that she must have written to you, let you know that she was coming to London. She'd have wanted to catch up on all your adventures in the big city.'

'She thought that I'd done well for myself. She was thinking she might try London for herself, she and her young man, after Miss Philippa got married, for she'd be out of a job then. Mrs Ferguson doesn't like Jeannie.'

'Rather, Mrs Ferguson doesn't like Philippa being so fond of her maid, isn't that it?'

'It is. Jeannie said— How do you know Jeannie, Mrs Collins? I don't think she's ever mentioned you.'

'I'm very worried about Jeannie, Heather.'

A fresh fall of tears dripped onto the table. 'Jeannie is a— She can take care of herself much better than I can.'

'Is that what it came down to, Heather? A

choice, Jeannie or you, when you couldn't pay Mr Watkins?'

'He sent a woman to see me. Mrs Jardine, she called herself. She said that I must—that I must—that I must pay my debt back to Mr Watkins by...' Heather covered her face with her hands and sobbed. 'I can't say it. Don't make me say it.'

'Then I'll say it for you. She told you that you must work off your debt in her brothel,' Kirstin said, in a clipped tone very different from the gentle one in which she had hitherto spoken. 'And you, Miss Aitken, were so desperate to escape her clutches that you handed your friend on a plate to her instead, am I right?'

'I thought that— I wasn't sure that they'd find her. I thought that maybe she'd get away—that Mrs Ferguson would...'

'If Jeannie had somehow managed to escape from whatever trap you set for her, don't you think you'd have heard from her by now?'

'She doesn't know where I am. Nobody does.' Heather was pale, shaking, her voice tremulous. 'She thinks I'm still working at the big house where I was first employed. One of the girls there, she brings me my letters.'

'And has there been one from Jeannie to let

you know she's in London? No, of course there hasn't.'

'Who are you?'

'I am here at the behest of Mrs Ferguson. This gentleman here is Philippa's uncle.'

'Philippa? What has Miss Philippa to do with this?'

'Miss Philippa, being so fond of Jeannie, tried to save her, and in the process was abducted with her.'

'Merciful heavens. Dear God, what have I done?'

Heather began to sway in her chair and would have toppled to the floor had not Cameron caught her. He set her down on the bed, which was tucked under the eaves of the room. Though her eyelids fluttered, she remained in a deep swoon. He stared down at her slight frame, torn between pity and fury.

'There's no point in being angry with her,' Kirstin said, getting to her feet. 'She was faced with a terrible choice. Self-preservation almost always wins out, in my experience.'

'What should we do with her?'

'Were you thinking of handing her over to the authorities?'

'No! I meant how might we help her? If we

leave her like this, she's like to fall further down the road to ruin.'

Cameron turned to the wan figure, now trying to sit up on the bed. 'Listen to me, Heather Aitken, I've no time to deal with you right now, but if, God willing, we find Philippa and Jeannie safe and well, I might consider offering you gainful employment in Glasgow. I'm promising nothing, but you had better make sure you don't do anything stupid in the meantime. Do you understand?'

Brushing aside Heather Aitken's startled promises and belated thanks, he took Kirstin's arm, hastening back out into the close, down the stairs and out into the alleyway, where he tossed a sixpence at the boy waiting across the road.

'I'm assuming you will be able to track down this Mrs Jardine for us?'

'It should be easy enough, if she is a madam. That was an extremely generous offer you made, Cameron. Especially in the circumstances.'

He turned to Kirstin, halting momentarily. 'I understand why you tend to see things in black and white, but in my experience there's many shades of grey in between. The instinct to survive at any cost—if you'd been raised as I was, you'd understand.'

'You're right, I can't imagine, though I am

absolutely certain that you would never choose to protect yourself by betraying someone else.'

'No more than you would,' he said.

She stumbled. Catching her, he caught a glimpse of her face, which had been concealed by Mrs Collins's bonnet, and was startled to see a tear tracking down her cheek, But before he could say anything a shadow across the way caught his eye. Cameron snarled at the man, who immediately ducked into the nearest doorway.

'We need to get out of here. I think we've overstayed our welcome.' Grabbing Kirstin's hand, he began to run, hurling the pennies from his purse at the clutch of waiting urchins until they reached the relative safety of Holborn.

You would never choose to protect yourself by betraying someone else.

Kirstin's own words played over and over in her mind as she prepared for her expedition to Mrs Jardine's brothel that night. A few days ago she would have had no hesitation in agreeing with Cameron, but now, sickeningly, she was forced to admit that it was not true. Though she truly believed that she was doing the right thing for Eilidh, and for herself and for Cameron too, every day that she kept his daughter a secret from him was still a betrayal. She was denying him his right to choose for himself whether to acknowledge her or not.

Which a growl of frustration, Kirstin turned to the mirror and began to hook the row of tiny buttons which fastened her full-length black pelisse. Since leaving St Giles that morning, she had been over and over this in her head a hundred times. Cameron didn't want children, but if he discovered he had fathered Eilidh he would feel obliged to take on a paternal role, and the life Kirstin had worked so hard to build for herself and her beloved daughter would come crashing down.

Cameron might want Eilidh to live in Scotland. As her father, he would have the law on his side, and the right to do so. Eilidh was not—she would never, ever think of her daughter as a—a—she would never allow her to be stigmatised for her unconventional birth, but Cameron would not tolerate what he saw as a huge disadvantage. He'd want to give Eilidh his name, which would mean he'd be forced to *marry* Kirstin, and even if it was to be a wife in name only, for the sake of their child, Kirstin could never tolerate such an arrangement. She would be Cameron's property. He would own her and her daughter, even her business. It simply didn't bear thinking of.

Though Eilidh would have a father.

But Eilidh didn't need a father any more than Kirstin had needed a mother. One loving parent was more than enough. So to think of her keeping his daughter a secret from him as a betrayal was quite illogical.

'Extremely illogical,' Kirstin said aloud to her reflection. The words lacked conviction. She, who prided herself on her honesty, was finding this abstention from the truth deeply uncomfortable.

With a sigh, she did up the last of her buttons, put on her hat and her gloves. The transformation was complete. The Procurer, not Kirstin, stared back at her from the mirror. It was odd, seeing her alter ego like this after what felt like a long gap, though it had still been only a few days. She felt confined, somehow, constrained, as if her true self had been bottled up, buttoned down, hidden under The Procurer's mourning black disguise.

Checking her watch, she saw that the hour was approaching eleven. Butterflies began to flutter in her stomach. Putting her own concerns firmly to the back of her mind, she headed for Cameron's suite.

'Do I pass muster?' Cameron asked, throwing his arms wide. 'Am I the proper rakish dandy?'

He was dressed for a night on the town, in a tight-fitting tailcoat of olive-green, with a high collar and a double row of silver buttons. His shirt points were high and starched, his neck-cloth much more intricately tied than was his wont, and set with a diamond pin. Buff-coloured pantaloons showed every contour of his muscular legs, and a pair of highly polished Hessians completed his toilette.

'Your shoulders and your calves are all your own, and I don't think you're wearing a corset to nip your waist in,' Kirstin said, trying not to stare at the way his pantaloons clung to thighs which were clearly shaped by muscle and not padding. 'So, no, you're not a typical dandy, but you do look very much the man about town.'

'And you look as if you are about to attend a funeral. All you need is a black lace veil.' Cameron eyed her with one brow raised. 'A very stylish funeral, if there ever is such a thing. Or—I don't know—there is something about the fit of that coat thing you are wearing. You could be a widow or a—don't take this the wrong way—but a very, very expensive...'

'Courtesan?'

He laughed uncertainly. 'Is it deliberate? It is extremely alluring. You don't look at all like yourself.'

'How am I to take that!'

'Alluring, yet untouchable,' Cameron said. 'As if you are made of jet and alabaster. Usually, you leave me in no doubt that you are flesh and blood. Then you are alluring, and almost irresistible.' His smile faded as he studied her. 'You are nervous?'

'Yes,' she admitted, taken aback. 'If we find them, Cameron...'

'Then we will get them out of there.'

'But how? Such places as Mrs Jardine runs will have men on the door. You will be one against two, perhaps more.'

'Kirstin, when this madam realises that Philippa is gently born with influential connections she'll be desperate to be rid of her.'

'If she has Philippa, don't you think that she'll already know these things?'

'Are you thinking that she might already have rid herself of her?'

'I'm sorry, but the same thing must have occurred to you, surely?'

'Aye, of course it has.' He ran his fingers through his hair, wreaking havoc with his carefully smoothed crop. 'I could see her pressing Jeannie into service, but Philippa—it's far too risky for her. I doubt she'll be there. God's honest truth, I don't want to think about where she'll be if she's not. But we're going to find out, Kirstin. Are you up for it? Because if you're not, I can do this on my own.'

'No.' She gave herself a shake, put her hand on his arm. 'We're in this together, remember? We will find her. Failure isn't an option.'

His own words quoted back at him conjured up the ghost of a smile. 'Right, then,' Cameron said, 'let's get on with it.'

Mrs Jardine kept a discreet house in Margaret Street near Cavendish Square, a well-established business aimed at the exclusive end of the market. Her boast, in the circles where such things were boasted of, was that she could cater for any taste, however outlandish, if the price was right, and provided it was not downright illegal. Though the boundaries of the law, as interpreted by Mrs Jardine, could sometimes be stretched, for a premium.

Admission to her house was strictly by means of introduction by a previous client, but the matter was too urgent for them to consider the delay of even a day while Kirstin found one such, so she watched from the shadows as Cameron attempted to bluff his way in.

As expected, there were two men guarding the door, dwarfing even Cameron's large frame.

Though they closed ranks, blocking his way, they made no attempt to manhandle him. He spoke to them. She couldn't hear what he said, but she could see the impact of it on the watchdogs who did not, contrary to her expectations, simply hustle him out into the street. They stood impassive. Then they separated slightly. Then they conferred. Then one of them departed, returning a few minutes later with a well-dressed woman, presumably Mrs Jardine herself. Cameron spoke again. Kirstin caught the flash of his smile. And then he was ushered in and the door was closed behind him.

Kirstin's heart was pounding, her mouth dry. She had been in dangerous situations before, but not like this, and she had always been alone. Tonight she was part of a team. One, possibly two innocent young girls might be somewhere in that house, desperate to be rescued.

She counted out the minutes carefully, until the agreed fifteen had passed. Then she crossed the road and rapped on the door demanding, in the imperious voice of The Procurer, to be taken immediately to Mrs Jardine on a matter of extreme urgency.

Cameron slipped a banknote to each of the doormen as he followed Mrs Jardine into the house. In the brightly lit hallway, he saw that she was younger than he'd thought at first, not more than forty, and had been a beauty in her day. She was not, as he had in his naivety expected, either painted or raddled, but there was a gauntness to her—the hollow cheeks, the deep-set eyes and the twig-like arms were indicative of poor health.

'Mr MacDonald,' she said, 'I must tell you that this is most unusual.'

'Aye, I know that, and I'm right grateful to you for making an exception for me.' He responded to her rasping tones in the soft lilt of the Highlands. 'I've only the one night to spend in London before heading off to India, and I heard that Mrs Jardine's was the premier facility in all of London.'

'And faced with a long sea voyage to India,' Mrs Jardine said wryly, 'your need is urgent.'

'Very urgent.' Cameron attempted what he hoped was a shy smile. 'I've never been in such a place as this,' he said, in all honesty, 'but I'm hoping it will more than cover my requirements.'

He'd had the banknotes ironed. They rustled enticingly as he handed them over. Mrs Jardine did not count them, nothing so vulgar, but he saw the very slight lift of her brow, and knew from the fact that she immediately slid them into a pocket in her gown that she wasn't going to turn him down.

'It depends what you are after, Mr MacDonald,' she said, 'but that will do nicely for a start.'

'I'm fresh from the Highlands,' he said, still smiling, 'but I'm not wet behind the ears. I reckon that's more than enough, whatever my proclivities.'

A dry little laugh which turned into a hacking cough greeted this remark. 'I refuse to believe a man with your looks and wealth could possibly be as inexperienced as you claim, but that is no concern of mine. I have a business to run. Tell me your pleasure, and we can both get on with our evening.'

'Call me sentimental, but I'm after a lass from my own neck of the woods. A lass to remind me of the home I'm leaving behind, fresh as the Highland air, if you get my drift?'

'I sincerely hope you are not asking me to provide you with a virgin, Mr MacDonald.'

'Could you, for a price?'

'No,' Mrs Jardine said baldly. 'Let me give you the benefit of my vast experience of the world,' she continued sardonically, 'to one who claims to know nothing of it. If someone tries to sell you a virgin, you can be certain that the flower has already been plucked. Such girls are rarities, and never available on the open market, not even from such exclusive houses as this.'

'Where, then, might one look?'

He knew the moment he spoke that he'd been too eager. Mrs Jardine narrowed her eyes. 'I think it might be better if you looked elsewhere for your entertainment tonight.'

She made to hand him his notes, but Cameron shook his head, pushing the money away. 'Away, now, I was only curious. Like I said, all I'm after for tonight is a wee Highland lass to remind me of home.'

The madam pursed her lips, studying him for long, anxious moments. Cameron remained smiling encouragingly, until she shrugged, sighed. 'Very well. I do have such a girl, as it happens, arrived from the north quite recently. Are you averse to red hair, Mr MacDonald? I know that some men…'

Though his belly lurched, he remained calm. *Jeannie*, he thought, *dear heavens, it can only be Jeannie*. 'As it happens, I have a particular predilection for redheads, Mrs Jardine.'

'First floor. Second room on the left. Luckily for you she is free. It's a quiet night. You have half an hour.'

He could feel her eyes on him as he made his way up the stairs, but his mind was already on the girl behind the door. She would be frightened, terrified, even. He'd have to reassure her, explain who he was. Half an hour to calm her, to find out where Philippa was, and to come up with a plan to get her out of there, and Philippa too if she was here. And all the time, Kirstin would hopefully be keeping Mrs Jardine occupied. If things went to plan.

When he reached the top of the stairs, the corridor stretched before him, six doors on either side. Was there a girl behind each? Were they willing, or had they no choice? He understood now, a little, why Kirstin was forced to see the world in black and white. Those few she could assist. The vast numbers she could not. He hadn't realised until now how invidious it must be for her to make such momentous decisions.

As he passed the first door on the left, his footsteps slowed. He stopped outside the second one. Should he knock? Aye. He did so. There was no answer. He turned the handle, easing the door open. She was sitting on the bed with her back to him, a slight figure wearing nothing but a shift, with bright red hair rippling down her back. He felt sick.

'Jeannie?' he said, closing the door and leaning his back against it.

'You can call me whatever you fancy, sir,

since you're paying for the privilege,' she said, turning round. Not a Highland accent but pure Glaswegian.

'I'd like to call you by your real name, lass,' Cameron said, 'what is it?'

'Moira.'

'Moira! Oh, Cameron, your heart must have sunk to have your hopes dashed like that,' Kirstin said.

It was very late, late enough for dawn to be imminent, and they were once again in Cameron's suite.

'It was a blow, I'll admit it.'

He was sprawled in a wing-back chair, having discarded his jacket, the high starched collar of his shirt wilting, the carefully tied neckcloth askew. There was a bluish shadow on his cheeks, and darker shadows under his eyes. He looked utterly dejected.

Sitting across from him, still in her tight-fitting pelisse, though she had taken off her hat and gloves, Kirstin was bone-weary. What would it be like for them to retire to bed together? To lie wrapped in one another's arms, to feel the reassuring beat of a heart, to drift to sleep still entwined, to wake slowly to the comforting warmth of another body, and to know that all it would take would be the gentle caress of a sleepy kiss to…?

'It would be better if we talked in the morning.'

Her eyes flew open with a start.

'You're exhausted,' Cameron said, 'we should…'

'No, this is too important. I'm perfectly fine.' She sat up, wide awake now. 'So, once you were convinced that Jeannie wasn't among the other girls, what else did you learn from Moira?'

'That two other girls had arrived a few days after she did, one a redhead like her. But they were kept apart from the rest of them, and were there only for one night. I asked her where she thought they'd gone, but she clammed up. I reckon she knows something, but she was too feart—so that's it, that's all I have. I hope to heaven you're going to tell me you have been more successful?'

'A little. More importantly, it ties in with what you were told.'

'Kirstin!' Cameron leaned forward eagerly. 'I knew you wouldn't let me down. Go on.'

Moved by his faith in her, she allowed herself to lean over and touch his hand. 'We will find them, I promise.'

Too late she realised she had broken her own rules, but she was well past maintaining The Procurer's carefully neutral front, incapable of pretending that this contract was like any other. She desperately wanted to find Philippa and Jeannie, not only for their own sakes but for Cameron's. She couldn't bear to see him so tormented. 'We will find them,' she said again. 'I promise.'

He gripped her hand. 'But how?'

'There is a club. A club so secret that not even I, with all my contacts, have heard tell of it. One whose members are so powerful and influential that, even though I threatened her with closure, and being sent to gaol for several counts of abduction, Mrs Jardine was still too frightened to talk about it.'

'Could you have her place closed down?'

'The Procurer could.'

'Tell me more about this mysterious elite club,' Cameron prompted.

'They convene six times a year at a secret location for the ritual deflowering of certified virgins,' she said, her horror when Mrs Jardine had confessed this still raw.

She saw her own disgust writ large on Cameron's face.

'There are precedents. Hellfire clubs such as the one founded by the Earl of Sandwich in the last century, where gentlemen of distinction met to indulge in what seems to me common debauchery dressed up as solemn ritual.' Kirstin made no attempt to keep the scorn from her voice. 'From the little I could winkle out of Mrs Jardine, these men will pay a king's ransom for an unsullied maiden, and are ruthless in protecting their anonymity.'

Cameron was staring at her in open disbelief.

'I know,' she continued, 'I found it difficult to credit too, but Mrs Jardine's terror was genuine, believe me.'

'Why, then, would she choose to hand Philippa into their clutches?'

'She had a choice.' Kirstin's voice hardened. 'When she discovered that her henchmen had captured not only a servant but a young girl of breeding, she was horrified. She could, of course, have done the decent thing and let Philippa go, but that would have put her nefarious trade at risk, so she chose to profit from her unexpected windfall instead.'

'We have enough on her to close her down.'

'Which is why she confessed to me what she had done. But we have bigger fish to fry at the moment.'

'Aye.' Cameron thumped his leg with his clenched fist. 'Though it sticks in my craw, we've far more important things to worry about. What the hell do we do now?'

'You're going to have to leave it with me again,' Kirstin said. 'It won't be easy. The fact that I have never heard of this exclusive club means that its members must be from the very top echelons of society. Members of the Government, the aristocracy, perhaps even minor royalty. But I have a few grateful clients who move in such circles. They may be able to shed some light.'

'If you're right about this club's attitude towards anyone who crosses them, they'll have to be very grateful clients indeed.'

'Trust me, they are,' Kirstin said, with more confidence than she felt. 'In the meantime, I did find out one piece of relatively good news. This club meets every second month, on the first Saturday. The sacrificial lambs are kept in a safe house somewhere, and they are exactly that—safe—until the allotted date. Philippa was not taken until after the last meeting. It is thirteen days until the next one, so we have almost two weeks to find her.'

'Do you think Jeannie is still with her?'

'All I know is that the pair of them were taken together, but clearly Philippa would be by far the most valuable. Whether Jeannie will feature in whatever despicable ritual they plan to enact, I have no idea. She could have been sold on, or more likely sent abroad, I'm afraid, to guarantee her silence.'

He swore under his breath. 'It disnae bear thinking of, does it? So we'll not—for tonight.' Getting to his feet, he held out his hand. 'We're both gubbed.'

'Gubbed?' Kirstin laughed softly. 'I've not heard that expression before, but it describes exactly how I feel.'

He pulled her into his arms and she did not resist, surrendering to the comfort of his reassuring bulk, wrapping her own arms tightly around his waist.

'We'll find them,' she said grimly.

He kissed the top of her head. She tilted her face up, and he kissed her lips. A soft, gentle kiss. Then he let her go.

'We will. Together, we're a match for anyone. Goodnight, Kirstin.'

Chapter Eight

❧

'Thank you for putting me in touch with the Marquis of Glenkin, it was an inspired idea,' Cameron said over dinner the next night. 'I met with his man of business today and, having pored over the books, I'm more than happy to take his various trading interests off his hands.'

'Ewan inherited his father's estate in Argyll about seven years ago, and it takes up a lot of his time, which is an issue now he has a growing family of three boys. He will be delighted to be relieved of the burden and to know it is going to be in safe hands.'

'So you get to help your old friend, while I get to expand my little empire, and everybody wins. Genius! I take it that he's the one who keeps you supplied with your precious tea? How do you come to know a marquis?'

'He was once a mere student of philosophy

and mathematics. My father taught him. I've known him for ever.'

'Well, I appreciate the introduction. I'll continue to keep you in tea by way of thanks.'

'There is no need. I was happy to—'

'I'd like to, Kirstin.'

She bit her lip, lowering her eyes to her dinner, shifting slivers of roasted pork from one side of the plate to the other. Cameron waited, knowing that she was debating with herself on whether or not to explain her apparent ingratitude. When she did, he rather wished that she had decided not to.

'When we've found Philippa,' she said, 'there will be no reason for us to remain in contact.'

'Unless we wish to.'

Emotions flitted across her face, but too quickly for him to read them.

She shook her head. 'That is not possible, whether we wish it or not.'

Not possible. An odd choice of words. Why wasn't it possible? He had already worked out that the blame could not be laid at The Procurer's door, for it was obvious that Kirstin and The Procurer were one and the same. He had been waiting for her to trust him enough to tell him her secret, but he was growing impatient.

'Tell me how you got on today.'

Kirstin pushed aside her plate. 'I have been trying to track down someone who can tell us about this secret society and, I'm sorry to say, so far with little success. Either the men I have spoken to really know nothing, or they are like Mrs Jardine, too afraid to speak out. There is what I can only describe as a wall of silence regarding the existence of this club, which confirms what we already surmised—that the membership consists of very influential men.'

Cameron pushed back his chair. 'It's driving me up the wall to have to sit about twiddling my thumbs while Philippa is locked in some room or attic somewhere, wondering what the devil is to become of her—or, worse, imagining the ordeal she's to face, if they've told her why she's there. And as for Jeannie, she could be anywhere.'

'It might not feel like it, Cameron, but we are making progress. I promised we would find them, and we will.'

He leaned his forehead against the cool of the windowpane. Lights winked from the houses across the street. A carriage pulled up at the hotel, and a doorman hurried out to help the old gentleman who descended from it unsteadily.

'You can't know that.'

'Come on, no defeatist talk, remember?'

He turned to face her, unwilling to keep up his

charade of ignorance any longer. 'You've clearly exhausted your own contacts. Don't you think it's time you admitted defeat, Kirstin, and asked for help from the very top?'

'What do you mean? I don't know anyone who has better—' She broke off, her eyes suddenly wary as she realised the import of what he had asked her. 'You mean The Procurer?'

Cameron said nothing. He had deliberately left her with two choices. She could lie, or she could confess. He dearly wanted her not to lie, but if he had been a betting man he'd have put the odds no higher than evens. Her expression remained quite impassive, but he knew her well enough. She had lowered her lids to hide her eyes. Her hand had strayed to her empty wine glass, twisting it around on the tabletop. When she gave that tiny little nod that told him she'd reached a conclusion he felt slightly sick.

'You have guessed, then,' she said.

Her tacit admission took the wind out of his sails. Taken aback by how much it meant to him, but feigning indifference, Cameron shrugged, returning to the table, pouring the dregs of the wine into their glasses. 'What have I guessed?' he asked, determined not to make it easy for her.

'That there is no— That I...' Her hand shook

just the tiniest fraction as she took a sip of wine. 'You know that I am The Procurer.'

When he nodded, she laughed, an odd, strangled sound, and then drank the last of her wine. 'How did I betray myself?'

'By being you,' Cameron said, unable to resist smiling at her. 'You are so very much your own woman, you don't behave like someone who is answerable to another. I was never convinced that you could be anyone's assistant. And then there is your own assistant. Mar...? Margaret? Marjory? Marion?'

'Marianne. You thought it strange that an assistant should have an assistant, I suppose?'

'It wasn't only that. You spoke of her with such assurance, with the air of one accustomed to command.'

'What else gave me away? How long have you known?'

'My suspicions have been growing with every passing day. The way you talk about The Procurer from such a position of intimate knowledge of her methods and philosophy, almost as if you can read her thoughts, which of course you can. You are probably not aware, but latterly you have almost lapsed into speaking in the first person when referring to her. There's one thing that puzzles me, though.'

'What is it?'

'Why are you here, Kirstin? I mean, why you in person and not another woman? My understanding of The Procurer is that she is a—a puppet master—or should that be mistress? You told me yourself, her business is to match women—other women—with her clients. So why didn't you do that with me?'

'Do you wish that I had done?'

'No.' Impulsively, he leaned across the table to touch her hand. Her own gesture. 'Don't fob me off.'

She smiled crookedly, twining her fingers around his for a moment, before pulling her hand away.

'That first meeting in the confessional was meant to be our last.' She pushed her chair back with a sigh, wandering restlessly to the window, where she stood gazing out, her back to him. 'I was curious about you, but I had no intentions of taking on your case. But when you explained why you had come to me, I knew I had to help. I fully intended assigning someone else, as I always do, but when I discussed the matter with Marianne she pointed out in passing that I had the perfect set of skills to assist you.' She turned back to face him. 'It was the right decision, Cameron. There really is no one with better contacts to help deal with such a delicate and sensitive issue.'

She had not answered his question. He knew it. She knew it. She would not lie, but it had already cost her very dear to trust him this far, and there was a risk that if he pressed her, she would simply clam up.

A discreet tap at the door brought the servant with their tea and coffee, buying Cameron some thinking time. When they sat down by the fire, he decided to quit while he was ahead.

'I'm fascinated,' he said, 'will you tell me how you came up with the idea of The Procurer in the first place?'

She smiled at him gratefully, and he knew he'd done the right thing.

'It's not a tale that I've ever told anyone.'

'Then honour me by making me the first.'

Kirstin sipped her tea, trying to compose herself. The initial shock of realising that Cameron had found her out had given way to a strange kind of elation. He had not been incredulous, he had not been sceptical, in fact he'd hardly even been surprised that she and her alter ego were one and the same. She was, despite herself, flattered, but she was also wary.

He had apparently let her off the hook by asking her for The Procurer's history, but that didn't mean he wouldn't come back to his question as to why she was here. For a fraction of a second she considered telling him the truth, but it was the kind of inexplicable impulse people felt when standing on a ledge, the urge to leap into the abyss. If he asked again, she would have to fob him off. She hoped he wouldn't ask again.

'It was Ewan, the Marquis of Glenkin, who gave me the idea,' she said, 'albeit inadvertently. He was my first unofficial case, so to speak. He was desperately trying to avoid a marriage parade, and he needed a woman to pretend to be his affianced bride to get him off the hook.'

Remembering the day Ewan had come to her, distraught, and recalling her own excitement as the idea had formed in her mind of a radical solution, Kirstin settled down to tell Cameron the tale.

'I had no idea that Ewan and Jennifer would actually make a match, thinking only that my friend could sore use the fee she earned to set herself up independently, but that's what they did. And as far as I know they are blissfully happy to this day,' she concluded some time later. 'Ewan jokingly said I should consider becoming a matchmaker, and that's what I do—

match problems with solutions, though marriage is never the intended outcome.'

Cameron smiled. '*Making the impossible possible*. It's an excellent selling point.'

'It's more about matching extraordinary skills to extraordinary requirements. The Venetian case I mentioned, for example. The young woman from St Giles, the card sharp. My client required her to help bring about the downfall of a certain man in order to avenge his father's death.'

Cameron's jaw dropped. 'If you are trying to shock me, you've succeeded. How did it turn out?'

'The young woman went to Venice about three months ago, and as far as I know is still there, so I don't yet know.'

'You don't worry sometimes that you are sending some of these females you rescue—?'

'Who rescue *themselves*.'

Cameron looked troubled. 'Who, in order to rescue themselves, have to place themselves in real danger, by the sounds of it.'

Kirstin stiffened. 'You think I ask too much of them? That I take advantage of their desperation, their lack of alternative options?'

'No!' Cameron swore under his breath. 'I don't think you either cruel or heartless, but I do wonder if you expect others to live up to your own very high standards. You would admit that the service you provide is unique. I'm merely trying to understand it better.'

It was obvious that he was speaking in earnest, but Kirstin was torn, because *not* explaining herself, her thoughts, her actions, to anyone, ever, and most particularly since coming to London, was one of the founding tenets that had sustained her. She would not be judged, yet here she was, contemplating exposing herself to Cameron's scrutiny, hoping he would see things her way.

'I'm sorry. I ask too much of you,' he said contritely, interrupting her thoughts. 'You have already entrusted me with a secret which no one else in London possesses—save presumably this Marianne of yours—I have no right to ask for more.'

'No. I want to speak. Now that you know, I may as well tell you the whole story.'

And so she did, from the beginning, the words tumbling out. She told him of her early successes, her near failures, and the outpouring was such an immense relief that she wondered why she had never, until now, felt the urge to speak. Cameron listened, saying very little, though his eyes never wavered from her.

'So, you see, the service I provide truly is

unique, and my reputation for never failing has been extremely hard-earned.'

'Which is why you can charge such a premium,' he said, 'and, more importantly, why you have to be so certain that you have identified the right woman for the task.'

'Exactly. I do ask a great deal of them, but I go to a lot of trouble to ensure that they are suited in the first place. Finding the ideal candidate can sometimes be the most time-consuming aspect of any case.'

'I'm not surprised,' Cameron said wryly. 'Not only must she be deserving of a second chance, but possess the rare skills necessary for the task. Have you ever failed?'

'In the sense of not finding a perfect match?' Kirstin pondered this. 'There have been occasions when my client's requirements seemed impossible to satisfy, but I have found that there are many ways to look at a problem. What they think they require and what will actually work are often quite different. The harder task for me is to assess whether the female concerned has the nerve and resolve to succeed.'

'And that is the real key to your success. Your impeccable judgement. Some might even call it intuition. That's what makes you preeminent. You conduct face-to-face interviews with the candidates on their own turf. You know by the time you meet with them that they have the skills, but you assess their moral fibre and whether they, like you, are prepared to risk all or nothing. Have I that right?'

She nodded, unable to speak because a very inconvenient and illogical lump had formed in her throat.

'You don't like to think of yourself as a philanthropist, but you are a bit of a crusader, in your own way, aren't you? These women who get a second chance, you feel strongly about the injustice they have suffered.'

Her cheeks heated. 'Don't make a saint of me, Cameron.'

He laughed. 'Saints are heavenly and ethereal creatures. You have much more earthly qualities. Thank you for trusting me with your secret. You know it will go no further.'

'Of course I do.' Kirstin looked at the clock, startled to see that it was almost midnight. 'I had no idea it was so late.'

Cameron yawned, getting to his feet and rolling his shoulders. 'I visited Louise today. I didn't tell her much, only that we knew Philippa was alive and as yet unharmed. Louise's friend is back from Paris. She's told her what has happened. I think it was a relief for her to confide in someone.'

'And a relief for you, knowing that someone is taking care of her?'

'If—*when* we find Philippa, Louise will be grateful. She may or may not stop blaming me for blighting the family by my presence, but there will be no more to it than that, Kirstin. Do you honestly think that a woman who would go to such lengths to keep her daughter's disappearance quiet for fear of scandal, would welcome a bastard half-brother into the family with open arms?'

'Don't use that word! She ought to be proud to call you her brother.'

He snorted. 'So proud she still refers to me as Mr Dunbar. What is your plan for tomorrow?'

'I must give all those I have contacted at least a day to mull over my request—I am asking quite a lot—so I don't have any plans as such. What about you?'

'Nothing in particular. In that case, would it be permissible, do you think, for us to escape for the day?'

Kirstin hesitated for only a few seconds. 'Yes,' she said simply. 'We are unlikely to get another such opportunity, for once we find Philippa—'

'Why don't we stop worrying about what happens after we find Philippa? Or even, if it's possible, let us stop thinking about Philippa and Louise and Jeannie completely, just for a wee while, and simply enjoy each other's company. What do you say?'

'I'd like that very much.'

She got to her feet, meaning to say goodnight, but the words died on her lips as her eyes met Cameron's. She stepped into his arms. She lifted her face. And their lips met.

How delightful kissing could be. Just kissing. Though these were not just kisses. The carmine she used on her lips mingled with the honeyed taste of the wine they had drunk. His hands slid over the silk of her gown as he pulled her tight up against him and his breath was a soft, shallow zephyr on her cheek.

She touched her tongue to his, her hands curling into his shoulders, her body arching against him, kissing him more deeply, making no attempt to hide her arousal. The hard length of him was making her belly clench with wanting.

She shuddered when he touched her, his hands on her bottom, sliding up the rustling silk of her gown to the side of her breasts, frustrated by the barrier of her corsets. He buried his face in the hollow of her neck. He kissed the swell of her bosom, licked into the valley between her breasts. She slid her hands under his coat, flattened her palms over his buttocks, urging him closer.

Cameron wrenched his mouth away, panting. Kirstin stared at him, his pupils dark with desire, his cheeks flushed, knowing she must look every bit as dishevelled.

'It's not remotely that I don't want to,' he said.

She smiled at that. 'You have made that perfectly obvious. And I—I won't pretend that I am exactly reluctant either. But you're right. We have shared enough intimacies and revelations for one night.'

'Then let us save some for another time.' He kissed her again, gently this time. 'Goodnight, Kirstin.'

Kirstin slept deeply, waking very early in a warm glow of well-being and with a mild case of butterflies in her tummy. It took her a moment to work out why. She had absolutely nothing to do today, save spend it with Cameron.

She jumped out of bed, pulling on a wrap, and pushed back the heavy curtains. It wasn't yet light, but the sky was clear, suggesting it was going to be one of those cold, dry, crisp winter days so rare in London.

Pulling the bell for tea, she threw some kindling into the embers of the fire in her sitting room while she waited for it to arrive, which it did with satisfying speed, for the hotel kitchens knew her habits by now.

Pouring the first very welcome cup, Kirstin curled up on the hearth rug beside the fire and stared into the flames. She wrapped her arms around herself, trawling her mind for doubts, for regrets, for fears that her confession would be used against her, but she felt nothing save a huge sense of relief. She neither needed nor wanted approval, but she could not deny that Cameron's admiration and his understanding were adding to her sense of well-being.

And then there were the kisses. And the tacit promise of more than kisses to come. She sipped her tea, relishing the memory and the anticipation of what else might happen. There could be no harm in her admitting to herself how much she enjoyed Cameron's company. There was so little time left to them, most likely no other opportunity like today, to take a moment out of time together.

Her face fell momentarily. She would never see him again once they found Philippa. But that, she reminded herself, was the point of her being here.

Why don't we stop worrying about what hap-

pens after we find Philippa? Cameron had said last night. Sound advice.

Kirstin turned her mind instead to how they might make the most of the fine winter's day that stretched ahead of them.

Cameron stared around himself in astonishment as Kirstin reined in the perfectly matched pair of black high-stepping horses, drawing the phaeton she had driven expertly to a halt. The mansion before them was built of red brick and white stone, turrets looming high at each corner, and the pedimented entranceway was a colonnaded porch approached by a broad flight of steps.

'Where are we?'

'Osterley Park. The country home of Lord and Lady Jersey,' Kirstin said, pushing aside the rug and jumping lightly down from the high carriage before he had a chance to help her. 'Though they are not in residence, as you can see.'

Indeed he could, now that he looked more closely, for all the windows were shuttered, the double doors at the top of the steps barred. 'What are we doing here, then, other than trespassing?'

She smiled her enigmatic smile, though there was a gleam in her eyes. 'Patience, Cameron, all good things come to he who waits. Remember, I'm The Procurer. I make the impossible possible.'

Kirstin handed the reins over to a groom who had appeared from around the side of the house. The man seemed to be expecting them, Cameron noticed.

'Shall we?' she asked, as the carriage was led away.

He took her arm, allowing her to lead them along a path which headed out of the courtyard and through some mature woodland, giving himself over to the unexpected pleasure of a day which, she had told him at breakfast, required nothing more of him save that he enjoy himself, which made it pretty much a unique occasion, as far as he could remember.

The sky was a perfect winter blue above them, the sun dappling the path ahead through the bare branches of the trees. Kirstin, wearing a long woollen coat of peacock-blue, trimmed military-style with black braiding, and a jaunty little military cap, nestled more closely into his side as they walked.

'How come you to know Lord and Lady Jersey?' he asked.

'I am not particularly acquainted with the Earl. Lady Jersey is one of the patronesses of Almack's, the club known as the marriage mart by the *ton*. They call her Silence, for she is said never to stop talking. Some make the mistake of thinking such prattle must be quite indiscreet.' Kirstin slanted a mischievous smile up at him. 'I know better.'

'She is one of your previous clients, I must presume?'

'Not directly, but she had a vested interest in being of assistance to one,' she corrected primly, her eyes twinkling. 'As to the detail, I'm afraid my lips are sealed.'

'With a kiss?' Cameron said, unable to resist.

She gave a little gasp as he pulled her roughly up against him and opened her mouth to his. Wrapping his arms around her, he was immediately aroused by the way she melted into his embrace, by the touch of her tongue to his. He closed his eyes as their kiss deepened, the scent of her perfume, her soap, mingling with the earthy smell of leaf mould, the chill air causing little puffs of cold breath to emerge as they dragged themselves apart, gazing dazed into each other's eyes. Then she smiled that smile that made his groin tighten, and the only thing that prevented him from dragging her back into his arms was the tiny shake of her head.

'Patience, remember?'

She took his hand, leading him along the path

quickly now, to where it emerged at the side of a large ornamental lake with a small island at its centre. A rowing boat was tethered to the jetty, its oars already set in the rowlocks. He jumped in without hesitation, helping Kirstin aboard, suddenly consumed with such simple joy that he understood what people meant when they said they wanted to bottle a moment and keep it for ever.

Unhooking the rope, pushing off with one of the oars, Cameron began to row towards the jetty visible on the island. Casting off his hat and gloves, he gave himself over to the pleasure of rowing, long, clean strokes, the oars entering the water at the perfect angle, the boat skimming smoothly along with barely a ripple on the lake's surface.

'You've done this before,' Kirstin said.

'Just a few times,' he replied, laughing. 'I taught myself to row on the stretch of the River Clyde at Flesher's Haugh at Glasgow Green when I was about ten, in one of the Humane Society's boats—they're the people who rescue people from the water. Even then I must have had an idea of making my living from the sea. I earned a few coppers at the docks once I'd got proficient enough, skiving off school when I could, ferrying sailors back to their ships.'

'I'd willingly pay to watch you exert yourself,' Kirstin said with a wicked smile.'

Her overt appreciation of his body, the way her eyes lingered on his thighs, on his arms as he worked the oars, was arousing. While he'd grown tired of his face and his physique drawing admiring looks from women, he'd happily have Kirstin admire him day and night if he could return the favour. He'd thought such base attraction shallow, found it unsatisfying, and it was where there was nothing else.

Would he desire Kirstin so much if she was not an out-and-out beauty? No question but that the answer was a resounding yes. Because he desired Kirstin. The woman behind the beautiful exterior. He wanted her more than he had ever wanted any woman.

Tingling with anticipation, Cameron rowed with purpose, pulling up to the jetty on the island as the sun disappeared behind a bank of cloud. Tying up, making the oars safe, he helped Kirstin ashore.

'What now?'

She made a show of consulting her expensive little enamelled watch. 'Luncheon?'

Laughing at his bewildered look, for all he could see were trees and shrubs, she pointed him at a track beside a box hedge.

'This way.'

The folly was painted brilliant white. An exotic open-air temple sat atop a bow-fronted frontage. Bemused, he followed as she led the way confidently up a flight of wrought-iron steps into the main room. It was painted forest-green, the lavish cornicing picked out in gold, the same design and colour reflected in the rug which covered most of the floor.

Astounded, Cameron saw that a fire was burning in the white marble hearth, and a meal had been set out under silver platters on the table in the bow window. A bottle of champagne sat chilling in a bucket of ice placed on a silver tray, and two crystal flutes were set on a convenient side table by the sofa.

Shaking his head in wonder, he mouthed one word to Kirstin. 'How?'

'Magic,' she replied, with a catlike smile.

He threw back his head and laughed. 'I'm inclined to think there's a more pragmatic explanation!'

She closed the door, tossing her hat and gloves onto a chair, and began to unbutton her pelisse. 'It occurred to me in the early hours of this morning that I have never once used my contacts to satisfy a personal whim rather than a business imperative. I decided to make an exception in this case.'

She slipped out of her pelisse and placed it on the chair.

'Then I'm very flattered,' Cameron said.

She chuckled. 'You should be.'

He opened the champagne, pouring two frothy glasses, handing one to her. 'A toast,' he said. 'To The Procurer, for working her magic. And to Kirstin, for a magical day.'

'It is not over yet,' she said.

Cameron touched his glass to hers. 'You're right about that.' Waiting only for her to take a sip, he set both of the flutes down. 'It's not over…not by a long chalk,' he said, pulling her into his arms.

Their kisses made Kirstin feel as if she were quite literally melting. There was, as Cameron had said, a magical quality to the day which surpassed her every expectation when she had planned it in the early hours of the morning. Only because he knew her secret had she dared to weave such magic. Though if he ever found out her deepest, most precious secret…

Guilt flickered on the edges of her mind. Cameron thought he knew her. He *did* know her, better than anyone knew her. This was a moment out of time, to be savoured later, when there were no more such moments. She would not spoil it with such thoughts.

Sipping champagne between kisses, the cold wine made her mouth tingle, and the taste of it lingered on their lips as they kissed again. They were languorous kisses, kisses which could go on for ever and ever, enhancing her sense of anticipation. She forgot all about the real world, forgot everything save her need for more of this.

Their kisses were intoxicating, creating a mutual haze of desire which banished hesitation, creating an urge, a need to carry on and on and on. Cameron was kissing the nape of her neck, trailing kisses along her shoulder as he eased her chemise over her arms, his hands cupping her breasts through her undergarments. Her corsets were unlaced, and he kissed her shoulder blades. The ribbon of her chemise was undone, and it dropped to the ground with her petticoats, leaving her clad only in boots, stockings, and pantalettes.

He turned her around to kiss her breasts, taking his time, pressing tiny fluttering kisses over every inch of skin, making her toes curl inside her boots with the delight of it, never wanting it to end, straining not to lose control.

She tugged at his coat and he shed it, kicking

it aside. His waistcoat followed. And then his shirt. They dropped to their knees, their mouths clinging, their hands roaming. His muscles were taut, his chest heaving under her flattened palms. She pressed her mouth to one nipple, making him moan, then to the other, seeing her own determined grip on control reflected in his eyes.

He eased her back onto a heap of pillows and took her nipple between his lips, his hand on her other breast. It was the sweetest of tortures, making her writhe, pant, moan. She was fast reaching the point of no return, only a last shred of sanity intervened.

'Cameron.'

He sat back abruptly, startled by the peremptory tone in her voice, swearing. 'I'm sorry. I thought…'

'No, no. It's not that I don't— But we can't, in case…' Her face was flaming. 'It was wrong of me to mislead you, to let you think…'

His smile dawned slowly. It was sinful. 'I know we can't take any risks,' he said. 'I have not brought the means to protect us with me, and I presume even The Procurer does not think of everything.'

Her cheeks burned. 'I was not planning this when we set out this morning.'

'We can't safely indulge ourselves,' he said, with another of his sinful smiles, 'but you can.'

'What do you mean?'

He eased her back onto the cushions, laughing softly. 'Can't you guess? No? Then let me show you.'

He untied the ribbon which held her pantalettes in place. 'Trust me,' he said, when she made to protest, pulling them down over her legs, easing her thighs apart.

And then he began to kiss her again, but this time his lips touched flesh which had never been kissed before. The bare skin of her leg above her garter. Upwards his mouth worked, to the soft flesh of her inner thigh. And then inwards, between her legs. She cried out with surprise, and then with guttural pleasure at the unexpected delight of it, at the way his mouth and his tongue teased and tensed her, licking into the most sensitive parts of her, stroking her to new heights of pleasure.

She wasted a tiny moment wondering what it was, exactly, he was doing, and then she abandoned thought, opening up to the sheer delight of it, arching under him, her fingers clutching at the cushions in an effort to make this new pleasure last and last, and then toppling over suddenly, and with force, her climax rippling through her, wave after wave after crashing wave.

Utterly lost in the moment, every instinct urged her to take him inside her. She tugged at his shoulders, pulling him on top of her, pressing pleading kisses to his lips. He responded with deep kisses, his fingers twining through her hair, long escaped from its pins, but when she fumbled for the buttons on his breeches Cameron rolled away.

'There's a point when even my self-control will falter, and I think we've just about reached it,' he said, getting to his feet, holding out his hand to help her up. 'Please don't fret,' he added, kissing her again. 'I found that every bit as pleasurable as you did.'

'I doubt that.'

He tilted her chin up, forcing her to meet his eyes. 'I mean it.'

And she could see, astonishingly, that he did. 'Thank you?' she said doubtfully,

He laughed, kissing her soundly once more before letting her go. 'No, thank *you*. Now, I think we should put some clothes on and sample some of this food before it spoils.'

'You're right. Monsieur Salois, the Duke of Brockmore's renowned French chef, will be less than impressed if we don't do his dishes justice.'

* * *

They had climbed a spiral staircase to the rooftop temple to watch the sun sink over the lake before finally quitting the island. On the drive back, wary of danger from highwaymen and roadside blaggards lurking in the growing gloom, Cameron sat on watch, armed with a pistol which Kirstin had produced from a secret panel in the phaeton. Nothing should surprise him about her now, but she was still capable of astounding him.

When they arrived at the hotel, the carriage and horses were handed into the care of another groom, this one clearly Kirstin's own, for he drove the equipage off rather than heading for the mews belonging to the hotel.

'Thank you,' Cameron said, turning to her at the door of his suite, bowing over her hand. 'For a perfectly lovely day.'

'It doesn't have to end here.'

'I don't want it to, but—are you sure, Kirstin?'

'It is a matter of taking appropriate precautions,' she said, and he was surprised to see her blushing. 'You mentioned that you have...'

'I do.' His heart was already galloping, but he forced himself to ask her one more time. 'Is that the only thing you're worried about?' When she nodded, he pressed her hand. 'Give me a minute. I'll join you directly.'

When he did, Kirstin had already taken off her pelisse, bonnet, and gloves. She locked the door behind him. Her hand trembled as she did so.

'Are you sure you're not having second thoughts?' he asked her.

'Not second thoughts, but I can't help feeling nervous,' she admitted reluctantly.

'You're not the only one.'

'It's silly, isn't it? A lot of water has flowed under the bridge since the last time.'

'Kirstin, I'm not interested in reliving the past. I don't want to make love to the woman I met six years ago. I want to make love to *you*.'

She thought this over. He waited. She gave that little nod of hers. Then she came to him, wrapping her arms around his neck. She smiled at him. *That* smile.

They kissed again, but there was none of the languor of those earlier kisses. These kisses were purposeful, urgent. He ran his fingers through her hair as they kissed, pulling out the pins as she unbuttoned his waistcoat. He shed it with his coat onto the floor.

Their kisses had an edge to them now, a raw hunger that could not be sated by kisses alone.

Still kissing, leaving a trail of clothing behind them, they staggered together to the bedchamber. He began to unhook her gown. She tugged at his shirt, smoothing her hands over his chest, pressing her mouth to his throat, licking him, making him moan. Her gown pooled at her feet. She stepped out of it and they moved towards the bed.

He stopped thinking as he helped her out of the last of her clothes, lost in the sheer delight of sensation, his mouth on her nipples, watching her eyes flicker shut as he sucked, licked, stroked. She unfastened the buttons at the front of his breeches. He kicked himself free and she stared at him blatantly, examining his chest, his belly, down to his erection.

She reached for him, running her hand up the length of him, curling her fingers around him, making his breath ragged, making him harder, thicker, pulsing in her hand. Then they were on the bed, her legs wrapped around him, their mouths meeting in another deep, hungry kiss, and he slid his fingers inside her. She was so wet. So tight. He stroked her. She moaned. Arched. Muttered his name. More than ready. As he was.

He quickly sheathed himself. She wrapped her legs around him. One last deep kiss, tongue thrusting, and he entered her, pausing, breathing deeply, clutching at the ragged remnants of his control. She tightened around him as he eased further into her, her eyes wide, watching him shudder, feeling him pulse, and then he began to thrust, slow, harder, hard, fast, and she became a wild creature beneath him, her body finding a rhythm with his, matching him thrust for thrust. She cried out as she climaxed, and then he came with a hoarse cry, falling on top of her, his chest heaving, his arms tight around her, before his mouth found hers in one last, delightfully sated kiss.

Chapter Nine

Kirstin watched as her daughter's left hand curled around the pencil, her expression one of intense concentration. Cameron was left-handed. 'Corrie-fisted', he called it, though he could write a passable script with his right hand, having been forced to favour it at school.

Eilidh glanced up, smiled distractedly, and went back to her sums. The little kink in her hair was sticking up as usual. It was the same kink that Cameron had. And her hair, which Kirstin had always thought reminiscent of her own, was also the exact colour of Cameron's. Marianne was forever saying that mother and daughter were the image of each other, but, looking at her afresh, Kirstin could see that the firm line of her daughter's chin did not come from the Blair bloodline but from…

From her father.

Kirstin felt slightly sick. She wouldn't ever be able to look at her precious daughter again without seeing Cameron. Every time she examined the clever, carefully detailed drawings Eilidh made, she would be reminded that she had inherited her artistic ability from her father. And she would wonder, as Eilidh grew older, which of her skills and ambitions and preferences were her own, and which had been derived from the man who would never be part of her life, whose identity she would never be aware of.

A man who decidedly did not want children. A man who would resent his own child for curtailing his freedom.

You can't miss what you have never had, he had said bitterly, referring to his own lack of a father. But the words rang hollow, even though she was still adamant that Eilidh didn't need a father, and equally sure that Cameron didn't want a daughter.

Kirstin stared down at the unread newspaper on her lap. The consequences of that first night with Cameron had been so momentous as to make her reluctant to repeat the experience. Her occasional dalliances with other men had been unsatisfying, but yesterday had proved once and for all that she was not, as she had assumed, beyond passion. When Cameron had left her in the early hours of this morning she had lain awake, replaying every touch, every sensation he had aroused, already longing for more despite the pleasant sated ache of her body.

Such passion could only be transitory in nature, but they did not even have the luxury of that small amount of time. She would miss him, the only person in her life who knew who she was and why her life had turned out this way, for she had told him far more than she had ever confessed to Marianne. Cameron truly understood her. Save that there was something fundamental about her he didn't know.

Guilt gnawed at her as she studied her daughter. She was withholding a fact that he didn't want to hear and it would destroy both their lives if she told him. Her guilt was therefore illogical. Yet it refused to be quelled. But it would, in time. One more thing to inure herself to.

The clock struck the hour and Kirstin smoothed her daughter's hair affectionately. 'Time for tea, young lady. Marianne said she would bring a chocolate cake.'

'Are you staying for tea, Mummy?'

'Yes, darling, but then I have to go out.'

Eilidh nodded solemnly. 'Business,' she said, matter-of-factly, making for the stairs. 'I know.'

A delighted whoop told Kirstin that the cake

had not been forgotten. Marianne appeared in the doorway and, seeing the question on Kirstin's face, immediately shook her head.

'Not a peep from anyone on the list you gave me, sorry.' She picked up Eilidh's workbook, flicking through the pages. 'Not a single mistake, as ever. She has a real head for figures.'

'Of course—she is her mother's daughter!' Kirstin said, more vehemently than she'd intended.

'Have you a headache?' Marianne asked, giving her a strange look.

'No. Sorry. I had hoped that we would have news today, that's all.'

Marianne sat down at Eilidh's desk, her slight build only just too big for the chair. A frown drew her fair brows together. 'It's horrible, thinking of those two girls locked up somewhere.'

'Assuming the pair of them are still together. I'm aware I'm asking a great deal of you, Marianne, expecting you to look after the business as well as Eilidh in my absence.'

'I like to think I've earned your trust.'

'More than that. I rely on you.'

'I've been thinking you could rely on me a great deal more.'

'What do you mean?'

'You're turning business away all the time. I

could help, Kirstin. Not replace you, never that, but I could become more involved.'

'But what about Eilidh?'

Marianne hesitated. 'You're not going to like what I have to say.'

'Not if you're going to suggest—again—that I send her to school.'

'You know that I'm right.'

'No,' Kirstin said flatly. 'I won't discuss this.'

'Hear me out,' Marianne persisted. 'If you are still convinced I'm wrong then so be it, but you know that I've got Eilidh's best interests at heart.'

'I don't doubt that. Go on, then, say your piece.'

'Eilidh is a very bright little girl. She needs to be pushed more. But it's not just that, Kirstin. She'll be six years old this year. She needs the company of other little girls, she needs to make friends. She needs to learn how to socialise in company other than ours. It's not normal, the way you closet her away.'

'It didn't do *me* any harm.'

Marianne raised a sceptical brow.

'I don't want Eilidh to be normal,' Kirstin said. 'I want her to be exceptional. I think she *is* exceptional.'

'You're probably right. As I said, she's very bright, but—but don't you see you're narrowing her horizons by keeping her isolated from the world? You're not protecting her, you're making her an outsider.'

A lump formed in Kirstin's throat. Tears burned her eyes. She knew, had always known deep down, that this moment would arrive, but she couldn't face it, not yet.

A child should not be condemned for the lack of a piece of paper declaring her parentage.

How adamantly she had spoken those words to Cameron. How certain she had been.

True, but unfortunately neither society nor the law would agree with you, he had replied.

She knew in her heart that he was right. His was the voice of bitter experience after all.

'No respectable school would take Eilidh,' she said grimly. 'And even if they did…' She pressed her hand to her eyes. 'I couldn't expose her to that. Don't ask it of me.'

'You know, you could pretend,' Marianne said gently. 'About Eilidh's father, I mean. Put a ring on your finger, call yourself Mrs Blair. You already dress like a widow most of the time.'

'But it would be a lie,' Kirstin said wretchedly. 'A tacit admission that I had done wrong. That Eilidh was a sin. I would be giving in, don't you see?'

'Sometimes there's no such thing as right and

wrong. Sometimes there's no place for principles. Sometimes there's simply doing what is
for the best.' Marianne got to her feet. 'Whether
you permit me to take on a more significant role
in your business is entirely your decision. But
regardless, Kirstin, I urge you to consider sending Eilidh to school, for her sake, if not yours.'

'I'll think about it. After this case is complete.'

Marianne touched her arm. 'We won't let it
come between us, you will do as you see fit, but
I owed it to my conscience to speak out.'

'And I'm grateful.' Kirstin smiled wryly. 'I
think.'

She picked up the newspaper which had fallen
on the floor, and was in the process of folding it
up when a notice caught her eye.

'Marianne!' She scanned the notice again, her
heart lifting. 'Marianne, look at this. I think I
may finally have found the key to unlock access
to the secret club.'

Kirstin had been gone all day. If she'd had
good news to report he'd have heard by now,
surely. All this waiting around was driving Cameron up the wall. It left him with far too much
thinking time. He was a man who preferred action to words, but he hadn't even dared leave
the hotel, lest Kirstin return. He'd answered

every scrap of correspondence. He'd drunk far too much coffee. He'd paced the floor so many times he was surprised there wasn't a path worn in the carpet.

As the clock struck six, he closed his eyes wearily, but the moment he did images from last night started playing out, frustrating him in a very different way. He'd been abstinent for too long, that was what it was. He'd forgotten the sheer joy of release, the bone-deep satisfaction afterwards of lying together, skin to skin, slick with sweat.

Aye, right! He had not forgotten because it had never been like that before. Cameron groaned. Last night had had nothing to do with abstinence. Last night, and yesterday afternoon on the island too, had been all about Kirstin. When they'd made love, whatever kind of love they had made, it had been about more than their bodies uniting—not that he'd be such an eejit as to say there had been a meeting of their minds too. What the hell? It had been special, and it was as simple as that.

Cameron rubbed his chin. He needed a shave. And he needed to think about what all this meant. They had their own lives, the pair of them, they lived in very different worlds, and he'd meant it when he'd told her he was happy with his. But now he wasn't so sure. He had a sneaking suspicion that Kirstin had filled a gap he hadn't even known existed. He had a sneaking suspicion that he could easily fall in love with her if she let him.

'Eejit,' he said, aloud this time, just to make sure he was listening to himself.

How could he fall in love with a woman he barely knew? All very well that she'd admitted she was The Procurer, but he still hadn't a clue how she lived, or even where she lived, and each time he'd tried to ask her she'd turned the conversation.

When he took over the tea business from the Marquis of Glenkin he was to send supplies to her place of business, for God's sake! Why was she so obsessively secretive? It couldn't possibly be because she didn't trust him. So what the devil was she hiding?

Twenty-five minutes later, Kirstin walked through the door. She was wearing another crimson gown, this one patterned with large blowsy roses. Silk, it was, of the finest quality, Cameron reckoned, and yards of it too, in the tiny pleats that formed the skirt which swished provocatively as she walked. The bodice, in contrast, was tightly fitting and low-cut, showing off the creamy perfection of her bosom and the long line of her neck. She never wore jewellery. He'd noticed that before. Her clothes were her one extravagance.

'I have news,' she said, helping herself to a sherry.

Her words pushed all thoughts of the future to the back of his mind. His heart leapt. 'Someone is prepared to talk?'

'None of the people I contacted have stuck their head above the parapet. But that doesn't matter. Look at this.'

She handed him a newspaper. He studied the paragraph which had been circled, announcing the coming out ball of Lady Beatrice, the eldest daughter of the Earl and Countess of Crieff. A name had been underlined twice.

'"The Right Honourable Griffith Griffiths, His Majesty's special envoy, who has lately been in Lisbon on business of the greatest import, will be granted the honour of partnering the debutante in the opening dance."' Cameron gave a snort of laughter. 'His parents seem to have been singularly lacking in imagination when they named him. Presumably he has been earmarked as a prospective son-in-law. How can you be so certain that this Griffith Griffiths will be willing to help us?'

Kirstin beamed. 'Don't ask me to explain, but

I will ensure that he does. Now all we have to do is find a way to gain access to Lady Beatrice's coming out ball. How do you feel about playing a second cousin twice removed, come all the way from the Highlands?'

Dinner arrived at that moment. Cameron waited impatiently as the waiter set out the various covered dishes, fussing over their placement on the table. Then there was the wine to be opened, decanted, tasted. And then he was distracted, as usual, by Kirstin's careful pondering over each dish, the way she studied everything first before making a small selection and arranging it carefully on her plate. She opted for the fish tonight, and a helping of her favourite winter greens. An odd combination. He had a bet with himself that she'd go back for the veal pie.

'Well?' she prompted, once Cameron had filled his own plate with a large slice of pie. 'Do you fancy playing a Highlander?'

'I'm a Glaswegian. I won't wear a skirt. And I'm wondering why we have to go to such a palaver in the first place? Can't we simply find out where your man is putting up while he's in town and call on him?'

'The ball is tomorrow night, and he is guaranteed to be there. We won't get a better opportunity. He may turn out be our only hope,' Kirstin said, becoming agitated. 'You have no idea how many strings I've pulled, how many favours I've called in, only to be met with a wall of silence. And all the time the clock is ticking.'

'You're right, you're right. So a Highlander I will be, though where I'm to find a plaid in London...'

'As a matter of fact...'

Cameron burst out laughing. 'I might have known you'd be one step ahead of me.' He lifted his glass to toast her. 'Here is to Laird Garrioch and his good lady.'

Kirstin, in the act of helping herself to a slice of the veal pie, looked up, eyebrows raised. 'Garrioch?'

'Of Garrioch House. The best lies are the ones containing an element of truth. Now, shall we discuss tactics?'

The next night Kirstin wore a simple white evening gown of satin with a gauze overdress, its front panel and the deep border of the hemline embroidered with white wild flowers. The plaid sash, fashioned by an accommodating Madame LeClerc from the offcuts of Cameron's outfit, was formed of tight pleats, worn over her shoulder and across her body, fixed at the waist with a large silver brooch. Her hair was simply dressed, a ribbon formed of the same plaid threaded through it. On her feet were white slippers. Long white evening gloves covered her arms.

Eyeing herself dubiously in the mirror, Kirstin fancied that she looked like a ghost. A Scottish ghost, mind you. She smiled. Rolled her eyes. And made for the door. She was very much looking forward to seeing Cameron in full Highland regalia.

He whistled silently as he opened the door to her. 'Laird Garrioch is a lucky man.'

Kirstin dropped a quick curtsey. 'Thank you kindly. I rather think Lady Luck favours his wife.'

Cameron bowed, but his smile was mocking. 'I've never worn a kilt before, and I hope to heaven never to have cause to wear one again.'

'At least this outfit doesn't smell of wet dog.'

'I should hope not, after what I shelled out for it. I had the devil of a job putting it on, though I was shown the correct way to fold and fasten it several times. You wouldn't believe how complicated it is. I'm wrapped up like a parcel.'

'Then let me examine the goods,' Kirstin said, making a show of inspecting him.

His evening coat was black and beautifully fitted across the breadth of his shoulders, conventional enough, though it had no tails. The high points of his shirt collar and necktie were pristine white, showing off his tanned face, his freshly shaved jaw. A plain black waistcoat was adorned with a single gold fob on which he wore his pocket watch. There were two plaids. The first was, like hers, draped over his shoulder and across his body, though it was much wider, and held in place by a large silver pin. The second plaid formed the kilt, falling to just above his knee, held in place with a large silver-buckled leather belt. He had not gone to the lengths of acquiring a claymore or a dirk, but there was a sporran fixed to the belt, and another silver pin affixed to the front of the plaid to weight it down. Knitted stockings and buckled shoes completed his outfit.

'Turn around,' Kirstin said, 'let me check the pleats at the back.'

He did as she asked, though his expression told her he knew perfectly well she wasn't interested in the pleats. Just as she'd hoped, the plaid swung out to give her a tantalising glimpse of thigh which she knew from last night was well-muscled.

'Well? Do I pass muster?'

She smiled, letting her appreciation show. 'I would not recommend that you take part in the country dancing, however, unless you wish the young ladies to faint.'

Cameron gave a bark of laughter. 'There's no chance of me dancing. I've two left feet.'

'I doubt very much that anyone will be interested in your feet.'

'We're going to stand out like a pair of sore thumbs, the two of us.'

'Which is exactly the point. It will be easier for us to bluff our way in to the ball if we make no attempt to blend in. That's precisely what you'd expect someone without an invitation to do.'

Cameron sighed theatrically. 'Fair enough. I bow to your expertise in the art of subterfuge. What am I to call you, Lady Garrioch?'

'I hadn't thought. Fiona? Mhairi? Annis?'

But he shook his head to each of these. 'Isla. I think that would suit,' he said eventually.

'Remote and forbidding, just like its island namesake, you mean?'

'No, unique and breathtakingly beautiful. What about me?'

'Let's think,' she said. 'What about Conlan? I was once told that in the Gaelic that means hero, or a man admired by all. Most apt.'

Cameron grinned. 'Isla and Conlan. A bit different from Euphemia and Caleb. Though I think we're every bit as loving a couple, don't you?' He slid his arm around her waist. 'In fact I'll wager we've not been married very long at all. Still in the early stages of—' He broke off, his face becoming serious. 'Look at the time. The carriage will be waiting.'

Kirstin's stomach immediately began to flutter with nerves as she picked up her evening cloak.

'Griffiths is to lead the Crieff girl out in the first dance. It's likely his own dance card will be full at least until the first supper. That will be around midnight. We've timed our arrival to be in the worst of the crush, so Lord and Lady Crieff will be less inclined to make a fuss in front of the rest of their guests. Once we're inside...'

'Kirstin.' Cameron put a finger to her lips. 'We've been over this a dozen times. There's no need to go over it again.'

'No. No. You're right. Only...'

'It is vital we get it right. You think I don't know that?'

'Of course you do.' She managed a shaky smile. 'And we will. If we can just get Griffiths alone, I know that I'll be able to persuade him to talk.'

'You are sure?'

Her nerves began to fade. A steely determination took over. 'Oh, absolutely certain. Now,' she said, softening her accent to a lilt, 'are you ready to play the charming Highlander, Conlan, my hero?'

'I certainly am, *mo ghràdh, mo chridhe,*' Cameron replied in a perfect soft burr. 'It means *my darling, my heart*, in case you're wondering. It's useful, isn't it, that I've a boatswain from the Isle of Lewis?'

'Why would a boatswain teach you such endearments?'

He took her hand, tucking it into his arm. 'Och, you never know when they'll come in handy.'

The ball to launch the Earl and Countess of Crieff's eldest daughter into society was being held at their town house in Mayfair. It was easy to spot. A long queue of carriages and sedan chairs was parked outside and blazing braziers illuminated the entrance. As they had hoped, Cameron and Kirstin were subsumed into the long line of guests making their way up the staircase from the reception hall to the first floor, where the Earl, his Countess and their daughter waited to greet them.

Cameron's attire was attracting a great deal of attention, most of it consisting of sidelong glances, though there were a few more brazen stares and several quizzing glasses raised. De-

ciding that Conlan, Laird of Garrioch was the
kind of man who enjoyed the limelight, Cameron returned stare for stare, supplementing
them with a smile, a haughty frown, or a wink,
depending on which took his fancy.

'There will certainly be no fading into the
background now,' he told Kirstin as they reached
the top step. 'Are you ready, my wee Isla, to face
the music?'

'Divide and conquer,' she said, stepping forward with not a trace of the nerves she'd shown
earlier, and dropping into a deep curtsey before
their host. 'Lord Crieff, my husband has told me
so much about you that I feel we already know
each other. How do you do?'

The startled Earl extended his hand automatically. 'I'm sorry...'

'My lovely wife, Isla, Lady Garrioch,' Cameron said, stepping forward. 'We're not long
wed, which is why news of our nuptials has not
reached you from the Highlands yet. And this
must be your good lady.' Cameron turned to the
Countess, taking her hand and pressing it to his
lips. 'I have heard so much about *you*, my lady,
and none of it did you justice. It is an honour to
meet you at last.'

'At last?' Lady Crieff flashed an enquiring
look at her husband, but Kirstin had placed her-

self at such an angle that Lord Crieff could no longer see his wife. 'You are...?'

'Conlan, of course,' Cameron said, 'Laird of Garrioch.' He leaned forward conspiratorially. 'We are on the last leg of our wedding trip, Isla and I. We've been away from the castle these last three months, where I know your invitation to the Scottish branch of the family will be waiting, and I said to Isla it would be right rude for us not to come along to pay our respects. I can see from the way your husband has taken to Isla that I'm right.'

Since Lady Crieff could still not see her husband, she had no option but to smile and nod. 'You have been on the Continent for your trip?'

'Indeed, indeed,' Cameron said, 'but I'll not bore you with the details while you've so many other guests to welcome. I'll just introduce myself to wee Beatrice—my how she's grown—and then I'll get out from under your feet. Lovely to meet you after all this time. Isla?'

He waited until Kirstin had dropped a second curtsey, then took her arm and, with the scantiest of greetings to Lady Beatrice, they were past the first hurdle.

'Well?' Cameron whispered as he led Kirstin into the crowd of the ballroom, nodding and smiling and making his way determinedly into the middle of the room.

'Fortunately, the Earl is not the brightest,' she said. 'He assumes I am some sort of distant cousin of his wife's.'

'And she thinks I'm *his* cousin—or she pretended to think so,' Cameron said, with a slight frown. 'I wouldn't count on her not following it up with him if she gets a chance. We'd do well to keep out of her way.'

'Fortunately, her time will be taken up with playing hostess at least for the next couple of hours,' Kirstin said. 'Where will we—?'

'Here, for the moment.' Cameron edged them closer to the floor, where couples were beginning to amass for the first dance. 'I want to get a look at our prey.'

'At last.'

It was after midnight and Cameron was getting impatient. Despite informing Lady Crieff, the first time she'd managed to track them down in the crowd, that neither of them wished to dance, she had quite determinedly foisted a partner on Kirstin, forcing him to take refuge in the retiring room set aside for gentlemen. Now, having observed their target escorting Lady Beatrice down to supper over half an hour ago—definitely a match in the making there—they were finally putting their pincer plan into action.

As Griffith Griffiths got to his feet to fetch more champagne, Cameron moved in, grabbing the man firmly by the arm and thrusting it behind his back.

'What the devil? Let go of me this minute or I'll…'

'Haud yer wheesht.' Cameron spoke in a low growl, in the broad accent of the Glasgow docks. 'A moment of your time is all I ask.'

'And if I refuse?'

'That wouldnae be wise.' Cameron tightened his grip. 'Do we understand one another?'

The other man gave no answer, but he made no further protest as Cameron marched him out of the dining room, keeping him close enough so that no one could see he was being forced, smiling genially.

Griffith Griffiths was about his own age. Fair-haired, with pale blue eyes, he had the look of a well-bred horse that passed for handsome amongst his class, and the sense of entitlement that always made Cameron grind his teeth.

'I don't know who the devil you are…'

'The Laird of Garrioch.'

Griffiths snorted. 'Lord Crieff's cousin from the Highlands? Or is it your wife who is Lady

Crieff's cousin? Beatrice wasn't very clear—and for a very good reason, I suspect.'

They were in the small corridor outside the parlour he and Kirstin had found earlier. Cameron came to a halt in front of the door, gazing coolly down at his captive. 'Whatever it is you suspect, you're about to find that you're well off the mark.' He rarely had need to use this tone to any of his crew, but when he did, it never failed him.

It did not fail him now. Griffiths turned chalk white and began to shake. 'What…?'

'If you co-operate, there will be no harm done.'

'And if I don't?'

'Best to co-operate,' Cameron said, throwing open the door.

It was a small room, chilly, the grate empty, the only light coming from a candelabra set on a marquetry table. Kirstin stood in the shadow. Cameron closed the door behind the pair of them and let go his hold on Griffiths, but the man had no sooner realised he could run than Kirstin stepped forward and his jaw dropped.

'You!'

Kirstin indicated one of two chairs set out at the little table. 'Sit down, Mr Griffiths.'

As Griffiths did as he was bade, and Kirstin

took the chair opposite, Cameron retired to lean the weight of his shoulders against the door, partly to ensure they were not disturbed, and partly to give Griffiths the illusion of intimacy. Until they'd had him captive here Cameron had not permitted himself to reckon their chances of success, but now, his heart thudding, seeing the profound effect Kirstin's mere presence elicited, he began to hope.

'What are you doing here?' Griffiths was staring at Kirstin as if he had seen a ghost.

Her smile was the sort which could make the blood seem to freeze in the veins. 'I came to see you. You do not need me to remind you that you are very much in my debt, I take it?'

There was not a trace of bravado left in the man. Casting a frightened look over his shoulder at Cameron, he simply shook his head.

'Nor do you need me to tell you that one word from me in Lady Crieff's ear will put an end to any pretensions you have to her daughter's hand.'

'No. Please, madam—'

'There is a club,' Kirstin interrupted. 'A *gentlemen's* club which specialises in deflowering virgins. You know of it.'

A statement, not a question. Kirstin waited. Her face was completely impassive but there was a hardness in her eyes that Cameron had not seen before. She had glossed over the details of The Procurer's methods when telling her stories, and he had been too caught up in her revelations to consider the lengths she must have gone to in order to succeed. Now he saw very clearly how ruthless she could be.

There was a sheen of sweat on Griffiths's brow by the time he had decided to answer. When he spoke, it was in a whisper. 'The Erotes Club. Men from the highest echelons.' Griffiths swallowed audibly. 'Some of the most powerful men in the land.'

'And why do these powerful men require virgins?'

'They represent Diana. The most powerful virgin. The ritual celebrates a demonstration of power.'

'By men over women. You mean they are violated? It strikes me as a flimsy pretence to allow jaded degenerates to indulge in depravity.'

Griffiths, his head sunk onto his chest, nodded. 'I'm not a member.'

'You hardly qualify,' Kirstin said disdainfully. 'Where do they keep the girls?'

'What?'

'Where do they keep their victims, Mr Griffiths?'

'I don't know. I...'

'For a diplomat, you are a singularly unconvincing liar. Listen carefully to me,' Kirstin hissed. 'There is a young lady, about the same age as Lady Beatrice, being held by these men. Like Lady Beatrice, this young lady is an innocent in every way, and I venture, like Lady Beatrice, she has only a very vague notion of what to expect on her marriage night. As you sit here prevaricating, she is hidden away in some attic or cellar, terrified. Imagine, if you can, your intended bride in the same situation. I do not ask you to save her from her fate. I ask only that you give me the information to allow me to do so.'

Seeing Griffiths glance over his shoulder at Cameron, Kirstin gave a brittle little laugh. 'And let me assure you,' she said, 'that whatever fate the Laird over there has threatened you with will only be the first painful step in your fall from grace.'

'If I tell you, do you promise never to come near me again? Never to ask, never to mention...'

'Yes, to all those things.'

'How do I know I can trust your word?'

'You already know the answer to that, Mr Griffiths. I am The Procurer, and there is no one more trustworthy in the whole of London. Unless I am crossed.'

Chapter Ten

In order to avoid any further encounter with their inquisitive hostess, they slipped out via a side door which opened onto the mews, completing the short distance back to their hotel on foot. It was almost two in the morning, but Kirstin was wide awake and so too was Cameron, judging by the alacrity with which he accepted her suggestion that they have a nightcap.

Shivering, for she had left her cloak behind, she crouched by the fire, coaxing the embers into life, sinking onto the rug with her back against a chair, watching as he discarded various bits of his Highland outfit with some relief until he wore only his shirt, cravat, kilt and stockings. She unfastened her own sash and put it on the chair behind her.

Cameron seated himself on the hearthrug beside her, handing her a glass of sherry. 'I have no idea what you have on Griffiths, but you scared the living daylights out of him. I wouldn't like to get on the wrong side of you.'

'Don't say that.' She stopped as her voice began to quiver and took a sip of sherry. 'Sorry, I'm being silly. It's been a very difficult night.'

'And you were formidable. Come here.'

Cameron took her glass from her, setting it down beside his on the hearth. Then he pulled her into his arms, tucking her head onto his shoulder.

'We got what we needed, Kirstin. We now know who runs that club, and we know where the girls are likely being held, all thanks to you.'

'I couldn't have done it without your help. I was terrified that Griffiths either wouldn't or couldn't spill the beans.'

'Well, you covered it up so well that even I didn't notice.' He dropped a kiss onto her head, his hand stroking her back. 'As I said, you were formidable. We'll find the girls now. I'm sure of it.'

She looked up. 'It won't be easy. We can't expect to just stroll in and take them away with us.'

'I know these men are secretive for a reason. They have a lot to lose if their activities are exposed, so we must expect the place to be well-protected. We'll need a plan of attack. Tomorrow, I'll watch the house, get the lie of the land. Maybe as soon as the next day I'll be able to hand Philippa back to her mother.'

'And it will be over.'

She would never see Cameron again. She had known this, right from the first day she'd walked into this hotel suite she'd known it, but for the first time she felt the chasm that would be his absence.

'It will be over,' Cameron agreed. 'And when it is, Kirstin, I thought we might—'

'No.' Whatever it was he was going to suggest—another night, another week, another month—it would be both unbearable and utterly untenable. 'No,' she said again, 'this is it, Cameron. This is all we have.' She twisted around to face him. 'So let's make the most of it.'

She waited, tense and yearning, willing him not to dispute the point, knowing that if he did they would not even have tonight, knowing that if she kissed him he would not resist, but reluctant to persuade him in that way.

He studied her in the firelight, his fingers tracing the plane of her cheek, her jaw, making her tremble. 'I have never wanted anyone as much as I want you,' he said softly.

'It is the same for me,' she said.

No lie. She would miss him so very much.

But still she forced herself to wait until he kissed her. When he did, she was momentarily overwhelmed, closing her eyes on the tears which filled them, telling herself it was the culmination of everything making her feel that way, not Cameron. And then surrendering to the sweet, sensual delight of their lovemaking.

It was utterly unlike what had gone before. This time she was acutely aware of their time together ticking away, and she wanted to remember every moment, to etch the memory on her mind for ever. Every kiss was to be savoured. The way their mouths adapted to each other, the slow sweep of their tongues, the sweet dragging ache inside her that their kisses aroused.

She tugged at the knot of his cravat, casting it aside, burying her face in the warmth of his throat, licking into the hollows at the base, tasting his soap, the faint tang of salt, her chin tickled by the soft hairs of his chest. She pulled his shirt out from his belt. 'Take it off.'

He did as she asked. 'Now you,' he said.

But she shook her head. 'Only you,' she said, smiling wickedly, inspired by the way he had kissed her on the island. 'For now.'

She pushed him, a gentle nudge, and he lay back obediently, his eyes lambent with desire. She leaned over him and began to kiss him, tracing the shape of his body with her mouth, licking, kissing his shoulders, his chest, hard muscle, smooth skin, rough hair. She could hear his heart beating wildly. She pulled out her hairpins, letting the thick curtain of her hair trail over his chest as she kissed downwards, tracing the shape of his ribcage with her hands, licking into the dip of his belly, hearing the sharp intake of his breath, the soft muttering of her name, her own heart hammering.

The belt which held his plaid in place stopped her kisses. She sat up to unfasten it, kneeling between his legs. He had kicked off his stockings. Teasingly, deliberately slowly, she ran her hand up one leg, calf, knee, thigh, her fingers just brushing the thick length of his arousal. His chest was heaving. His eyes were fixed on hers. He was utterly in thrall, hers to do with as she pleased. Save that all she wanted was to please *him*.

She dragged her eyes away, returning her attention to the plaid. It was wrapped several times around his body. Deciding against unravelling it, she pushed it roughly aside. He was completely naked underneath. And completely aroused. She touched him, feathering her fingers along the length of him, fascinated by the silky skin, the hardness beneath. She heard him swallow as she curled her fingers around him. Then, driven by the unstoppable urge to know him, she dipped her head and began to lick.

His body became absolutely rigid. Instinct took over as she took him carefully into her mouth. Cameron groaned. She drew him in deeper, astonished at the responsive throb. Fascinated, she explored him with her mouth and her hands, astounded at his response, at her own. He wasn't the only one throbbing. She ached for his touch.

'Kirstin.' His voice was hoarse, a plea.

She lifted her head.

'No more. I want—wait.'

He struggled to his feet, pulling her with him, the plaid unravelling behind him, and wrapped his arms tightly around her. He was completely naked. She was almost fully dressed. She pressed herself against him, thinking to tease, but it was she who moaned in frustration. When he kissed her she moaned again, her head spinning with desire, her whole body taut with barely leashed passion.

'Yes,' he said, though she hadn't spoken, 'I think we've waited long enough.'

Scooping her into his arms, he strode through to the bedroom, setting her down by the bed. The pair of them made quick work of her clothes, falling onto the bed locked together kissing wildly, limbs tangled, hands stroking, clutching, urging.

His fingers slid easily inside her, making her gasp and clench. 'Hurry,' she said, 'hurry.'

He laughed, a throaty sound that sent a frisson down her spine. 'A moment, just one more moment.'

There was the briefest of gaps while he sheathed himself, though it felt like an hour, and then he pulled her back into his arms, rolling her on top of him, easing himself into her slowly, slowly, slowly, but even so she was so aroused, so near the edge, that his first careful thrust almost sent her over.

She tightened around him. He closed his eyes. And then she moved, and he moved with her, fast, hard, deep, each driving the other to completion, her climax triggering his, his hoarse cry mingling with hers as she fell on top of him and their lips fastened in one last deep kiss.

Lying in Cameron's arms, chest to chest, her head beside his on the pillow, their legs tangled, Kirstin was confused by the surge of emotion that brought her to the brink of tears. She put it down to the culmination of momentous events, the strain of her interview with Griffiths, the fact that they were so close to finding Philippa—and to saying goodbye for ever.

Though she would happily have lain there, listening to the beating of Cameron's heart, falling asleep in his arms, she forced herself to get up, turning her back on him and searching for her clothes.

'The hotel staff will be up and about soon,' she whispered, hearing the rustle of the bedclothes as he sat up. 'Try and get some sleep.'

'What about—?'

'We'll talk tonight. I will spend the day trying to collate any additional information I can glean to add to the details Griffiths has provided, and by then, following your observation of the house, you should have a good insight into the challenges involved in rescuing the girls.'

Throwing her gown over her head, she made for the door, bidding him a hasty goodnight and closing it softly behind her before he could say anything more.

Her own bed was cold. Huddling under the covers, Kirstin closed her eyes, but sleep was the furthest thing from her mind.

When they found Philippa she would have made good on her promise and completed the terms of her contract. So why was she worried, rather than excited? As always, Eilidh was at the centre of it. Cameron didn't want a child. Her child didn't need a father, and even if she wanted one—well, Kirstin most certainly didn't want a husband. She'd made many, many sacrifices for her daughter, but that was one she would never make.

Even if the husband was Cameron?

She sat up, plumped her pillows and threw herself back down on them. No, not even then! She would miss him—but working together, being quite alone together in this hotel, it wasn't real. And, yes, in the last few days it had become increasingly clear to her that she'd miss him enormously. But there was nothing to be done about that, was there? When she returned to reality she would see there was no place for him, so the sooner she returned the better.

And that was an end to it. The explanation for those irrational tears. So now she could get some sleep, because tomorrow was a hugely significant day.

Kirstin closed her eyes, taking slow breaths, counting in, holding, counting out. It was the way he'd looked at her, she thought hazily. As she'd unbuckled his belt. So trusting. And the way it had felt...what she had done afterwards. Such a shocking thing to do. Yet all that had been in her mind had been to please him. To show him just how much...

* * *

Cameron didn't bother trying to get to sleep after Kirstin left. Making love to her tonight hadn't been a revelation, more of a confirmation. As he lay back, his hands behind his head, the taste of her in his mouth, the scent of her on his sheets, a slow smile crept across his face.

He loved her.

He had never been in love before, never come close, yet he knew without a shadow of a doubt that he loved Kirstin. He felt it in his bones. They were meant for each other.

Fate had brought them together six years ago, but neither of them had been ready to fall in love. The timing had been wrong, so fate had patiently waited and brought them together again when the time was exactly right. He knew it now. It was just a question of persuading Kirstin.

His smile faltered. It wouldn't be easy. She was so determined not to see all the things which were suddenly so clear to him. The reason neither of them had married in the years since they'd first met was because no one else could measure up. That was why their lovemaking was so perfect. It was illogical. It was irrational. But that didn't mean he was wrong. He loved her. He couldn't feel like this if it was one-sided. He couldn't.

Why would she not countenance the possibility of a shared future together? Was it his illegitimate status? But she'd been vehemently dismissive of those who condemned him for that. Was it because *he'd* been vehement that he'd never want to marry? No. It came back to those words of hers. *Not possible*, she'd said. *That is not possible, whether we wish it or not.*

Why the devil not? They both had businesses to run. They were both accustomed to living alone, answerable to no one. At present, they were settled in two different countries. But all of those things were mere practicalities that could be resolved, weren't they? None of them made a future together impossible.

Cameron pushed back the covers and got out of bed, pulling on his dressing gown. He was missing something. There was something crucial she wasn't telling him. But what the devil could it be to make it impossible for her to consider a future in which he played a part? He *loved* her, dammit! And he was sure she could love him, if only she would allow herself to. What was stopping her?

He rang the bell for breakfast and shaving water. It arrived with an express from Tommy Devine, confirming what they now knew, that the maid's footman suitor was still in Edinburgh and innocent of any involvement. The young man had been wondering why he'd not heard from Jeannie, Tommy wrote, and when he'd discovered that she'd not written to any of the servants at the Ferguson household he'd become more worried still.

Cameron folded the missive, frowning. Louise hadn't taken account of servants' gossip, thinking only to silence Philippa's betrothed. He'd better warn her to do something about it, or all her efforts to suppress a scandal would have been in vain. Ought he to tell her that they knew where Philippa was being held?

Draining his second cup of coffee, he decided against this. A vaguely positive report would be best until they had firm news.

It was not yet eight o'clock, but Cameron was eager to be out and finally taking action—even if it would involve a deal of *in*action. He would have plenty of time, while watching the address Griffiths had given them, to think about Kirstin and to plan how to persuade her they had a future. He loved her so much. Far too much to let her go without a fight. There was a barrow-load of obstacles in their path, but he had always liked a challenge.

A foolish grin crept across his face. He was in love. He, Cameron Dunbar, had fallen deeply and irrevocably in love for the first and last time in his life. Who'd have thought it? Certainly not he.

Pulling on his greatcoat, and picking up his gloves and hat, he opened the door of his suite just in time to see a flash of red pelisse disappear down the stairs. Kirstin was going about her business very early too.

Without thinking, he followed in her wake. She walked quickly, and with purpose. If she'd looked back she'd have seen him. He made no attempt to hide himself, but nor did he try to catch up with her. She headed east, obviously a well-trodden route, for she knew the best places to cross, and never once had to check her bearings.

She was going home, Cameron realised with some trepidation. She had been so very careful never to reveal where her home was, she would be furious if she thought that he was spying on her. Which was exactly what he was doing. But some instinct made him decide to continue to follow her all the same.

The house was on Russell Square. Cameron stopped by the railings. A front door painted glossy black was thrown open as Kirstin approached the shallow steps. A little girl came bounding down, wearing a white pinafore, her coal-black hair in pigtails.

'Mummy!' she cried, throwing herself at Kirstin. 'We didn't know you were coming to see us.'

As Kirstin stooped to hug her daughter, Cameron had a clear view of the child's face. His heart lurched. She looked to be about five years old. He knew without a shadow of a doubt that she was his. He knew it in his bones and in his heart.

He looked on, dumbstruck, until the pair made their way into the house. The door closed. His stomach heaved and he lost his breakfast in the meticulously tended shrubbery of Russell Square.

The morning was turning grey, cold and damp, the kind of day that soaked a person through without it raining. The kind of cold that got into a man's bones. Heedless of it all, Cameron walked, heading south in the general direction of his quarry, the house on Half Moon Street. But it was not the future which occupied his mind, it was the past. His head reeling, he made for the quiet of St James's Park. How could Kirstin have kept such a secret from him? A child! *Their* child! He counted out the years and the months. If he was right, she would be six years old in September. *Was* he right? How could he be sure?

Kirstin had told him it was safe, he remembered. He had been careful all the same. But he had not been sheathed. He gazed sightlessly out at the canal, where a group of ducks were circling to keep warm. And then it struck him. The proof was staring him in the face. If the child wasn't his, Kirstin would have no reason to keep her existence a secret. Therefore she had to be his.

He had a daughter.

Now, finally, he understood Kirstin's use of that word *impossible*. Now he understood why she'd been at such pains to reveal so little of her home life. But why had she kept her child a secret from him in the first place? She could have found him. She hadn't even tried. Why the hell not? She had denied him a say, had decided he'd no right ever to know his child and, what was more, she'd decided that his child had no right to know him.

Seething, he strode along the banks of the canal, crossing into Green Park, his fists clenching and unclenching, walking faster and faster along Constitution Hill, oblivious of the astonished stares of the few hardy souls braving the weather.

Reaching the entrance to Hyde Park, he slowed, his anger began to fade, and reason returned. Six years ago Kirstin had known almost nothing about him. She had not judged his suitability to be a father, she had judged him—what? Unnecessary? Irrelevant? No. She had simply made the question moot, and by doing so had spared him.

And herself?

Cameron took a seat by the Serpentine, oblivious of the drizzling rain which had started to fall. Now the initial shock had begun to fade, he tried to see the situation from Kirstin's point of view. Six years ago she'd been so excited, so full of plans, and confessedly terrified too, of the bold step she'd taken, leaving Edinburgh behind in search of a new life in London. To find that she was pregnant, with no one, never mind a husband, to support her...

He cursed long and fluently under his breath. What she must have gone through. The strength of mind, the resolution—and to have kept her daughter too, when she could easily have given her away, just as his own mother had done.

The tiny glimpse he'd had into their domestic life this morning had made the loving bond between Kirstin and her child obvious. He smiled wryly. It explained The Procurer's ethos—her first test must surely have been to save herself. And what a job she'd made of it. He could see now too, where the ruthless streak which had made Griffiths crumble had its roots.

If only he could have spared her some of what she must have endured, or even helped her, at least.

And, pray, how did he think he could have done that? Cameron forced himself to take a good hard look at himself. Six years ago, how would he have felt if Kirstin had got in touch? He knew what he'd have done, and that was married her, there was no question, but would doing the honourable thing have made either of them happy?

The answer to that was extremely unpalatable but it had to be faced. He would have resented having both a wife and child foisted on him, for they'd have kept him at home. And Kirstin— would she have consented to marriage? And, if she had, would he have permitted his wife to become The Procurer?

'Permitted,' Cameron muttered. Knowing Kirstin now, he would neither wish nor try to order her life, wouldn't dream of deciding what she could do or what she wanted to do. But back then…? Though he'd love to think otherwise, honesty forced him to admit that he'd have tried to force her into a conventional marriage, would have tried to make himself a conventional husband and father. He shuddered. They would both have been miserable.

Droplets of rain gathered on the brim of his hat had started to trickle down his back. Cameron stood up, shaking the folds of his greatcoat. Deep in thought, he began to retrace his steps, heading for Half Moon Street where he would spend the day on watch. There was no point in going over what had happened or what might have happened six years ago, because it was done. What mattered was the future.

He loved Kirstin. He wanted to marry her. He wanted to spend the rest of his life with her. And his daughter.

Good grief, he had a *daughter*! Tears stung the backs of his eyes. He slowed, almost overwhelmed with the love which surged through him like a physical force. He had a family. He would move heaven and earth to be with them. Whatever sacrifices he had to make to shape his world to Kirstin's he would make. He would convince her—

Doubt clutched at him, stopping his thoughts in their tracks. What if he was wrong? What if she didn't care? Saw their time together as nothing more than a brief dalliance? It was possible, even if he didn't want to admit it, for a person to love and not be loved in return.

But this was neither the time nor the place for navel-gazing. He had a niece to rescue! As he turned off Curzon Street, Cameron forced himself to put Kirstin and his new-found daughter to the back of his mind.

Half Moon Street was, according to Kirstin, a rather mixed bag of a district. There were several town houses occupied by those who either disdained the grander and stuffier parts of Mayfair, or were considered unsuitable by the residents. There were genteel apartments for those whose income could not run to a town house. There were several gentlemen's lodging houses, for the street was conveniently close to the clubs of St James's. And there were a few discreet houses occupied by a few select ladies kept by gentlemen with the means to support two households for very different purposes.

The house which Griffiths had described was halfway down on the left-hand side of the street, with a red door and a knocker in the shape of a lion's head. The lower windows were barred, though so too were the windows in several other of the buildings. The windows of the attic and the second floor were shuttered, but those on the ground and main floor were curtained. The rooms behind were dark.

Frustrated, Cameron looked around for a place from which to spy, but each house abutted the next. He could not stand there all day without raising suspicion. So he'd have to find a hiding place.

'You did *what*?' Kirstin exclaimed.

It was very late by the time Cameron returned, but she had held back dinner for him.

'I hired a room in the lodging house diagonally opposite,' Cameron said, helping himself to a leg of chicken. 'A room at the front, of course. With an excellent vantage point.'

'How did you explain the fact that you had no luggage?'

'I told some tale of it having been lost in transit. The landlady didn't believe a word of it, of course, but she was happy to go along with it when I supplemented my tale with a very generous down-payment. I'll go back tonight, get my money's worth out of that room.'

It was wrong of her to be disappointed. Guiltily, Kirstin set aside her own inappropriate ideas for how the rest of the night might be spent. 'You'll not see much in the dark.'

'No.' Cameron frowned down at his chicken

as if it had offended him. 'How did you spend your day?'

'That's the second time you've asked me that. Is there something wrong?'

'No. Yes. No.' He pushed aside his plate, uncharacteristically leaving it half-full. 'Kirstin, I— Never mind, it can wait.'

'What can wait?'

He stared at her, clearly torn, then shook his head. 'Now is not the time,' he said.

She had the impression he was talking to himself rather than her, for he stared down at his plate again for some time, shifting his dinner about abstractedly.

Finally, he gave a sigh. 'What were we talking about?'

'You are determined to return to Half Moon Street. In the dark. Even though you won't see anything.'

'But I might.' He sighed again, and gave himself a little shake. 'No, I'm definitely going,' he said firmly. 'I want to keep an eye out for any comings and goings,' he added grimly. 'We've no idea how many poor lasses are locked away behind those doors.'

'It's not likely to be more than one or two. What I have managed to extract from my sources, using what Griffiths told us, is that the *gentlemen* of the Erotes Club are very discriminating.' Kirstin gave up pretending to eat. 'They number minor royalty amongst their members. To think that such men— It's disgusting.'

He drummed his fingers on the table, frowning deeply. 'If they find out that you've been sniffing around, they will ruin you without compunction. If they are as influential as you say, they'll know who The Procurer is and where to find her. However we go about breaking into that house, you can't risk being involved.'

He looked exhausted, with circles under his eyes, his jaw dark with stubble. 'They could just as equally ruin you,' Kirstin said, reaching across the table to clasp his hand.

He tightened his fingers around hers. 'It's *my* niece we're rescuing, *my* promise to Louise Ferguson that we're honouring. Two young lassies, Kirstin, and a mother at her wits' end. Compared to that, my business doesn't matter.'

'I made a promise too, remember? To you, Cameron. I'm not deserting you at the last minute.'

'Kirstin, you can't risk all you've worked for.' He pushed back his chair, pulling her to her feet and wrapping his arms around her. 'I can't let you do that,' he said, sounding oddly desperate. 'After everything you've— No, I won't let you.'

She reached up to smooth back his hair, puzzled by his vehemence. 'Then we'll have to make sure that we don't get caught, because I'm coming with you. No,' she said, putting her finger over his mouth when he made to protest, 'listen to me. Philippa doesn't know you, Cameron. How is she to know you have come to save her, not take her away to endure some horrible fate? It will be much better for her if there's a woman there to reassure her—and Jeannie, too, if she is in that house.'

'I hadn't thought of that.'

'And as for those in charge of the Erotes Club—yes, they could ruin us both, I'm not denying it, but we could ruin them too, if we have to.'

'Expose their—their private peccadillos to the public, you mean?'

'Exactly. *If* we are caught—and we won't be—then we can threaten to expose them. They have even more to lose than we do.'

His arms tightened around her waist. 'They don't. Kirstin, I—' He broke off, biting his lip, shaking his head at her enquiring look. 'Another time. I must go.'

'We'll find a way to get Philippa back safely. We are so close…'

'I know. It's not that.'

'Then what?'

'Not now. We'll make a rescue plan in the morning. Try and get a good night's sleep.'

A longing to spend the night sleeping wrapped in his arms assailed her. Not to make love, but simply to sleep. She yearned to smooth away his frown and his worries, and to wake up to his kisses, his tender smile...

Kirstin untangled herself from his embrace and bestowed her professional smile on him. 'The sooner we act the better, for the sake of those girls.'

And for the sake of her own peace of mind too. She could not allow herself to become too attached to Cameron. Feelings clouded one's judgement. She could not permit that.

'Until the morning.'

She nodded, was about to head for the door, but somehow found herself wrapping her arms around him instead, pressing a fleeting kiss to his lips. 'Good luck.'

There was a distinct and inexplicable wobble in her voice. Afraid as much of the emotion in her voice as of Cameron's noticing, Kirstin fled.

They had spent the morning planning and preparing. Now, on the brink of leaving for Half Moon Street, Kirstin was trying not to panic.

'You really think this will work? Wouldn't it be easier to hire a couple of thugs?'

'Easier if we want all hell to break loose.' Cameron turned from the mirror, where he had been adjusting his cravat. 'And that's exactly what we're trying to avoid.'

'I know that.' She managed a strained smile. 'Don't worry. I won't lose my nerve.'

'That is one of few things I'm not worried about. Come here, sit down for a minute.' Cameron patted the sofa, clasping her hands in his when she sat down beside him. 'The more time we can buy ourselves between spiriting the girls away and our little ruse being discovered the better, right?'

'Right.' It was foolish to be reassured simply by the clasp of his hands and a warm smile, but she was.

'So we will persuade this Mrs Allardyce woman Griffiths says is the housekeeper that we've been sent by her employers, the Erotes Club. The mention of the name should be enough to convince her we are legitimate visitors.'

'But if she is cautious and insists on checking first?'

'Then I will point out how foolish she is being to risk upsetting her paymasters by contacting them unnecessarily when discretion is all. And if that doesnae work,' Cameron said in his broadest Glaswegian growl, 'then I'll batter the life out of the two thugs on the door, and you can take care of the lassies.'

Kirstin shivered. In his guise of a rough Glaswegian, Cameron made her feel fragile, helpless, when she was never any of those things, and he made her feel completely safe, sure that he would never let any harm come to her, though she was in no need of a protector.

'It is to be hoped that we can avoid any physical violence,' she said, unable to prevent herself from pressing a kiss to his knuckles.

'If there is, then you've chosen the perfect disguise, Nurse Grey.' He smiled wickedly. 'I'm tempted to get myself a wee bit bloodied just so you can be my ministering angel.'

'Oh, no, Dr Black, you are quite mistaken, I am no ministering angel,' Kirstin replied in Nurse Grey's clipped tones. 'I'm the stern, cold-baths-and-plenty-of-fresh-air kind of nurse, who tolerates no malingering.'

'But who also has a wee soft spot for Dr Black?' Cameron winked.

'Dr Black, I think you are trying to distract me from the task in hand.'

He kissed her softly. 'Is it working?'

Kirstin sighed, smiling reluctantly. 'Yes. I am much better now. Shall we go?'

He narrowed his eyes, scrutinising her for some moments. What he saw obviously satisfied him, for he nodded, getting to his feet and pulling her with him. 'Aye,' he said curtly. 'Let's get this business done.'

Chapter Eleven

Half Moon Street was eerily quiet in the middle of the afternoon. The pavements were deserted as the hackney carriage pulled up in front of the red door of number nine. Dr Black, in a long cloak, with a tall hat, carrying an old-fashioned swordstick in the guise of a malacca walking cane with an embossed silver top, descended first. Nurse Grey, in a plain brown wool dress and short cape, with a white starched apron and cap to match, emerged behind the good doctor, carrying his bag and keeping her head lowered.

Though Kirstin's heart was hammering, her mind was completely focused on the task in hand, taking her lead from Cameron.

A sharp rap of the knocker revealed a tall, well-built woman of about forty, dressed in a housekeeper's garb. Her smile failed to meet her eyes.

'Yes?'

'Mrs Allardyce.' Dr Black had the plummy, booming, confident voice of a man sure of his station in life and his welcome. 'I take it we are expected? I am Dr Black,' he said, upon receiving a blank look, 'and this is my assistant, Nurse Grey. Please resist making the obvious comment, it has been done to death.'

Taking advantage of the woman's confusion, he pushed passed her into the hallway with Kirstin scurrying behind. The two thugs who guarded the house and its precious contents stood, arms folded, at either side of the stairs, like grotesque and oversized newel posts.

'Gentlemen,' Dr Black said, with a careless nod.

Mrs Allardyce, meantime, had recovered her nerve. 'I am afraid you are under some misapprehension, Dr Black,' she said coolly. 'There is no one here who requires the services of a medical man.'

Cameron clapped his hands together and tutted with just the right amount of condescension. Kirstin, still hovering in the background and taking covert stock of the place, wondered who his role model was, certain that he had one.

'Well, now, Mrs Allardyce,' he continued, dropping his voice to a confidential stage whisper, 'I sincerely hope for your sake no one here is ill, since it is your job to keep them fit and well, and that would constitute a dereliction of duty.' He smiled benignly. 'Rather, it is a matter of my verifying that they are up to specification. For the coming experience. If you take my meaning. This is the first occasion the goods in question have been sourced from a madam such as Mrs Jardine, so the powers that be prudently wish to satisfy themselves as to their suitability.'

'I am not sure I can allow...'

'Now, I am very sure that you don't want me to disclose in front of these fine gentlemen here precisely who sent me, for your—let us call him your benefactor—would not wish his name to be bandied about, would he?' Dr Black's smile became menacing. 'He pays you a great deal for your discretion. You would not wish me to cause him to think that his money has been badly spent.'

Kirstin was not surprised to see Mrs Allardyce wither, but the woman had not earned her trusted place in this hellish house for nothing. She did not dismiss the thugs. Instead she opened the door of a small parlour and indicated that Dr Black should follow.

Kirstin hesitated, but a tiny shake of his head informed her that Cameron wanted her to remain where she was. The door was left open, giving her a view of Mrs Allardyce and Cameron, she remonstrating, he standing his ground, shaking his head, saying little. Though Kirstin's hearing was acute, she could make out only the odd muttered phrase.

The two thugs made no pretence at uninterest, their attention fully focused on the confrontation. Taking advantage of this, Kirstin studied each of them, noting the unmistakable outline of cudgels under their rough coats. To deter unwanted visitors, no doubt. Her mouth was dry. How many girls had been incarcerated here, locked away, kept fed and watered, physically unharmed, but in mental turmoil? What kind of state would they be in when they were finally taken to meet their fate? And what happened to them afterwards? Some of the many questions she had been unable to obtain answers to. With this case, she had for the first time reached the limits of The Procurer's influence.

The booming tone of Dr Black made her start. 'A wise move, Mrs Allardyce. Your caution does you credit, but I fear you might undermine your position were you to trouble your superiors with a spurious query as to my credentials. They are not the type who like to have their actions questioned.' Cameron was shaking the woman's hand. 'I shall inform His Grace that he is being very well served indeed. Now, if you will call off these gentlemen...?'

A nod from Mrs Allardyce and the men stood aside. 'Nurse Grey, if you will bring my bag we will complete our task and be gone.'

He began to stride up the stairs, so Kirstin hurried after him. Cameron paused for a mere second at the top of the landing on the uppermost floor to swear under his breath.

'That was one hard nut to crack, but she decided discretion was the better part of valour. Philippa is in the room at the end of this corridor. Jeannie is with her.'

'They have cudgels, both men,' Kirstin said.

'Better that than pistols.' Cameron raised his voice. 'Hurry along, Nurse Grey, I'm a busy man. I don't have all day.'

There were two doors on either side of the hallway in addition to the one in which Philippa was being held. All four of the rooms, to Kirstin's utter relief, were empty. She knew that any attempt to release other victims would put Philippa's safety at risk, it was something they had both discussed, and a conclusion painfully reached. But she knew that Cameron would have been still tempted, and as for herself—well, she was simply glad not to be put to the test.

'This is the one, Nurse Grey,' Dr Black boomed, throwing back the first bolt.

As he stooped to open the second bolt Kirstin saw that his hand was shaking, fumbling with the mechanism. She touched his arm. Their eyes met briefly. He gave a firm nod and pulled back the bolt, opening the door just wide enough for the pair of them to step through, before shutting it again and leaning his back against it.

The girls, one with raven-black hair, the other with a tangled mop of bright red, were huddled together in the furthest corner of the room. They were dressed in white shifts, barefooted, but while Jeannie's face was a picture of utter terror, Philippa was trying desperately to compose herself.

'What do you want?' she asked, and though her voice trembled there was a touch of her mother's hauteur in her tone. Louise, Kirstin thought, had been very wrong in thinking her daughter lacked spine.

There was no time now for explanations, all that could wait until the girls were safe. 'Philippa,' Kirstin said calmly, 'my name is Kirstin. This man with me is Cameron. We've been sent by your mother, Mrs Louise Ferguson, to take you home.'

Jeannie whimpered and would have come forward, but Philippa caught her, pushing the maid behind her, glaring at Kirstin from under fierce brows exactly like her mother's.

'Why hasn't my mother come herself? We haven't made any trouble. We've eaten our dinners and we've kept quiet and we've not made a fuss, exactly as we've been told to do. So if the ransom has been paid why hasn't Mama come to fetch us?'

Ransom! So this was how the girls were kept in line—with the promise of release. At least they had been spared the agony of knowing their real fate, but it was a hideous lie to feed them.

'Philippa,' Kirstin said urgently, 'there has been no ransom demand. Your mother has had to resort to other methods to rescue you. I cannot explain right now, there is no time, but believe me, your only chance of escape is with us, right now.'

'But they said—'

'Dr Black?' Mrs Allardyce knocked on the door. 'Have you completed your preliminary examination?'

'Get on the bed,' Kirstin said, in a tone which brooked no argument.

Cowed, the girls did as she bade them, watching wide-eyed as she removed a fiendish-looking pair of forceps from the doctor's bag and held them out for Cameron, who had hurriedly cast off his cloak and gloves. Jeannie gave a shriek at the sight of the instrument, and even Philippa whimpered. No need to tell them to look as if they'd been traumatised, Kirstin thought darkly, recalling her own first glimpse of one of those fearful implements.

She pulled out a towel spattered with pig's blood from the bag and draped it over her arm. 'Philippa, your mother has a miniature of you which she keeps in a blue enamel case,' she whispered. She tried desperately to recall what Louise Ferguson had been wearing at their one and only meeting. 'And she has a ring, rose gold, with five garnets set in the shape of a cross. And a gold locket, oval in shape.'

'It has a lock of my father's hair in it. Who *are* you?'

Kirstin heaved a sigh of relief. 'Please do as we ask, say nothing, and you will be with your mother very shortly.'

Philippa nodded. 'Jeannie, did you hear that?' she asked her maid gently. 'Hush, now, do as they say, and we'll be home soon.'

'Take this,' Kirstin said, pushing a second gruesome towel into Jeannie's hands. 'Hold it here,' she said, 'as if…'

'Dr Black! If you do not open this door…'

'Now, now, Mrs Allardyce, I was trying to preserve the girls' dignity.' Cameron waved the forceps in the woman's face. 'Our very important little miss passes muster, as far as I'm concerned, but I would prefer the absolute certainty a very quick second opinion would provide. Unfortunately, we have a little bit of a problem with her handmaiden. Nurse Grey?'

Kirstin obligingly held up the gruesome towel. She pointed to Jeannie, clutching the second towel in her lap, hoping that Mrs Allardyce was the squeamish type and not inclined to question the exact nature of either Jeannie's complaint or Dr Black's examination.

'Not a handmaiden at all,' Dr Black said, tutting, 'but soiled goods, I'm afraid. You see what a wise decision it was to call me in? She'll make a full recovery, but she's of no use to your benefactor. I'll take her with me, find her a more appropriate home.'

He tapped the side of his nose, then clapped his hands together. 'Nurse Grey, young ladies, let us be off. The sooner we are gone the sooner we will be back.'

'This is most unusual,' Mrs Allardyce protested. 'I am not at all sure…'

'Ah, but you will be, with the benefit of a second examination,' Dr Black said. 'An hour, two at the most, and I'll have her back to you. Better safe than sorry, that's what I say. I've no more desire to upset our paymasters than you.'

Kirstin hurriedly wrapped her short cape around Philippa, while Cameron held out his cloak for Jeannie, placing himself between the girl and Mrs Allardyce so that she did not see Kirstin grabbing the bloodied towel and shoving it back into the bag along with the forceps. Jeannie could barely stand, but Philippa whispered something reassuring in her ear and pushed her forward.

Kirstin led the way, with Cameron at the rear, the two girls sandwiched between them. She fought the urge to run, heading down the stairs at a stately pace, aware of Dr Black still making booming small talk, though the roaring in her ears prevented her from taking in a word.

The thugs were in position at the bottom of the stairs. Kirstin made for the door. One of them rushed in front of her. She had just enough time to wonder frantically if she could lift the heavy doctor's bag high enough to hit him square in the face when he opened the door for her and stood back.

The carriage was waiting. The driver, seeing them, jumped down from the box and lowered the steps. Kirstin discovered that she could still find solace in prayer as she stood back to let Philippa and Jeannie in. She climbed in after them.

Dr Black bid Mrs Allardyce a last fruity adieu and a promise that her helpfulness would be extolled. Then Cameron leapt into the coach, slammed the door shut and it was over.

When they had arrived at the house where Louise was staying Kirstin had firmly refused to leave the coach, not wishing to intrude on the reunion. She completed the business of covering their trail by paying their driver to lose his memory, returning late to the hotel and a note from Cameron, informing her that he was staying for dinner with Mrs Ferguson.

The following morning she received a second note, informing her that he would be wholly occupied for some hours assisting Mrs Ferguson—still Mrs Ferguson, not Louise—complete her travel arrangements north with all possible speed. Understandable, and extremely wise, Kirstin thought. Louise wished to thank her in person, but Kirstin decided against this. Seeing Cameron's face as they'd left Half Moon Street had been all the thanks she needed.

So she wrote her own note, informing Cameron that she was taking a walk in Hyde Park and would see him at dinner. The weather co-operated with her desire for fresh air and solitude, a chill breeze making the few clouds which dared to blot the clear blue winter's sky scud along. The park was virtually deserted. It was too cold for nursery maids and their children, too early in the year for the hoi polloi to take the air and show off their horses, their toilettes and their mistresses, so Kirstin had nothing but the ducks and a few hardy souls taking their daily constitutional for company.

She wandered aimlessly, trying to conjure up the satisfaction of a job very well done, which she had every right to, but signally failing. The case was over. Philippa and Jeannie were both safe and would recover fully from their ordeal in time. Cameron had made good on his promise to Louise, the debt he believed he owed her paid. And Kirstin had made good on her promise to Cameron.

Their time together was almost over. Tonight would be her last in the hotel, for there was no reason to linger there. Tomorrow she would go home to Eilidh, and Cameron—most likely Cameron would escort Louise and Phillipa safely back to Edinburgh.

It was over. There was no point in crying or feeling sorry for herself, especially when she had exactly what she wanted, a happy outcome for the case, and for her the reassurance that she had made the right decision all those years ago, when Eilidh had first been given into her arms.

She would miss Cameron. Dreadfully at first. But it would pass. And she would have no cause to question her decision again. Nor ever to see him again either.

She halted at the edge of the Serpentine, staring blindly at the murky waters as she tried to get herself under control. There was still tonight. They would be together tonight. They would make love tonight. One last time. She would make it memorable. And when morning came—

But she wouldn't think about the morning.

'Kirstin.'

She whirled round. 'Cameron!'

'You didn't call,' he said. 'Louise was very disappointed. She couldn't understand why you were so reluctant—but in the end she wrote you a note.'

'You know that it is my policy to remain in the background.'

'I thought this case was different. Obviously not.' He offered her his arm. 'Shall we walk? It's cold standing here.'

She sighed, doing as she was bade, and they began to follow the path around the Serpentine. She didn't have to explain herself. Yet she couldn't resist. 'I have already broken a great many of my own rules in taking your case on. It *is* different from any other, you're right about that.'

'Then why won't you see Louise?'

'Because she doesn't owe me any thanks. Her gratitude should be directed at you. You're the one who rescued Philippa.'

'We achieved that together, you and I.'

'But I wouldn't have been involved at all if not for you.' She glanced up at him, smiling faintly. 'From the beginning you've put the safety of those two girls over everything. I know you think that it was a—a form of reparation, but you didn't commit a crime, Cameron, simply by being born.'

'So you stayed away in order to ensure that Louise had to heap every scrap of her gratitude on me, is that it?'

'And did she?'

He laughed. 'Almost, but not quite. She was almost effusive. I even got a hug—well, a light patting, which is the next best thing.'

'Did she explain who you are to Philippa?'

'She did.' His expression became serious once more. 'That is one very brave young lassie, Kirstin. She didn't say much about what they'd been through, and insisted that they were never in fear of their lives, well-cared-for, all that, and Louise was happy to swallow it.'

'You think Philippa is protecting her?'

'Ironic, isn't it? Philippa's not one to blow her own trumpet, but I reckon she was a tower of strength to Jeannie.'

'What will happen to her? Louise blamed her for what happened...'

'I reckon she still does, though she dare not say it for fear of upsetting Philippa. In the short term, all Jeannie wants is to go home to her mammy in North Berwick.'

'And what about Philippa's engagement?'

'That decision, believe it or not,' Cameron said, 'has been left in Philippa's hands. She, clever girl, has chosen to take her time deciding.'

'Goodness, but Louise has changed her tune.'

'She's had a lot of time to think, she told me.'

Kirstin raised a brow. 'She seems to have told you quite a lot.'

'Aye.' Cameron smiled briefly down at her. 'Whether it's relief, gratitude, or whether this whole horrible experience has genuinely altered her view of life, she does seem to have warmed to me.'

'Cameron!' Kirstin stopped in her tracks, beaming up at him. 'That is...'

'Hold your horses. She's not ready to call me brother yet, not by a long chalk. Though Philippa is already calling me Uncle Cameron. Which, let me tell you, sounds mighty strange.'

'I think that where Philippa leads, Louise will follow. I'm so pleased for you.'

'We'll see.'

They turned at the dog leg of the Serpentine and began to head back on the other side of the lake.

'Do you think the members of the Erotes Club will come after us, after yesterday?' Cameron asked.

'I doubt it. I'm not naïve enough to think they'll abandon their activities, but at least we've forced them to cancel their next meeting. Considering all you have achieved, you don't seem particularly happy.'

'For someone who has played a pivotal role, I could level the same accusation at you. I owe you a huge debt of gratitude in addition to a large fee.'

'I don't want your money, Cameron.'

'Don't be silly, Kirstin, you've earned it, and I signed a contract…'

'I don't want your money. I did this because— Oh, it doesn't matter.'

'It matters a lot.' He stopped as they reached

the gates of the park. 'I've wondered from the beginning why you took my case on when The Procurer's business is to find other people to make the impossible possible, not to do it herself. So why am I the exception?'

That look of his, the way his eyes bored into her very soul, made her want to flee. And why was she getting the impression that this was a plea, rather than a question? What did he want her to say?

'I met you because I was curious. I took on the case because I was the best person for the role and time was pressing. I stayed because I desperately wanted to help find Philippa and Jeannie.' All of which was the truth, but not even half of it.

And none of it, evidently, was what Cameron wanted to hear. 'Is that it?' he asked.

'I knew how much finding them meant to you,' Kirstin elaborated a little desperately, 'and—and I—you deserve to be given a second chance. Your sister—I was sure that if only she could forget the past she would realise how fortunate she is to call you her brother.'

He smiled wryly. 'So you did it for me?'

'I—yes. I did it for you.'

She couldn't tell if that satisfied him or not. He looked up at the sky, which was darkening, the sun now completely obscured behind thick cloud.

'Looks to me like we might be in for snow. We should head back to the hotel.'

'I sincerely hope it's not snow, else your journey north—'

'Oh, I'm not escorting Louise.' He took her arm and began to walk quickly in the direction of the hotel. 'I promised I'd visit as soon as was convenient, but now is not in the least convenient. I've business of my own to attend to.'

'Ewan's tea business?'

But Cameron, increasing his pace, seemed not to have heard her.

The evening gown Kirstin wore for her last dinner with Cameron had an underdress of scarlet satin paired with an overdress of sarcenet decorated with silk flowers in every shade of red, the leaves picked out in silver. The neckline was square, the sleeves simple caps, the hem weighted with a border of red and silver beading. It was an outrageously expensive and wildly extravagant gown, one she was unlikely ever to wear again, though the result was worth every penny.

Kirstin painted her lips with carmine, added a light dusting of powder to her nose, and adjusted the velvet ribbon in her hair. Crimson slippers and a new pair of long white evening gloves completed her toilette.

'You look absolutely ravishing,' Cameron said, bowing low over her hand.

'Thank you.'

In a dark blue coat and waistcoat, with tightly fitting fawn pantaloons and a pair of gleaming Hessians, Cameron had dressed with care for this, their last night. *Their last night.* She mustn't allow herself to think of it like that.

'You look very dashing.'

'Thank you. Sit down, Kirstin. I've asked them to delay serving dinner.' Taking a bottle from a silver bucket, he began to twist the cork. 'I thought we'd forgo our sherry. Tonight calls for a celebration, a toast.'

He seemed tense. Watching him pour the champagne into crystal flutes, Kirstin was becoming nervous.

He sat down beside her and touched his glass to hers. 'To you,' Cameron said. 'Kirstin Blair, a woman who makes the impossible possible.'

'Cheers,' she said, immeasurably touched and also reassured. She took a sip of the golden liquid, relishing the way the bubbles melted on her tongue, and sighed with pleasure. 'This was a lovely idea.'

But Cameron's smile was perfunctory. He set his glass down, untouched, and Kirstin had a horrible conviction that the night was not going to go to her plan. Her fingers tightened around the stem of her own glass. Cameron's throat was working, a sure sign that he was having to steel himself to say something, and she was absolutely certain that, whatever it was, she didn't want to hear it.

'Cameron...'

'Kirstin.'

The look in his eyes made her heart flutter, then pound. She sat frozen to the spot, allowing him to remove her glass and take her hands in his.

'Kirstin, when I told you that I never dreamed of marriage, I meant it. But that was because I'd never met the right woman.'

'No.' She tried to pull her hands away, but he held her tightly.

'Listen to me,' he said urgently, 'please hear me out.'

Feeling quite sick, she realised that if she did not, the break between them would never be final. Besides, it was every bit as vital to make the break clean for him too. And it would be a test, she thought grimly, of her own resolve, which she could use as a talisman against any future regrets.

'Go on,' she said.

'Six years ago—' He broke off, cleared his throat, released her to take a deep gulp of his champagne. 'Six years ago,' he began again, 'I met the right woman. You.' He smiled at her softly. 'But the time wasn't right for us. You were only just setting out to make a life for yourself, and I—well, I hadn't a clue whether I was coming or going, after that meeting with Louise. So we went our separate ways. And we lived our own lives, the pair of us, and made a success of them.'

'Exactly, Cameron, which is why—'

'When the fates brought us back together this time,' he interrupted, 'we were ready. I didn't know it that first night here, Kirstin, when I went on about my freedom to roam the world and my liking for having things all my own way, but I very quickly realised. You are the one I've been waiting for. You are the only woman for me. I love you with all my heart.'

'No.' Her own heart was beating so hard that she could hardly breathe. 'No, Cameron. Please, I can't...'

'You assume you can't, because you've not thought about it. Think about it now, Kirstin.

I'm not asking you to marry me straight away—
though that's what I want. And I'm certainly not
asking you to give up all that you've worked so
hard for. All I'm asking is that you think about
it, that you give us a chance to see if we can create a whole new life together. Will you at least
think about it?'

'No!' Panic-stricken, she jumped to her feet.
'No, Cameron, I can't countenance that.'

'Why not? Don't you care for me?'

'You know I do, but—I told you. I told you
right from the start that we could not—that we
could never— Our situations are far too different for us ever to find any compromise we could
be happy with.'

'You can't know that if you don't try.'

'I don't need to try,' Kirstin said wretchedly.
'I know it wouldn't work, it's impossible.'

'Why is it so impossible?' Cameron caught
her hands, forcing her to face him, to meet his
gaze. 'Can't you trust me with the truth?'

It was that same look he'd had at the park
gates earlier. As if he was pleading with her
to tell him something. An appalling possibility crossed her mind. But that was simply not
credible. She tried to think, tried desperately to
recall if she had said one single thing, made a

single slip which could have set him down that path, but there was nothing.

She shook her head. 'There isn't anything to tell.'

'You know,' he said gently, 'the one thing you're not any good at is lying.'

He knew. She had no idea how he'd guessed, but he knew. She was finding it difficult to breathe. She must have laced her corsets too tight. The room was too hot. The need to escape was too strong to resist. Kirstin, who had never failed to face anything in her life, made for the door.

He caught her easily. He was smiling. Why was he smiling?

'Kirstin, my darling, I know we have a daughter. I know that she is the reason you think our being together is impossible, but you're wrong. I have never been so delighted…'

'Delighted?' She stared at him in utter disbelief. 'You told me that you never wanted children. You said that you would resent them, that you—you cannot possibly be delighted.'

'But I am. When I saw her—'

'When?' Cold anger cloaked her terror. 'When did you see her?'

'The morning after the ball. I was on my way out, heading to Half Moon Street, and I saw you.'

A faint flush tinged his cheeks. 'You *followed* me?' Kirstin exclaimed incredulously. 'You spied on me? You followed me to my home, the home that I have been at great pains to keep private.'

'For a reason I now understand fully.'

'For a reason which I never wished you to know.'

'But I understand that,' Cameron said urgently. 'You were determined to establish yourself, to make an extraordinary life for yourself. Despite what happened between us that night, you didn't know me, could have had no idea whether I'd ignore a letter informing me that I was a father or, perhaps worse, from your point of view, whether I'd force my name on you and dictate how both you and your daughter should lead your lives. Am I right?'

He was so correct that she was astonished and could only nod. 'You see now why it is impossible?'

'I see now why it was impossible six years ago. But now...'

'No,' Kirstin said flatly, 'nothing has changed. I am perfectly happy as I am, and perfectly capable of taking care of my daughter myself. I don't need you.'

Cameron looked as if she had slapped him. 'And my daughter? Isn't she entitled to a father?'

'She doesn't need one. She has no idea who you are, and that is how I intend things to remain.'

'But I love you.'

'That changes nothing,' she said ruthlessly, refusing to see the hurt she was causing, wanting only to escape, to protect her daughter and herself. 'I don't love you. I *won't* love you. There is nothing more to discuss.'

He was silent for a very long time. 'I notice you don't deny that she is mine.'

It was an agony not to relent, but she was fighting for her life. Even so, she would never tell such a dastardly lie. 'Of course she is yours,' Kirstin admitted shakily. 'Why else would I have kept her a secret?'

He studied her, his eyes hardening. 'I won't allow my daughter to suffer as I did for the lack of a name.'

'She has my name.'

'You know perfectly well what I mean. You are so determined to bend the world to the shape you desire, and heaven knows I admire you for it, even though there must have been many occasions when you've paid a heavy price for your uncompromising stance. But it's wrong of you to make our daughter pay the price for your principles.'

'*My* daughter does not suffer,' Kirstin said through gritted teeth.

'What does her school think about her mother, *Miss* Blair?'

'She does not attend school.'

His lip curled. 'So that's how you preserve her innocence? That's how you protect her, is it? By hiding her away? You can't do that for ever.'

'Don't you dare tell me what I can and can't do. *This* is why I did not tell you…'

'You're deluding yourself,' Cameron barked, making no attempt to subdue his anger any more. 'You can't keep her hidden away from the world for ever. The longer you lie to her…'

'I don't lie to her.'

'She may not be old enough to be curious yet, but one day she will ask about me. For such an intelligent woman, you're being incredibly stupid. I can't bear the thought of my daughter going through life tarred as a bastard.'

'She is not—'

'Don't kid yourself. That is exactly what they'll call her. She'll be ridiculed, she'll be bullied, she'll be made to feel that she is worthless. It will be a permanent stain on her character. I speak from experience, as you may recall from my choosing to confide in you.'

'It's not the same,' Kirstin protested, but her words lacked conviction.

'You know it is, which is why you've brought her up in splendid isolation, by the sounds of it. Well I won't stand by and let her suffer. I won't let her endure what I did.'

His peremptory tone made her rally. 'You have no say in the matter. After tonight, I never want to see you again.'

If her words hurt him, he recovered quickly enough. 'After tonight, I am absolutely determined to give my daughter my name.'

'Don't be preposterous. You can't force me to marry you, Cameron.'

'I won't have to. Logic and reason, those tenets you live by, will eventually make you realise that you owe it to your daughter to free her to go out in the world, and to protect her too. It's clear that you love her very much. Loving someone doesn't mean keeping them in a gilded cage, Kirstin. It means…'

He turned away, pouring a glass of champagne with a shaking hand, downing it in one. She watched, unable to move, almost beyond thought, never mind words. *This couldn't be happening.*

Cameron set the empty glass down. 'I'll give you a year.'

She stared at him blankly.

'Twelve months to think about what I've said, to come to terms with the fact that we're going to be married, and then I'll be back.'

'We're not going to be married.'

'You need have no fear that I'll force myself on you, or on my daughter either. I won't interfere with your precious life. I'll give the child my name—you'll allow me that, at least?—but that's it.'

'I would become your property. You would be entitled to my business—the law would give you it all, including my daughter.'

'Do you not understand me at *all*?' he roared, clutching at his hair. 'Can you not get it into your head that I'm not interested in owning you or changing you or— Dear God, Kirstin, have you really no idea at all what I feel for you? I wouldn't change a hair on your head.'

His hand reached out towards her, but he snatched it back. 'You think this is all about the child, don't you? You're quite wrong. It was about you, first and foremost—but there's no talking to you about that. I've done with spilling my guts. Think very carefully about what I've said. I'll be back in exactly a year from now to hear your answer.'

He opened the door for her. Distraught, she

walked towards it, wondering if her legs would carry her the short distance to her own suite and the sanctuary of her bed.

'Kirstin?'

She gazed up at him through a curtain of tears.

'Her name,' Cameron said wretchedly. 'I don't even know her name.'

'Eilidh,' she said, as the tears began to cascade down her cheeks. 'Her name is Eilidh.'

Cameron remained where he was, standing by the door, completely numb. A sharp rap roused him from his reverie. He wrenched it open, only to be confronted with two waiters and his very carefully ordered dinner. He sent them away, keeping only the wine, cursing his stupidity. After all, Kirstin only gave second chances to deserving females.

He loved her and yet he had lost her.

With a shaking hand, he poured himself a large glass of wine, gulping down the finest vintage the hotel had been able to provide as if it were ale. Kirstin was gone. Kirstin didn't love him. *Wouldn't* love him.

He stared down at the floor as if into a chasm. He'd get by without her. His chest tightened. He bit back a huge heaving sob. He'd survive. He poured himself a second, brimming glass of burgundy and tipped it down his throat. Another sob racked his body. No wine, no matter how fine, was a cure for a broken heart.

Cameron staggered to his bedroom, threw himself on the bed and pulled a pillow over his head.

He woke in the early hours of the morning with an aching head but a clear mind. He'd gone over and over what he'd said the night before, wondering if he'd got it wrong, but he hadn't. It was Kirstin who had made it all about her daughter, giving him no option in the end but to follow her lead. The child was all she cared about.

While he had been falling in love with her almost from the moment she'd stepped through the door of this very suite, she had never seen him as anything other than a—a dalliance. She didn't love him. She wouldn't love him. And there was not a thing he could do about that.

Heavy-hearted but resolved, Cameron rang the bell for shaving water and coffee, and set about packing. He would never be happy without Kirstin, but if what made her happy was to be free of him, that was what he'd give her.

Though on one point he was resolute. His daughter. Eilidh. It was a very different kind of pain, the knowledge that he'd never be part of her life. The only thing he could do was protect her from all that he'd suffered. Let her save the grit and determination she'd no doubt inherited from her mother for more worthwhile causes than defiance and covering up her hurt.

Sitting at the writing desk, Cameron dipped a pen in the ink and pulled a fresh piece of paper towards him. It was a curt note, businesslike in its tone, stating his terms. He folded the thick wad of notes he'd obtained from his bank yesterday and sealed it. Contract completed. Time for him to move on.

Picking up his portmanteau, he gave the porter directions for the rest of his luggage. No looking back at the room where he and Kirstin had made love. Or *he* had made love, to be brutally accurate. No looking back at the table where they'd dined together so many times, or the sofa where they'd sat, sipping sherry. He'd never drink sherry again.

Treading lightly, he pushed his note with some difficulty under the door of Kirstin's suite. Then he made his way down the stairs, paid their bill, and went out into a hackney, headed for the posting house to join his sister and his niece for their journey back to Scotland.

Chapter Twelve

Eight months later, October 1819

Kirstin made a final, wholly unnecessary check of the dining table. The silverware glittered, the crystal sparkled, the napkins at each of the four place settings were crisp and folded into the shape of fans atop the Royal Doulton crockery. She'd lived in this house on Russell Square for four years, and this was the very first dinner party she had hosted. A most extraordinary and momentous event, which had taken her three months to organise. She moved one of the decanters set out on the sideboard a fraction to the left, twitched the curtains, and left the room.

Her little enamel watch told her that her guests were due in half an hour. In the drawing room, champagne was chilling on ice, sherry and madeira had been decanted, and a variety of glasses and goblets were set out on a silver tray. Upstairs, Marianne was reading Eilidh her bedtime story. Her daughter had turned six two weeks ago. Another milestone she had deprived Cameron of.

Her heart lurched as it did every time she thought of him, which was constantly. Every time she looked at Eilidh she was reminded that her daughter was the product of two parents, reminded that one of them was missing out on every aspect of her life. Guilt was her constant companion. But it wasn't the worst of her burdens. Being in love and having thrown away the chance of happiness was the hardest to bear.

Kirstin sank into her favourite chair, resting her head against the winged back, closing her eyes. She'd finally acknowledged that she loved him that fateful morning when she'd woken up heavy-eyed in the hotel to find his note pushed under the door, though she had refused to act on that revelation.

She'd procrastinated for weeks, diverting herself by being insulted that he'd insisted on paying for her services when she had wanted to give them free, as a gift. With anger that he had spied on her, with outrage that he had dared to demand that she marry him, with indignation that he had dared to ignore her very clear declaration that they could have no future once Philippa had been found.

She had refused to allow herself to miss him. She had refused to take his vow to return seriously. It had been bluster. He had been hurt by her rejection. Angry at being thwarted.

But she knew Cameron too well to convince herself of any of those things, and the pain of recognising how her cruel words must have injured him was an agony.

He loved her.

She remembered the first time this fact had fully registered. She had been in discussions with a client, too intent on the subject matter to notice that he'd served her coffee and not tea until she'd tasted it. Assailed by the aroma, and the memory of Cameron drinking his first cup of the day, as he always did, in one gulp, she had completely lost track of the discussions.

Cameron loved her.

He'd poured his heart out to her, and all she'd been able to think about was Eilidh. She'd thought that Eilidh was all he'd been interested in, too obsessed with her own fears to listen.

Cameron loved her.

Later that day, alone in her drawing room, Kirstin had mustered the courage to reflect on their time together. The memories, kept buried for weeks, had been frighteningly vivid, fresh and heartbreaking.

Cameron loved her. He loved *her*—everything about her. He knew who she was under her skin, and he didn't want to change her. He didn't want to put her in a gilded cage.

When you love someone... he'd said, and though he hadn't ever finished that sentence she knew now what he meant. He'd set her free by leaving her, as she'd asked him to do. When he came back it would not be to trap her or to change her. He'd asked so very little of her. How her jibes, her determination not to listen must have hurt him. She'd give almost anything to take them back.

She had known she could not undo the harm done, but she had been determined to find a way to apologise. It would have to be something extraordinary. Something unique. A gift that no one else could give.

The idea which had come to her had been so obvious it had taken her breath away, though how she was to achieve it, she'd had absolutely no idea. But she had known she would find a way.

Because she loved Cameron.

It had come to her like a simple truth, one she had not once tried to deny in the weeks and months that had followed. She loved him with all of the heart she must have convinced him she didn't possess. She loved everything about him, and it was just as he'd said to her, she wouldn't change a hair on his head.

She'd cried then, wretched with guilt and with loss, for it had all seemed so impossible. Even if she hadn't killed his love that night, even if he did still love her, despite her best efforts to stop him, what difference did it make that she loved him back?

They led very different lives. He didn't want to change hers. She didn't want to be the reason he changed his, for then he would blame her if it went wrong, or he would resent her, and their love would twist and warp into something very different.

Eilidh, ironically, was not the problem Kirstin had always imagined, because Cameron was not the man she'd always feared. All he'd asked from her was the right to give his daughter a name. To legitimise her, in society's eyes, for her sake.

From a man who had never had a family, who had gone to such lengths to protect the family who had rejected him, that was a very paltry request. He'd asked for his daughter's given name, but he'd claimed no rights—on the contrary, had promised not to interfere. How much that must have cost him. How wrong she had been, how very wrong, to imagine that he'd take more if it was not given—Cameron, who always put everyone's needs before his own.

Kirstin was wrong to deprive her daughter of a father. She was wrong to deprive Cameron of his daughter. And he was right. She'd finally acknowledged the sickening fact, less forcefully put to her by Marianne too, that she could not force Eilidh to fight her battles against a judgemental society. It was selfish of her and very wrong. Logic and reason, as Cameron had predicted, must prevail.

Next February, when the year was up and Cameron returned—and she didn't doubt he would—she would marry him in name only, for the sake of their daughter.

But Kirstin didn't want to marry Cameron for Eilidh's sake. Yes, she wanted him to be a father, but she wanted—longed, yearned—for Cameron to be her husband. But, given they lived such different lives it seemed as impossible as ever. And yet she was just about to have dinner with three remarkable women who had achieved that feat for themselves.

Her pocket watch pinged the hour. A few seconds later there was a rap on the door. Her dinner guests had arrived.

She got to her feet, shaking out the skirts of her scarlet gown. No black apparel tonight for this momentous occasion, the first time The Procurer had ever come face-to-face with some of the women who had, with her help, rescued themselves. They had achieved it, all three of them, in the most surprising manner. She wanted, desperately wanted, to learn from their experience. To find a way to make the impossible possible, and so grant her heart's desire.

This was one dinner which would not be reported in the press, though it was hosted by one of the most powerful women in London, and her guests, in very different ways, wielded a great deal of power of their own. All three had, thanks to The Procurer's intervention, escaped very different tragic fates.

None of them knew each other. Kirstin had chosen them carefully. They were strong, feisty, in at least two cases, and extremely intelligent women. Each one had been determined to find a way to support herself and live independently. Yet every one of them had married the man The Procurer had despatched them to help.

Kirstin wanted to know why. She wanted to know how. She wanted to know if they were happy. She wanted to know if she could benefit from their experience.

'I am asking a great deal of you,' she said, when the champagne had been poured and the introductions made. 'Perhaps not as much as when we last spoke,' she said with a smile, 'but I am asking you to be completely frank. I'm aware I am breaking my own rules by asking you to share your history.'

'You've already broken your rules by revealing your true identity to us and inviting us into your home, Madam Procurer.' Madame Bauduin, whom Kirstin knew as Lady Sophia Acton, looked at her fellow guests for confirmation. 'I think I speak for all of us when I say that we are very much aware of the honour you do us, Miss Blair, and the trust you have invested in us.'

'And I also speak for all of us, I'm sure,' said fiery-haired Allison Galbraith, Countess Derevenko, 'when I say that anything we can do to assist you, we will do. We owe you not only our lives, Miss Blair, but our happiness.'

'No, you owe me nothing. Whatever you have achieved, you've achieved through your own efforts. I merely provided you with the opportunity.'

'Precisely—when no one else would.' Becky Wickes, the former card sharp who had very lately become the Contessa del Pietro, beamed.

'I'd like to propose a toast.' She raised her glass, and the other two women followed.

'To The Procurer, who makes the impossible possible,' they said, as one.

Deeply affected, Kirstin made no attempt to disguise her tears. 'Would that I could weave such magic in my own case. The one thing I am lacking and cannot have is…'

'Love,' Sophia said softly. 'The last thing I thought I was looking for, if you recall. I cannot imagine living without it now.'

'Being only recently married,' Becky said, with a wicked smile, 'I am not ashamed to say that it's the one thing I can't get enough of.'

Sophia chuckled. 'I've been married to Jean-Luc for almost a year, and I still feel exactly the same.'

'Three years and two little bundles of joy since I was married,' Allison said with a tender smile, 'and with every passing day I find myself more in love with Aleksei.'

'Miss Blair…'

'Kirstin, please.'

'Kirstin,' Sophia said, setting down her champagne flute, 'are you telling us that you are a victim of unrequited love?'

She had never said it aloud, but it was surprisingly easy in the company of these remarkable women, each of whom was quite transformed. 'I am in love,' Kirstin said, 'with a man called Cameron Dunbar. As to whether it is unrequited, there's the rub. He does—or rather did—love me, but I fear I have ruined everything.'

'And you would like to remedy that?' Allison asked.

Kirstin nodded. 'But his business is in Scotland. His life is travelling the world. And mine...'

'Is making the impossible possible,' Becky said, chuckling. 'What is it they say? Physician heal thyself?'

'That is exactly what she's trying to do,' Allison said. 'Ladies, The Procurer wants to learn from our experience. That's what you meant, isn't it, Kirstin, when you said you wanted us to be completely frank with you? I'm willing to bet that we swore to you that all we wanted was the chance to lead our own lives, and yet each of us opted instead for marriage.'

'Marriage *and* independence,' Becky said.

'Kirstin wants to know how that might be achieved,' Allison concluded. 'And the answer is, not without difficulty.'

'And a lot of compromise—which I confess did not come easy to me,' Becky added.

'I think that we would all do very much better discussing this over dinner,' Sophia added.

'Judging by the delicious smells, I think it has arrived.'

'Shall we?' Kirstin got to her feet. 'With your reputation for serving the best dinners in Paris, Sophia, I took the precaution of engaging Monsieur Salois for the evening.'

'The Duke of Brockmore's chef?' Sophia's eyes gleamed. 'I have heard great things about him. Ladies, we are in for a treat.'

November 1819, Oban, Argyll, Scotland

Cameron stood on the jetty where he had been deposited, gazing out at the Isle of Kerrera which was, presumably, his final destination. A small island—he judged it to be no more than four or five miles long—it was dwarfed by the majestic Isle of Mull and, as far as he could see, uninhabited.

Each step of his journey from Glasgow, every connection from post-chaise to ferry, and onwards by pony across drover's roads, had been carefully co-ordinated by the unseen hand of the person who had summoned him here. Unseen, but not unknown.

He knew of only one person capable of orchestrating such a complex trip. Though he had absolutely no idea why he was here, he had been certain, from the moment he broke the seal on her letter, that it was Kirstin he would be meeting.

A little boat was making its way from Kerrera towards him across the choppy waters of the sound, and Cameron's iron grip on his nerves loosened. He had steeled himself to wait the full year before allowing himself to contact her, but he had thought of her every day and missed her more with every passing moment.

Knowing her as he did, he was sure that she would agree to a marriage in name only for the sake of their daughter. Knowing her as he did, he was certain that she would wait until the very last moment to do so. He very much regretted his ultimatum, but she had left him no choice. He had been very sure that she would make good on her vow never to love him.

Then the letter had arrived, and with it hope. He'd tried to manage that hope, but now, as he stepped into the little boat and the taciturn boatman headed back towards Kerrera, Cameron surrendered. Kirstin wouldn't bring him all the way to an island on the Inner Hebrides to agree to a marriage of convenience. This wasn't about Eilidh. Nor was she bringing him here to tell him that she wanted nothing more to do with him.

His heart began to hammer as the boatman

beached the dinghy and pointed to the track which led up the slope and along the shoreline.

'It's about three miles' walk,' he said. 'You'll know where you're headed when you see it.'

With this cryptic comment he set off again, back to the mainland, and Cameron set off too, glad of the sturdy brogues he was wearing, along the stony track.

The views back to the little fishing village of Oban were spectacular, but he did not waste his time on them, focusing only on walking at a brisk pace which became almost a run. The path wound inland, up and over what he reckoned must be the southern tip of the island. A farm lay in the glen below him, but a wooden arrow pointed him along another path.

The castle loomed suddenly into view, perched on the cliffs—though it was more of a ruined tower than a castle, with half of its roof gone. The approach was a steep scramble down what must have once been a bridge, judging by the crumbling remains.

Kirstin was waiting in the empty doorway, wrapped in a thick black cloak, bareheaded, tendrils of her glossy black hair blowing in the breeze. She was trying to smile, but her eyes gave her away. His heart soared as he looked at her, her expression a mirror of all he'd been feeling himself, so full of hope and yet utterly terrified.

'You came,' she said, by way of greeting.

'Of course I did,' he said, pulling her into his arms. 'How could you possibly have doubted me?'

'After all that I said…'

'Let's not rake over it. I love you, Kirstin, and if you—'

She threw her arms around him. 'Oh, Cameron, I love you so much.'

'Of course you do,' he said, beaming like an eejit, wondering if his heart might burst.'

Kirstin's smile was dazzling. She reached up to smooth his hair. 'Of course I do,' she said softly.

He kissed her. Her lips were salty, with sea or tears or both. She was trembling in his arms, clinging to him as if he might vanish, and he kissed her again, soothing kisses, whispering that he loved her, would always love her, touched to the core by the very fact that this bold, brave, fiercely independent woman needed to be reassured.

'I love you,' he murmured, kissing her forehead, her tear-stained cheeks. 'I love you.'

'I love you too. I love you so much.'

His arms tightened around her. Sheer untrammelled joy filled him as their lips met again, tenderness heating to passion as their kisses deepened. Only the shattering of a slate, blown by a gust of wind from the roof, made them jump.

'Kirstin, my darling, could you not have chosen a more convivial place for our reunion?' Cameron said ruefully. 'Somewhere with a roof, at least, if not a bed.'

She laughed. 'I didn't bring you here to make love to you.' Her face fell. 'After all the terrible things I said to you, I couldn't even be sure that…'

'I thought we'd agreed not to go over that? You were frightened I'd take our daughter from you. You were frightened that I'd start making all sorts of demands…'

'I should have known better—' She broke off, biting her lip. 'I know better now.'

'And I know that we've a lot of talking to do, a lot of sorting out to do. It won't be plain sailing, Kirstin, and I'm not making any promises…'

'Oh, no, please don't. That is one of the things I've been warned against.' She smiled at his obvious confusion. 'You'll be astonished when I tell you who has advised me. But before we talk about the future, Cameron, please let me make up to you for the things I said. Not by making love to you—not yet, anyway—but by telling you why I have brought you home.'

He eyed the castle doubtfully. 'Home? It would take a great deal of work to make this into a home. Were you thinking we should buy it?'

She chuckled. 'I've already bought it. For you. Here, come in under what little shelter there is and read this.'

She ushered him through the empty doorway and into what was left of what must have been the great hall, under the remainder of the roof. The thick parchment she handed him was a deed of sale for the Island of Kerrera and all its goods and chattels.

'Why?' he asked, completely puzzled.

'Until the Jacobite Rebellion of 1745 this was the ancestral home of the Laird of Kerrera,' Kirstin said. 'Finlay Cameron, Laird of Kerrera, to be precise. He fought with Bonnie Prince Charlie at Culloden, and was forced to flee not long after, returning first to Dunbar Castle to rescue his wife and his baby son, Lachlan. They sailed for the East Indies, their passage having been arranged by Lachlan's best friend, a government man playing a very dangerous game.'

'Wait a minute, did you say Dunbar Castle?' Cameron interrupted. 'This is *Dunbar* Castle?'

Kirstin nodded, smiling. 'Finlay and his wife

never returned to Scotland, but their son, Lachlan, had grown up hearing such romantic tales of Dunbar Castle that in the early seventeen-eighties he made the bold decision to try to recover his ancestral home. He came first to Edinburgh, to make good on a long-standing promise to his father to seek out the man who had helped the family escape retribution for the Rebellion. John Campbell was dead, but his daughter Sheila was living in Edinburgh.'

'Sheila…' Cameron stared at Kirstin incredulously. 'That was my mother's name.'

'Sheila Ferguson. Née Campbell.' She caught his hand between hers. 'I know that Finlay wrote to her, for he kept copies of all his correspondence and left the copies behind at his home in the East Indies. I have those for you, Cameron. But when he sailed for Scotland the trail went cold. Clearly when they met they fell in love—for she must have loved him, to contemplate giving up her daughter and her husband for him. They would have planned to return, I would guess, to live in the East Indies as man and wife.'

'But my mother didn't elope. My father abandoned her—that is what Louise told me.'

'Your father came north, heading for Kerrera. He made it as far as Oban. The parish records show he died of the plague before he could either see the place of his birth or make good on the promise he'd made to the woman he loved. I'm so very sorry, Cameron. I doubt he even knew of your existence.'

'How did you manage to find all this out? How long has it taken you?' Cameron asked, utterly stunned.

'I started with your name. It was the one thing, you told me, that your mother gave you.'

'So I come from a long line of merchants. The sea is in my blood. I can't believe it—what you've done, it's impossible.' He laughed ruefully. 'Though not impossible for The Procurer. I don't know how to begin thanking you.'

'I don't want your thanks. I want…'

Kirstin drew a shaky laugh. 'It won't be easy, we both know that. We must make no promises we can't keep. We will have to compromise. But it's not about giving up independence, Cameron. It's about finding room in your life for someone to share it with, someone who respects you, and who loves you so much they wouldn't change a hair on your head.

'No, wait,' she said, when he made to speak, 'I'm not finished. I want you to be a father to Eilidh in much more than name. You've already missed out on so much of her life. She's *our* child, not just mine. I want us to be a family,

Cameron, all three of us, but before that there's something every bit as important I need to ask you.'

She dropped to her knees. 'I love you exactly that way. I know you love me too, in the same way. We can make it work as long as we have each other. Will you marry me, my darling?'

He was dumbstruck for all of a second. Then he dropped to the ground beside her, pulling her into his arms.

'You can have no idea, my love, of how very, *very* much I would like to marry you. Yes,' he said, kissing her. 'Yes,' he said, kissing her again, 'and yes,' he said, kissing her for the third time, but most certainly not the last.

Epilogue

Excerpt from the Town Crier, *December 1819*

The End of an Era!

We can exclusively reveal to you, our loyal readers, that today marks the end of the reign of the legendary London icon hitherto known only as The Procurer.

The woman who makes the impossible possible quite literally lifted the veil of secrecy from her most exquisite countenance today when she stood before the altar of St James's Church to plight her troth to Mr Cameron Dunbar, Merchant of Glasgow.

In true Procurer fashion, she has been harbouring an astonishing secret—they are tying the knot for the second time! The pair, it seems, made a match the first time

*around when they eloped to Gretna Green
seven years ago.*

*For reasons they would not entrust even
to someone as discreet as yours truly, they
kept their marriage private. Today, in The
Procurer's own words, they celebrated
their love for each other in public.*

*For the ceremony the bride wore a full-
length pelisse of crimson velvet trimmed
with swansdown, which perfectly complemented her striking beauty. Her adorable
little daughter, playing bridesmaid and
carrying a bunch of heather sent all the
way from the family's Scottish estate, was
identically dressed.*

*Both daring toilettes were created exclu-
sively for this momentous occasion by the
Bond Street modiste Madame LeClerc. The
groom, a Scot with rather splendid shoulders and an excellent pair of legs, was dis-
appointingly not clad in the kilt, though the
more observant among us noticed a sprig
of heather in his lapel pinned there, the
clearly doting father informed us, by his
little daughter for luck.*

*A light dusting of snow began to fall as
the happy family entered the church, much
to the delight of the youngest member of the*

party. A more romantic winter's day or a more romantic wedding cannot be imagined. I am not ashamed to confess that the magical scene brought a tear to my eye.

Mr and Mrs Dunbar are quitting London with their darling daughter almost immediately, and will retire for some unspecified period to consider their future plans.

Does this mean that The Procurer is lost to London for ever? Watch this space!

'Well, what do you think? Will the piece serve?' Kirstin asked.

Cameron set the scandal sheet he had been reading aside, shaking his head with amusement. 'I think it will serve very well, provided that no one checks the records at Gretna Green.'

'If they do, they will find all is in order,' Kirstin said, smiling at him. 'I am nothing if not thorough.'

He gave a hoot of laughter. 'I should have guessed.'

The door of the hotel suite was flung open and Eilidh burst in. Kirstin watched indulgently as her daughter threw herself into her father's arms. 'Daddy! Marianne says I have to say goodbye now. But you and Mummy will be back very, very soon, won't you?'

Cameron picked her up, hugging her tightly.

'Of course we will,' he said, 'and then all three of us are going to our new house to see in the New Year. Isn't that exciting?'

'In Scotland. Will there be lots of snow?'

'It will probably come up to your chin. We can go sledging.'

'Will Mummy come sledging too?'

Cameron cast an amused glance at a horrified Kirstin. 'No, Mummy will make sure we come home to a nice hot drink.'

'And will you still read me a story in the new house?'

'I'll read you a story every night, I promise.' He kissed her forehead. 'You know I'll really miss you?'

'Yes,' Eilidh said seriously, patting his head, 'but you'll have Mummy and I'll have Marianne and you'll be back quick as a flash.'

He laughed, setting her down reluctantly. 'Quicker than that. Now, go and kiss Mummy goodbye.'

The door closed on Marianne and Eilidh a few moments later. 'I know I'm biased, but she's an extraordinary wee lass. And in that,' Cameron said, pulling Kirstin into his arms, 'she takes after her mother. Have I told you lately that I love you with all my heart?'

'Yes, but I'm more than happy to hear it again.'

'I love you. With all my heart.'

'And I love *you*. With all my heart. And with all my body too.'

'You do, do you?'

Kirstin wriggled free of his hold. 'Come with me,' she said, urging him towards the bedchamber in their hotel suite, 'and I'll show you.'

'Oh, no, Mrs Dunbar,' Cameron said, scooping her up in his arms, 'I think we'll start married life as we mean to go on. Let me show *you*.'

She was laughing as he set her down by the bed, but then he kissed her, and the warmth of her laughter turned to the heat of desire.

The stunning creation of crimson gauze and silver spangles which Madame LeClerc had designed for the wedding ceremony was cast aside as Cameron kissed his way lingeringly down her body, making her pulses jump and flutter, slowly, deliciously slowly, building the tension inside her. He shed his own clothes carelessly, until they were both naked, and she was clinging desperately to the remnants of her self-control, and he was hard, panting, reaching for his sheath.

'No,' Kirstin said impulsively, catching his arm. 'I think we'll start married life as we mean to go on.'

'Are you serious?'

She gazed deep into his eyes, almost over-whelmed by the love which surged through her like a physical force. It terrified her, how close she had come to throwing it all away. 'You have no idea how much I love you,' she said. 'I am very serious, if it is what you want too.'

'Kirstin…' Tears filled Cameron's eyes. 'It is what I want. More than anything, I find. If we are fortunate enough a second time, I can think of nothing more perfect.' He kissed her deeply. Then smiled at her wickedly. 'Of course we may not be fortunate straight away. It may not even be possible.'

'Then I'm looking forward very much to try-ing to make the impossible possible,' Kirstin re-plied, pulling him towards her.

* * * * *

Historical Note

I've taken a few liberties with the timings of travel between London and Glasgow. It would probably have taken somewhere between two and three days, even travelling by the mail, but that was far too long for poor Philippa and Jeannie to have been in custody, so I cut their trials just a little short.

Osterley Park, which Kirstin borrows for her day out with Cameron, is a real place. It does have an island, but not the one in my book, which is based on Temple Island further down the Thames at Henley.

You might think that the Erotes Club is a totally over-the-top invention of mine. Absolutely not. I used the Hellfire Club of which Byron was reputedly a member, but there are many and assorted others to choose from far worse than the one I've written about.

If you're Scottish and of a certain age then the comedian Rikki Fulton's Reverend I M Jolly *Last Call* sketches would have been a highlight of your Hogmanay television. Cameron's Reverend Mr Collins is my tribute to him, and a little nod, too, to the fabulous Mr Collins, my favourite Jane Austen character.

If you're interested in reading Ewan and Jennifer's story—The Procurer's first case—then you can, for free! *From Cinderella to Marchioness* is available on the Harlequin website, along with loads of other fabulous free reads. The link is on my website.

Finally, if you're a regular reader of my books you'll know that I like to reuse my secondary characters. In case you're wondering, Madame LeClerc the modiste came to England from France with Serena in *The Rake and the Heiress*, and made a very important gown for Henrietta in *Rake with a Frozen Heart*. Monsieur Salois is chef for the Duke and Duchess of Brockmore in *Scandal and the Midsummer Ball* and *Scandal at the Christmas Ball*. I'm not done with either of them yet!

MILLS & BOON

Coming next month

THE EARL'S IRRESISTIBLE CHALLENGE
Lara Temple

'And so we circle back to your agenda. Are you always this stubborn or do I bring out the worst in you?'

'Both,' Olivia said.

Lucas laughed, moving forward to raise her chin with the tips of his fingers.

'Do you know, if you want me to comply, you should try to be a little less demanding and a little more conciliating.'

'I don't know why I should bother. You will no doubt do precisely what you want in the end without regard for anyone. The only way so far I have found of getting you to concede anything is either by appealing to your curiosity or to your self-interest. I don't see what good begging would do.'

He slid his thumb gently over her chin, just brushing the line of her lip, and watched as her eyes dilated with what could as much be a sign of alarm as physical interest. He wished he knew which.

'It depends what you are begging for,' he said softly, pulling very slightly on her lower lip. Her breath caught, but she still didn't move. Stubborn *and* imprudent. Or did she possibly really trust him not to take advantage of the fact that they were alone in an empty house in a not-very-genteel part of London?

It really was a pity she was going to waste herself on that dull and dependable young man. What on earth did she think her life would be like with him? All that leashed intensity would burn the poor fool to a crisp if he ever set it loose, which was unlikely. A couple of years of being tied to him and she would be chomping at the bit and probably very ripe for a nice flirtation. He shook his head at his thoughts. Whatever else he was, he had never yet crossed the line with an inexperienced young woman; they were too apt to confuse physical pleasure with emotional connection. It wouldn't be smart to indulge this temptation to see if those lips were as soft and delectable as they looked. Not smart, but very tempting...

Continue reading
THE EARL'S IRRESISTIBLE CHALLENGE
Lara Temple

Available next month
www.millsandboon.co.uk

LET'S TALK
Romance

For exclusive extracts, competitions
and special offers, find us online:

f facebook.com/millsandboon

🐦 @MillsandBoon

📷 @MillsandBoonUK

Get in touch on 01413 063232

For all the latest titles coming soon, visit
millsandboon.co.uk/nextmonth